Life Eternal

Aaron J. Booth

three
ravens

First Edition 2011

www.threeravensbooks.com
www.aaronjbooth.com

Cover design by Georgina Gibson

Library of Congress Cataloging-In-Publication Data
is available upon request

ISBN 13: 978-0-9844356-2-3
ISBN 10: 0-9844356-2-X

ACKNOWLEDGMENTS

I would like to thank Jess Rhodes, without whom this book might never have been written. I would also like to thank everyone at Three Ravens for making this all possible.

Chapter One

Rain lashed heavily on the domain of the dead. It was quiet; perfectly so, despite the frantic screams of the one man who stirred where all else remained still. Beneath the ground, the body of a man was consigned to the All-Father's embrace, beneath the ground that same man had awoken, scared and unsure.

The darkness was heavy and oppressive. Conrad could not piece together just where he was or how he had gotten there, all he knew was that it was black as pitch and a horribly confined space. He screamed more out of fear than expectancy of aid, yet he was certain his cries would be heard by no one.

The air around him felt thick and was laced with the pungent taste of death; it felt as though his tongue was coated in a glaze of putrescence.

It sickened him.

That was when the realization dawned. The foulness of the air, the darkness, the cramped space in which he had awoken. He was in a grave. His grave.

His mind swam with half-hidden memories that would not form. The image of a knife sliding between his ribs flashed to the forefront. He groped at his torso and found only unbroken flesh. He began to panic, fearing that he would suffocate and die a second death, but then he realized that his chest was not rising or falling.

He was not drawing breath.

He began to pound on the roof of his coffin with a grim determination; he could uncover the mysteries of his new life when he escaped his deathbed. At first, his blows struck weakly as his muscles roused themselves from what should have been an eternal slumber. The cramped conditions of the coffin offered little room for effective strikes, but after a few moments his fists were pounding the lid of the coffin with such force that he felt the wood begin to splinter and the first trickles of wet earth fall onto his still chest.

The earth felt soft above him as his fists tore through the wooden lid. He was fast becoming buried in soil soaked from heavy rainfall, but despite the great weight bearing down atop his body, he would not give in. He had survived death and was mere feet from salvation. His own grave could not hold him; death could not keep him down. A few feet of moist earth would not achieve what the Undergods themselves had failed in doing.

He fought with all his strength to get from off his back and into some sort of upward position to better claw his way out of the grave. His hands tore through the sodden soil and on into the night air.

The rain beat down against his cold flesh. He should have been exhausted from his exertions, yet he felt as refreshed as when he had first awoken. He found himself praying that his unnatural stamina would hold a few moments longer, as if he slipped back into the grave beneath, he could not be certain he would have the resolve to drag himself out again.

Grasping about the surface for purchase, all his roaming hands found was grass and sodden earth. Frustrated, he dug his fingers deep into the ground and tried to force his body up from the murky depths of his grave. He roared in anger, thick, wet lumps of soil seeping into his open mouth as he did so, making him gag.

His arms burned with a strength he had not known he possessed, his legs twinning their efforts as he desperately tried to swim his way to the surface through the thick layers of dirt.

With one final and almighty effort, Conrad hauled himself out of his grave and lay beside what was to be his final resting place. Light rain lashed down from the heavens, washing the thick layers of mud from his hair and burial clothes. He still could not get over the fact that he was not breathing, and was momentarily stunned to find that he was not panting for breath after his long climb from the depths of the earth.

Undoing his burial shirt, he stared in disbelief at where his wound ought to have been. Despite the almost total darkness that the midnight sky afforded, he could see nearly as well as if the sun were high atop its zenith. And what he saw was his own pale flesh staring back at him, minus the wound that ought to have killed him.

He had felt the smoothness of his skin back in the grave and had not believed it then. He had wanted to see it with his own eyes, but doing so had not made the situation any easier to understand.

Try as he might, he could remember very little from the night of his stabbing. His memories were fleeting and incomplete at best. Small jumbles of images presented themselves but made little sense. All he knew was that he had been stabbed between the ribs, that much was certain. He was unsure why he had remembered that, the most painful memory he had in life, when all others had deserted him, but was certain of its validity.

He pushed himself to his feet, not wanting to stay by his grave longer than was necessary. The last thing he wanted was someone stumbling across him tonight; he had no answers for himself let alone the curiosity of strangers.

With ease he made his way past the gravestones and the labyrinth of overgrown shrubbery. Due to his unnaturally keen eyesight everything was picked out in almost perfect black and white with the merest hints of color. He saw the moon emerge from behind a thick veil of cloud and at that moment he felt a certain kinship with it, for they had both emerged from oppressive darkness into the clear night.

His feet threatened to sink with every step as the rain played havoc with the soft soil underfoot. More than once he steadied himself with lightning-quick reactions moments before he was about to slide over. He ran his hands up and down the lengths of his arms, his fingers traced across lithe muscle. He had always been proud of his physique, but he had never been as toned as he felt now. His fingertips picked out every detail, every rise and fall of muscle beneath his sodden burial shirt.

It felt as if every part of his body was more awake than it had ever been. His senses were screaming out to him, showing him things that he had never noticed or would never have cared to notice in the past. His eyes picked out the smallest carvings on tombstones at twenty paces or the intricate markings of each individual tree. He could smell a plethora of different scents, but the smell of the grave was most prevalent.

The smell of his own dead flesh.

He noticed now that he was breathing again, yet it felt wrong, almost as though the action were somehow unnatural. It was easier than he had thought to simply stop breathing and keep himself from doing so. It shocked him, but he discovered that not breathing was commonplace; it was like blinking, it just happened. Yet to draw breath continuously took a conscious effort.

His stomach felt empty and a sudden pain flared within him. He had to eat something; his bursts of strength had no doubt used the majority of his body's reserves. Licking his dry, cracked lips, he thought of eating once again. But just as quickly as the thoughts comforted him, they began to turn his stomach. Images of meat and broths were repugnant to him. The urge to vomit became overwhelming.

His keen hearing alerted him to a sound far off back the way he had come. It was only the faintest of noises, a twig being stood on in the distance. It should not have been audible over the sound of the falling rain, yet to his ears it was as if it was the only sound in the world.

Casting a glance back over his shoulder, he kept expecting to see the silhouette of someone tending a grave, despite how foolish such a thought was what with the time of night and lashing rain overhead, yet he saw nothing. He kept his eyes transfixed on his own grave; perhaps someone had stumbled across the disturbed earth and had gone to alert the authorities of grave robbers?

No. Impossible. If that were the case, they would have made some sort of sound as they had left. He was not certain of himself anymore, but he knew just from hearing that twig snap that no man could leave and not be heard. Not unless the man in question did not want to be heard.

He was being played.

The twig had been snapped deliberately. Someone had wanted him to hear them and now they were toying with him. He was certain of it.

A rustling noise in some bushes prompted him to spin around with the speed and grace of a dancer. Yet again, he saw nothing, only rain.

"I could toy with you all night, I do so enjoy seeing the paranoia on the face of the newborns," came a smooth voice at his shoulder.

Conrad turned to look at the man who had been following him. He recognized him instantly, yet wherefrom he could not tell.

The man looked as though he was in his late twenties, yet his dark eyes gave away many more years than his face suggested. He was ruggedly handsome and had shoulder-length flowing hair that was black as a raven's feathers.

"You found your way out of your grave I see, you're fortunate they didn't bury you nearly as deep as I."

"Who are you?" Conrad asked.

The man feigned a look of shock. "I'm hurt, you mean to say you don't remember the one who made you what you are? You certainly spoke my name enough when I found you in the alley, bleeding your life away. You called my name and begged for my help. Even when I told you of the only way I could help you, you still begged. If anything, you begged a little harder. It never ceases to amaze me how quickly the cattle wish to cast aside their mortal coil and embrace eternity." The man walked past him and motioned for him to follow. "Come now, you won't want to be standing around discussing the finer points of your death come sunrise."

Conrad wanted to flee from the stranger, yet something in the man's words tugged at his curiosity and he found that, despite all of his will power, he could not refuse.

"You asked my name? Why, I wonder? What is the importance of a name? You mortals seem as transfixed on your habits of naming as is a moth to the flame. A name is but a word with as little meaning as any other, yet to your kind it is the focal point of your existence. Without them you would be lost. To us, you are all the same; you are all cattle and nothing more."

"Then humor me, tell me what your name is," Conrad said, frustrated at the man's lengthy speech.

"Very well, young Conrad. My name is Sallus Sovain. Now that the formalities have been dispensed, do tell me, how do you feel? How do you like what I have bestowed upon you?"

Conrad thought for a moment. Memories of his last night were slowly coming back to him as this man, as Sallus, spoke. He remembered trying to entice the favors of a young lady and being confronted by a group of men intent on the same thing. Someone had knocked him down and held him tight while another had plunged a blade into his side. He remembered the pain as the handle of the knife struck his ribs. Absent-mindedly one of his hands strayed for the wound that was no longer there. Once again, the realization of its absence surprised him.

A strange and unbridled anger, like nothing he had ever felt before, bubbled up from within him. They had left him to die in some back alley along with the vermin that would have no doubt picked his bones clean before anyone found his body. That was when he had seen Sallus, as he lay there trying to plug the wound with his thumb. That was when his weakness had been witnessed and his savior had seen the strength that could be gleaned from his rage.

Sallus had been sitting in a darkened archway further up the alley. He could have been mistaken as Conrad's twin were it not for the differing color of his hair. Where Conrad's was a sandy blonde that only served to highlight his good looks, the man had dark, jet-black hair that gave his handsome features a more sinister look to them. The dark-haired figure had been watching the struggle, had just watched as the men had tried to kill Conrad and had done nothing to save him.

He had told him his name and toyed with Conrad's emotions as he threatened to leave him to die with the rats. The memory of begging the man for help was still fresh. Sallus had then told him what he would have to do, but the pain had been too much and Conrad had not heard much of his speech. Certain that life was preferable to death, he had just agreed and continued to beg for salvation.

He had felt another pang of pain as Sallus had stuck his own finger into the wound only to pull it out and place it in his mouth, sucking it dry of the blood. On the verge of blacking out, Conrad had grasped at Sallus' collar only to have his hand beaten back and his head forcibly turned to one side.

The world then became a miasma of pain and light-headedness as Sallus sunk his teeth into Conrad's neck and drank deeply of his lifeblood. He thrashed weakly as the dark-haired creature gorged itself, hideous sucking sounds intermingling with hungry snarls. Death's icy touch was closing around him and, desperate to free himself of the suffering, he welcomed it. He had revised his notion that life was better than death and would have taken the calm of the grave over this agonizing life in an instant.

Sallus tore free from his fiendish embrace and sunk his teeth into his own wrist, tearing savagely with fangs as sharp as razors until his own black blood began to ooze thickly from the wound. Conrad stared on in horror as the vampire forced its dripping wrist into his mouth.

The blood had felt cold and impossibly thick as it seeped down his throat and into his stomach. The calms words that were said next had perhaps filled him with more fear than the vampire's actions: "We are one."

"Well? Do you intend to keep me waiting until sunrise for your answer? I do hope not, I'm not much of a morning person."

Sallus' words drew Conrad from his reverie. "I feel stronger and more alive than ever. I suppose, given that I now remember what you did to me, there could be no greater irony than feeling more alive than I ever have," he said.

Sallus laughed at Conrad's response. "There is poetic justice in unlife, wouldn't you say? Cast down from the world of the living and spat back from the dominion of the dead. Yet you feel more alive than the healthiest of men and have the touch of the grave about you while achieving that feat. The best of both worlds, wouldn't you say?"

"How is having the touch of the grave a benefit?"

"You take the eternity of rest that death offers with none of the slumber. To live forever and to do so as a young man is the dream of many and the realization of few. Your muscles will never deteriorate and your looks will never fade. You have the strength of a daemon and reflexes that a cat would be in envy of. There is perfection in death, and we are it."

"Perfection means to have no flaws, yet I smell the stench of my own flesh decaying. What is that if not a flaw? I do not intend to spend my days looking young only for my scent to give away how many years I should have been in the grave!" Conrad spat.

"Do you smell it on me? Do I smell as though I should have been slumbering in a wooden box for three hundred years? Do not fear, young one. The scent fades. Your flesh decays from the moment your life leaves your body and ceases to the moment your aura is dragged back into your lifeless husk."

"My aura? My soul?"

"No, a vampire has no soul, only an aura, or consciousness, if you prefer that term. With your soul goes your imprint on this world. Never again will you see your face when you gaze into a mirror. Such is the vampire's curse, to be forever young but not be able to enjoy our youthful visage."

****

It had been a full day since Conrad had clawed his way out of his grave and the hunger was setting in. It ravaged his stomach and ate away at the back of his mind, yet his supposed savior, Sallus, had made him wait.

The hours waiting out the day had felt like an eternity. Knowing what he would have to do in order to sate his hunger, he hated himself for what he had become. Yet, as unnatural as it should have felt, whenever he thought of sinking his teeth into the neck of a ripe young woman, his mind slipped into a moment of euphoria.

Sallus had explained that waiting until he was truly hungry, until the bloodlust took him completely, was the only way to go about one's first feeding. As Conrad stalked the gloomy streets of Cabblehiem he felt that sentiment ring true.

Nothing would stop him this night. Nothing *could* stop him.

He felt the watchful gaze of his sire upon his back. Sallus had said that this was a step best taken alone, he obviously had no idea as to how attuned Conrad's senses had become in such a short time. The thought of toying with Sallus crossed his mind, just as his sire had with him the night previous.

No. The burning desire to feed came above all other petty pursuits. The pain of hunger was too much to ignore any longer. He craved it. He needed it.

A group of young men stumbled drunkenly across the street. Hidden in darkness, Conrad watched. The desire for fresh blood suddenly became distant as his memories began to swim to the forefront of his mind. These men were not the ones who brought him low, but they were a reminder of his end and the fuel to his fire.

Seeing these men, he knew exactly where he would do his hunting this night. He knew where his first meal would be found.

Conrad had been denied the pleasures of that young woman in life, but in death he would have all of the pleasures that her flesh offered and more. Melting back through the shadows, he moved off in the direction of the *Broken Goblet*.

****

The tavern was as he remembered it, full to the brim with drunkards and whores. Each piece of meat had a different aroma to it. Conrad could smell the age and experience of each of the women.

The whores had a repugnant, heady scent about them. No, his first taste of flesh would come from something far less broken in.

Something unsoiled.

Finding one such rose amidst this sea of thorns would prove difficult, especially if he continued to lurk in the shadows and watch from afar.

Stalking the cattle while walking amongst them should have been simple, yet as he took his first step towards the *Broken Goblet's* door he felt trepidation within him. This was where he had spent his last night as a living man. What information he had prized from Sallus had been enough to make him wary. A second death would mean a complete death.

Unnatural strength burned through his veins in place of mere blood. The only fear to be felt this night would be that of the cattle when he set about his gruesome task.

Once more a stiff pain clawed at his stomach and tugged at his mind. His hunger drove him on where his fear of dying a complete death would have held him back.

Conrad slunk through the tavern's open door and moved amongst the living for the first time since his awakening. The heat that their bodies exuded was stifling in such close quarters; he had grown far too used to the cold touch of death.

None of their eyes darted towards him accusingly as he thought they might. To them, he was just another man in from the street looking for somewhere to drink and be merry. The poor fools had no clue as to how literal that thought was.

His senses were bombarded with the vulgar smell of the unwashed cattle; no doubt many had spent more time wasting their coin on cheap pleasures than they did at their own homes. A pity, for a dull night in would have saved their lives.

The gentle caress of a woman tickled against his cold flesh as she gently stroked her hands up and down his arm. He turned to see a sight that he felt a certain connection with. An older woman, her face painted so that she looked more youthful. He thought about how his looks would defy the ravages of time and then thought back to this wretch of a woman who had to do battle against age herself.

She smiled as he drew her in towards him, no doubt expecting a pile of coins for an evening's pleasure. He tilted her head to one side and stroked her neck with his nose, taking in her scent.

"You reek, woman," he said with disdain. "Your time will come, but you shall not be my first." The woman slapped him hard across the face for the insult.

"Oh, your time will come," he repeated.

Conrad left the woman to her own devices, making a mental note to ensure that she suffered for the slight against him. He wanted to bring her to heel for the affront there and then, but doing so would spoil his search for the young rose that he desperately sought now.

Men stumbled drunkenly past, knocking him as they went. None seemed to notice the lone man, barely moving as men twice his size barreled into him with drunken abandon. Those who took issue with being knocked to ground as they bounced off of him quickly remembered they had other things to do when they saw the emptiness within his eyes.

He was beginning to think his search would be in vain, that the young woman he craved would not show tonight. He had only ever seen her the once so he could not pretend to know her schedule.

As he slowly began to give up hope and grow content with the thought of settling for something far less perfect, he caught her scent. It was an aroma like no other. Her skin was laced with the finest of oils that oozed with the intoxicating fragrance of rose petals and lavender.

Immediately the woman turned to look at him, no doubt able to feel the oppressive weight of his lustful gaze. A look of recollection passed over her emerald eyes, he would have been insulted if it had not. Conrad had spent many hours vying for her attention like some dog begging at his master's heel. The thought sickened him. To think that he would make himself appear such a fool just for a night of passion!

But not now. There would be no more begging, not from him anyway. He fully expected that his victims would beg for their lives before he drained it from them.

The woman beckoned him with one of her deliciously pale, white hands. So pale he could almost see the blood coursing beneath.

He thought back to his last night as one of the cattle and scoffed at the woman. He would beg no further. She would have him at her beck and call no longer. He could see it in her eyes; the frustration. She was a lady too used to getting what she wanted and not well versed in being rejected.

Something about the way he refused her must have enticed her further. Did she enjoy this game? She would enjoy it for little longer.

She sauntered across the tavern, fighting off the advances of lecherous drunks as she did so. She had a stiff kick and a good eye for the soft spots in which to hit a man. Conrad was impressed, but then pretty women had been fighting off the amorous advances of young men since the dawn of time. She was just a student of the game, nothing more.

She stood before him for a moment or two, perhaps expecting him to slip back into the role of the begging sycophant, or perhaps taken in by his handsome features. When he refused to acknowledge her with anything more than a cursory glance, she spoke, absentmindedly toying with the ringlets of her auburn hair.

"Back for another try, eh?" she said, winking and clapping a hand down atop his. He noticed her wince as the warmth of her hand contrasted against the deathly cold of his.

Pulling his hand away from hers he replied, "Hardly, for I think tonight our roles are reversed."

"You think 'ighly of yerself. I don't get men who think I want them more than they want me." The woman's voice was common, frustratingly so.

He laughed quietly to himself. "It is you that sought me out across a crowded tavern, not I you."

"You're the only one that ain't drunk out his 'ead, don't look like you're lookin' for a good night is all. Got me all curious, it did."

"Did it now?" asked Conrad, laying a hand on her cheek. She winced once more at his cold touch. "What say I change your opinion of my not wanting a pleasurable evening? They have rooms above, yes?" he said, looking toward the ceiling.

The woman nodded excitedly.

It took little coaxing to have the woman lead herself to her own slaughter. She eagerly gripped him by the hand and led him off up the steep, wooden stairs of the tavern.

The hallway was narrow and on either side several doors lined the walls. She stopped before one of them, fished a key from her brassiere and thrust it into the lock.

Conrad's fine sense of hearing could pick up the faintest of sounds from the other rooms. Muffled moans of pleasure floated alongside the far more audible screams of ecstasy. The sounds almost caused him to despair, no one would think twice about the noises the woman made as he drained her of all that she was.

The room was spartanly decorated, but that did not matter, he barely noticed his surroundings. He only had eyes for her. She began to remove her clothes, but he stopped her with the simple gesture of holding up his finger. He beckoned for her to come closer.

As she drew in to his embrace, he ran his hands the length of her body and felt her shiver at every touch. He stopped as he reached her head. Gently, he tilted it to one side and brushed the hair aside with his free hand.

"You should have been as accommodating when we first met. You will regret your ignorance."

The woman withdrew a pace after hearing his words. Her eyes widened as horror gripped tight at her heart. What stood before her was no more the simpering young man desperate for her affection. Before her stood a gaunt, lifeless creature with a hellish glint in its cold, dead eyes.

Pulling her back toward him, he sunk his fangs into the throbbing vein of her neck. Sallus had been right, the feeling of his first feeding was indescribable, highlighted no doubt due to the starvation he felt.

Pleasure coursed through him, rousing his senses as her thick, warm blood gushed from her body and into his own. He had tasted blood before, his own blood. It had tasted metallic and vile. But this, this was nectar; this was finer than any wine he had supped. Finer than any sensation he had ever before felt.

Conrad gulped greedily, forcing himself onto her even more, as if the extra pressure might draw more blood.

Drawn from his meal by a fierce rapping on the door, he glared angrily at the source of the disturbance. He did not need to answer it to see who it was. His smell gave him away. Sallus. His scent, although not tinged with that of decay, shared none of the vigor that the cattle possessed.

Casting his rose down as unceremoniously as an old coat, Conrad wiped his mouth with the back of his hand. It had been a messy meal; her blood stained his white shirt and was seeping into the thin rug beneath his feet. He was annoyed with himself as he had been far too caught up in the intoxication of her blood to notice what, if any, sound she made as she died. It was something he had been so looking forward to.

The knock came once more.
"Do let me in, son of mine."

****

If it were possible to drown beneath the weight of a dying man's scream, the township of Cabblehiem would have been struggling for breath after the horrific slaughter at the *Broken Goblet.*

Sallus had made his way back down toward the drunkards and had taken a seat amongst them to take in the bloodshed in its entirety. He sat close to the door so that none could escape the wrath of his son-in-death.

The boisterous crowd had fallen silent as a few astonished gasps picked out the ashen-faced man bathed from lip to gut in blood, none of which looked to be his own. His sandy blond hair was tarred and matted with the sticky red substance and his cold blue eyes staring calculatingly at those before him. Their silence turned to screams as he grabbed the nearest woman by the hair and sunk his teeth into her jugular without remorse.

The mass of people struggled to gain any real sense of cohesion, scattering about in their drunken stupor like frightened children. Men and women alike were trampled beneath the feet of those fortunate enough to remain standing.

Those with any sense dashed for the windows, avoiding the equally pale gentleman who sat looking unperturbed by the doorway. Sallus allowed them to escape, after all a dead man could not fear you. He wanted the entirety of Libetha to fear him—survivors would be needed to spread the word. Any who came to close to the door, however, were killed without mercy. The vampire snapped their necks, their spines, or simply tore into their soft flesh with his bare hands, pulling great lumps of dripping wet meat free from their bones.

He cast his gaze back to Conrad; his son-in-death was drenched from head to foot in gore with a pile of broken and bleeding bodies strewn about his feet. The newborn had hold of a man in each arm and dashed their heads together with relish. Neither man rose to their feet again, their skulls caved in from the gruesome impact.

Conrad's eyes widened in shock as pain lanced through his back. He turned and grabbed the tavern's barman, pulling him close. A knife fell from the man's trembling hand.

"How rude," he said, grasping the man by his collar and throwing him forcibly back behind his bar, smashing an assortment of bottles as he struck the far wall.

"I think it time we moved on from this place, don't you?" asked Sallus, taking down a candle that was fastened to one of the walls.

"I'm not finished. He still lives!"

"The most enjoyable deaths are rarely the quickest," Sallus replied, tossing the candle behind the bar.

The flame fed off the alcohol and within moments a thick sheet of bright orange fire had risen to consume the bar. The screams of the barman were more potent than any they had heard that night, and they still rang out loud across Cabblehiem as the two fiends took their leave of the *Broken Goblet*.

Conrad and Sallus stood, bathed in the shadows of one of Cabblehiem's back alleys, watching as the townsfolk tried desperately to stop the fire from spreading and consuming their homes.

It did not take long for the *Broken Goblet* to be devoured entirely by the flames, and despite the best efforts of the townsfolk, the buildings that were attached soon followed. If it were not for the rain that began to fall deep into the morning, then perhaps the entire town would have succumbed to the vampires' assault.

"This night is the start of your unlife, young one. You have tasted flesh, and you have seen the strength you possess compared to that of the cattle."

Conrad nodded; he did not need to say anything in response. Sallus had seen what he could do, and he knew that Conrad reveled in his new abilities and the suffering they could bring. Despite his earlier thoughts of not wanting to devour the living or bring them pain, Sallus was certain that his son-in-death had wholly succumbed to the beast within.

"This is just the first of many such scenes, young one. Libetha shall pay in blood for what was done to me."

Sallus looked on at the fire as the rain slowly aided the townsfolk in putting it out. Conrad was his family now, and as such, Libetha was now his grudge to bear as well. One way or another, a member of the Sovain line would bring this foul, despicable country to its knees and feast on the cattle that called it home.

Turning their backs on the carnage they had wrought, the two fiends of the night faded into the shadows.

Chapter Two

A burning husk was all that remained of the *Broken Goblet*, a once prosperous and popular tavern amongst the locals of Cabblehiem. Castus had noticed the thick plumes of smoke that hung over the town even in the dead of night and had little illusion as to what had caused such destruction. As a Warrior Priest in service to the blessed All-Father, Castus had seen many such scenes of destruction. They were commonplace in his line of work.

His tracker, a vagrant by the name Giento, trudged along ponderously behind him. Castus had stumbled across the man back in Gurdalin, where he had been trying to sell himself as a mercenary to any who would list him to their cause.

Castus had told him he would pay a king's ransom if he could aid in laying low a creature of the night. At first, the man had looked skeptical, no doubt awed by the task the priest had laid before him. It had taken nothing more than the strings of Castus' purse to come undone, flashing the man a handsome pile of gold and silver coins to change his mind.

Giento had spun some great tale about how he could sense when the dread lords of the night were close at hand, he claimed he had crossed paths with them before and that he had never truly been rid of their touch. Castus had his doubts about the man's tale, but it mattered not to him. He had served the All-Father for seven years and rarely had his duties taken him far from Gurdalin. It was not that he wanted Giento's company; it was that he needed it if he was to find his way around the Empire that he loved so dearly and fought so hard to protect.

The fact that he relied on a man of such low standing to show him around his own lands ate away at him, but then a man of strength knew when to bury his pride.

The pair stood back, watching the townsfolk try to put out the fire. It would not help them any if they were to wade in and offer a helping hand, as for many people the Warrior Priests were something to fear. They were the embodiment of the All-Father's holy justice and very few men had a clean enough conscience not to be worried by their presence.

Castus looked to his guide. The man was huddled close to him, his eyes watching the shadows. He knew what they hunted and knew enough to be wary when taking refuge in dark places. Especially when the fiend had a hand in the events of this night.

"Do you sense him? Is he near?" Castus asked, he too watched the shadows.

"You don't need *me* to tell you that," Giento replied, his voice shaking. Castus expected that it was not solely due to the cold and the rain.

He could not blame him if that were the case. Castus had hunted this vampire for the better part of a year and had come to know of the fiend's name—Sallus Sovain. It was a creature of habit, and its habit dictated that it stay and savor the pain it had inflicted on its victims. The beast would be near, lurking somewhere, taking in the scent of fear and desperation like the sick parasite that it was.

There were few creatures in existence as abhorrent and unjust as a vampire. Castus knew the scene before them was nothing that man could not replicate. Men had burned buildings to the ground many a time, but what set the *Broken Goblet* apart from anything man had done would be the massacre inside. A part of Castus was thankful for the fire as, as threatening to the town as it was, it also ensured that none of those within would rise into unlife.

Too many times, in his priestly duties, he had been forced to dismember and burn the corpses of Sallus' victims over the past year. He was grateful for the respite. However accustomed to the duty of cleansing the dead he had become, no part of him would ever miss the task when his days of hunting this vampire came to an end.

"I think it best if we wait and talk to one of them townsfolk, ask 'em what happened 'ere before we start searchin'," Giento offered.

As much as he hated waiting, Castus had to agree. There was too much smoke, too many people running about panicked for any sort of search to be conducted easily. It would give Sallus the chance to find refuge, but he could not go far. It was mere hours before the sun came up, the creature would not risk skipping town for fear of being caught out in the open when morning came.

"We shall find a room for the night and ask our questions tomorrow, come first light," Castus stated.

"Find a room? You'll struggle to do that. That vampire of yours just set fire to the only place in town that offers a man a room."

The priest grumbled beneath his breath. He did not want to spend the night in the open as that was asking for trouble, especially when the creature knew it was being hunted.

"Then we shall bunk with one of the locals, no man may refuse the use of his home to a servant of the All-Father."

"Good luck with that," Giento sniped. "If you can find a man in his home tonight I'd be surprised. Fire's already catchin', see. They'll be too busy savin' their homes to make a bed for us."

"Then we sleep in the open," Castus barked. "You will take first watch."

"Sleep out 'ere?" Giento's voice was shrill.

"Do you have a better idea?" he asked dryly.

"There were some barns not too far back, how 'bout we try there for the night?"

Castus mulled the suggestion over for a moment. "Good idea, you have a flair for hunting vampires, vagrant. It is places such as those that the creature will make its lair. And if not, then at least we have a place to rest our heads for the night."

Giento's eyes widened in shock. He had tried to avoid the vampire but had unwittingly ended up suggesting a plan of action that could drive him even closer to it.

"Onwards, vagrant," ordered the priest, shoving his aide forwards as he did so.

Giento trudged off, leading the way towards the outskirts of Cabblehiem where the dim flickering light offered by the fire slowly faded into near total darkness.

****

Giento had barely slept a wink. Despite having searched the barn they had chosen to take refuge in and those surrounding it for any trace of the vampire, he had still been uneasy with the idea of sleeping. Just because they had not found it when looking did not mean it would not crop up after they laid their heads down to rest. He was not anywhere near as well-versed in knowledge of these beasts as he had had the priest believe and, as such, he was not all too keen on leaving anything to chance.

He welcomed first light and the harsh arousal he received from Castus. Although tired beyond comparison, he was alive. Though for how long he could not say. His lack of sleep would not put him in good stead if they did indeed need to confront Sallus later that night.

They had seen nobody on their short walk from the outskirts to the town centre, and that trend continued as they made their rounds of Cabblehiem. The townsfolk were no doubt sleeping after the events of the previous night. Giento could not help but feel ashamed of himself for not helping put the fire out, but as he looked into the eyes of his paymaster, he knew the priest felt no shred of guilt.

"Perhaps we should 'ave waited 'till noon, give 'em all a chance to sleep. Sun ain't been up for more than half an hour, and I bet they didn't get that fire under control 'till not too long back," Giento offered as he sensed the priest's annoyance growing.

"Then we shall rouse them from their beds. I would know what they know," Castus replied.

"After what just happened, can't you have a little compassion? Who knows how many died in there last night? Just give 'em an hour or two, let 'em rest," he pleaded.

"The events of last night should be all that is needed to make these people see that they need to help rid Cabblehiem of the evil that plagues it. Any man, woman or child who takes issue with being woken when the eradication of a vampire is at hand should be ashamed of themselves. No, we ask our questions now. The longer we have to find this beast before the sun sets, the better our chances will be."

Giento knew better than to push further when the priest was in such a foul mood. In truth, his main concern was not for the people of Cabblehiem, it had merely crossed his mind that it would be perfectly safe to try and gain a few hours of uninterrupted sleep while the sun was up. Perhaps if they found out what they needed in good time, he would still have the chance to get some rest before nightfall. He doubted it, but then he had learned that any hope while in the employ of the priesthood was slim at best.

He had not been working with Castus for long, but just from that short period of time he knew the man had a temper that seemed only to be brought on by this creature he hunted. It was as if he took everything the vampire did as a personal insult to himself. Giento watched as the priest stormed up to the nearest dwelling and thundered his fist on the wooden door. When no answer came he hammered at it once more.

"Open the door! In the name of the All-Father I demand you open this door!" Castus shouted, his cheeks burning a fierce red.

Giento pitied the poor fool on the other side. Most men were perturbed by the All-Father's most faithful at the best of times, and this was by no means the best of times. If it were him, he would pretend he was not home and pray that the madman thrashing at his door grew tired and wandered off to bother somebody else.

At length, the door did indeed open. It was answered by a tired-looking young man with scraggly red hair who could barely keep himself from yawning. His eyes widened as he took in the sight of the man at his door.

Tall and well-built with the distinctive earthen-colored trench coat worn by the priesthood and with his closely cut, short black hair and eyes that burnt with a passionate hatred, Castus looked anything but somebody wishing to help. Were it not for the trench coat and the symbol of his God that hung from his neck—a circular pendant depicting a pair of wings unfurling—he could have easily been misinterpreted as an enforcer of the Undergods rather than an emissary of the All-Father.

The man's face creased with worry, no doubt scouring his brain to think of what he had done that could warrant a visit from one of the priesthood. The man locked eyes with Giento momentarily. It must have been a stark contrast to see such a small, grubby-looking vagabond as the accomplice to a warrior priest.

"The events of last night, tell me what you know!" It was plain to see that Castus' forcefulness would get them nowhere. The man had taken a step back as the priest barked his demand. It had not made matters any better that Castus had closed the gap, following him into his home.

Over the course of his career as a sell-sword, Giento had spent some of his more enjoyable times at the *Broken Goblet.* Libetha had been a second home to him after leaving his home-country of Gremecia, and he found the smaller towns to be far more comfortable than the cities. He did not much fancy the idea of being in the employ of the priesthood forever, and when his time was through, he wanted to return to a more quiet lifestyle of drinking and enjoying the pleasures of local whores. Despite Cabblehiem's lack of a tavern, he did not want to find himself unwelcome here just in case he wound up staying in the town again somewhere down the line. With a carefree future in mind, he put his good health on the line and rushed to the aid of the homeowner.

"Come now, don't be so 'ard on the lad. If you want answers you gotta ask, not yell."

Castus spun on his heel to face him, and in that moment Giento suddenly realized that being alive now was far more valuable a thing than being welcome in Cabblehiem somewhere in the future. He braced himself and prepared for the worst, eyes squeezed shut.

A moment passed and he realized he was still standing. When a few more moments passed he opened his eyes, content that no blow was forthcoming. Castus was still glaring at him, but there was something different. His breathing had slowed and the hatred was gone from his eyes. The priest turned back to face the young man he had been berating and slowly took a step back out of the house.

"I apologize, my companion is correct. I am often far too quick to temper when great evil has been done under my nose. Please, tell me what you know of the events of last night and have my assurances that the creature responsible shall suffer greatly."

The sudden change in the priest's demeanor was almost unheard of. The man he had been shouting at looked equally shocked and not entirely certain whether or not he should believe the priest's apology was sincere. It would have been easier had Castus remained hot-headed, at least then Giento would know where he stood with the man. With a temper as random as the wind he would be far trickier to deal with.

"I…I…I got there…I…late. I didn't see anything. I just helped fetch some water. Please…don't hurt me." It was obvious that the sudden change of attitude had done little to reassure the man, Giento could hardly blame him. Castus was no doubt used to talking down to those he considered beneath him and as such afforded the common folk little in the way of respect.

It was not a thought he relished, but Giento knew he would have to talk with the priest when they were alone. He needed to alter his attitude towards the innocents and not let his hatred of the vampire cloud his judgment. As little as the prospect of dressing Castus down appealed to him, the thought of a knife in the dark from a vengeful local appealed even less. After all, if Castus truly offended someone, it was more likely that they take it out on his less imposing aide than the man himself. It was a cowardly way to get revenge, but it's what he would do.

"We ain't gonna 'urt you. All we want is whatever you know about the fire last night. Do you know anyone or did you hear anyone talkin' 'bout anythin' they saw?" Giento said, trying to calm the man down. None of what he said was the truth of course. What he really wanted was for the vampire's trail to somehow disappear and hopefully lead Castus to some safe part of the Empire where he might be able to lose him and make a new life for himself.

Unlikely, but beggars could dream.

It was difficult to say, but judging from the look on the priest's face it appeared as though he approved of the intervention. That was what he wanted, make Castus think he was all too eager to valiantly go off in search of this thing, it would make leading him to a far less dangerous place all the easier.

"There was talk. I heard people say there were a few who got out of the *Broken Goblet* before the fire took it."

A smile crossed Castus' face; finally, they were getting somewhere. "Do you know where these survivors are? I'd much rather spend my time questioning them than I would you."

Giento rolled his eyes, despite his notable change in attitude, the priest still did not seem to worry too much about being respectful to those he questioned.

"You'd be better off asking Harlen Wilks. He's our local lawman around here. He doesn't have a chapter house or anything, Cabblehiem isn't big enough for that. He lives on the road near the tavern."

"This entire town is patrolled by one solitary lawman?" Castus asked in disbelief.

The man nodded. "Cabblehiem's a quiet town. Everyone knows everyone. Most of the time we don't even need one lawman."

"Sadly, it appears at this time you need much more," Castus said, turning and walking off in the direction of the *Broken Goblet*.

Giento watched the poor soul they had interrogated sigh with relief. He envied him; he still had not figured a way to get the priest out of his life.

****

The *Broken Goblet* lived up to its name. The midmorning sunlight showed the devastated building for what it was: a brittle skeleton of the animal it had once been. The wood was blackened in places and not there in others. Great gaping holes marked spots where the walls had weakened and those still alive inside had thrown themselves at the building in a desperate attempt to break free of the inferno. The majority of the roof and second floor had collapsed inwards, leaving the jagged walls to stand like broken teeth.

The pair stood and surveyed the wreckage in silence. Two buildings either side of the tavern had suffered from the blaze also, the townsfolk were lucky not to have lost more than they had. Castus bowed his head in a show of respect and kissed the winged pendant around his neck. The feeling the tavern gave off was one of immense sorrow, it was almost as if the weight of the pain and suffering could still be felt now all was silent and still.

"May the All-Father give peace to their souls and allow their bodies eternal rest," Castus intoned, taking solace in the fact that whomever died in the blaze would indeed rest for eternity. "Come, vagrant, let us find this lawman."

It was not hard to find the lawman's abode. He was obviously proud of his station within Cabblehiem and as such had had a large white star emblazoned on his door. His home was no different to that of any other citizen: a small, shabby-looking, single-storied building built for function rather than fashion.

Castus strode towards the lawman's home, motioning for Giento to follow. He lightly rapped his knuckles on the wood of the door, a glaring contrast to his earlier handling of the situation. Wilks was a man of the law and Castus afforded them more respect than the common folk, it seemed.

The door was answered by a pot-bellied dwarf of a man with thin wisps of gray hair either side of his head and nothing on top. The man they had spoken to previously had not been joking when he claimed that Cabblehiem did not need more than one lawman. By the look of the man standing before them, it barely had that.

"A priest? Going by what I've heard in the last few hours, we certainly need the blessings of the All-Father upon this town." Wilks' voice was gruff and powerful despite his stature, for a moment Castus was hoping that this was one of the lawman's lackey's, however he wore the white star of office upon his chest.

"I have not come to this town to offer my blessings, I have come to rid it of the evil that haunts its streets and stalks its people."

Wilks nodded and stood aside, allowing Castus and Giento into his home. Both of them had been expecting a more well-kept home for the man in charge of policing the town than the hovel they were invited into.

Old boots and coats lined the sides of the hallway, the walls were in ill repair and visibly splintering or missing small chunks in places. Wilks' pride of his position did not seem to carry on past his front door.

The dwarf led them into what must have doubled as both the primary living area and the lawman's office. It was, unsurprisingly, as poorly kept as his hallway. A comfortable-looking chair on the far side of the room was the only well-looked-after piece in the lawman's home. It was obvious he did the majority of his work as lawman from his backside. Castus imagined the only reason an assortment of junk and rubbish had not found it was because Wilks rarely left it.

"You'll have to excuse the mess, I'm in the middle of reorganizing," Wilks said, his cheeks glowing a faint red after seeing the look of shock on the priest's face.

"So long as your work ethic isn't as slovenly as your housekeeping, I will take no offence."

Wilks offered a weak smile and rummaged around on top of his desk, producing several sets of notes, all of which were composed in such terrible handwriting that Castus simply shook his head and waved the man back.

"I was tired when I took these, can't make a whole lot of sense of them myself. Had been up all night helping with the *Broken Goblet,* you see," Wilks said.

"They are your statements?" Castus asked.

Wilks nodded. "All of 'em say the same or similar things. Most of them talk about a handsome young man with sandy-colored hair."

"This man, he was the instigator of the violence?" The color of the man's hair had caught him off guard. Sallus had hair of deepest black. Was he still on the fiend's trail? Or had he slipped onto that of another without realizing? "Are you certain his hair was not black?"

"*His* was most certainly sandy-colored. There's mention of another young man with black hair, though," Wilks shuddered. "It says he tore lumps of flesh off of people as they tried to get out the door. He's what drove the survivors out the window."

Castus breathed a sigh of relief. The black-haired man had to be Sallus; no mortal man could tear chunks of flesh from another with his bare hands, not with any great ease. But that begged the question, who was his accomplice?

"What was the other man doing to make the townsfolk flee?" He had his suspicions before he even asked the question. Vampires seldom kept company outside of their own kind.

"That's the worst of it...all the reports said he came from the second floor, bathed in blood. Then he grabbed a woman near to him and ripped her throat out with his teeth. His teeth, man! Gods above and below, what has come to my town?"

"The creatures that I hunt," Castus stated without emotion. "Now tell me, did any of the witnesses say they saw a direction in which the two men fled?"

Wilks shook his head. "None. Men running for their lives don't tend to look back."

The room fell silent for a moment as Castus began to ponder over what course of action to take next. Cabblehiem was a small town and theoretically there were very few places to hide that would remain unused by the townsfolk during daylight hours. They had already checked the barns during the night, which had eliminated three potential hiding spots for Sallus and his newfound ally. There could be scarce few left.

"You know this town better than most, yes?" Castus asked the lawman.

"Of course, I've lived here for fifty-six years. I know what's what and who's who."

"Are there any places that are left unused by the townsfolk? Any places that would grant a man shelter from the sun? Excluding the barns on the outskirts of town."

Wilks thought for a minute. Castus had not told the man there were vampires loose in his town and he did not intend to. He had mentioned a place that offered shelter from the sun and he would try not to divulge much more as to the nature of the beasts than was necessary. If Wilks thought he was hunting a man, a deranged madman at the worst, then he would do so. But who could say whether the lawman would lend his help if he knew he was stalking the undead?

"There's a storehouse that was used by the tavern. It's leased out by a couple of other small traders too. And there are a few wagons on the road past the temple, they don't get much use unless the merchant who owns 'em travels south to Tilbon. They won't be getting any use now I think about it, poor Tobias Gress is thought to be one of the men who died in the blaze." Wilks bore a pensive expression as he mentioned the merchant's passing; as the man they had questioned earlier had said, everyone knew everyone, and what with Wilks' position of lawman, he no doubt had a great many friends amongst the townsfolk.

"We can drive the evil from this town, but we cannot do it alone. Would you aid us in our fight?"

Wilks looked hurt, as though he thought Castus had assumed he would do nothing more than take a few statements, brush the whole incident under the rug and leave the mess for somebody else to clear up.

"Of course! That's why I wear this star," he said, fingering his badge of office. "You have me at your disposal."

"That is good to hear. I want you to gather as many able-bodied men as possible; arm them with silver and torches. I wish that you then divide the group, one half shall search the wagons and surrounding area and the other shall check the temple's graveyard." The graveyard would be a pointless search as the undead could not survive for long on consecrated grounds, but it would be foolish of him not to check all possible hiding places.

"The temple doesn't have a graveyard. The cemetery is on the other side of town. We had that before we had the temple, you see, and there wasn't room enough to build them side by side." Wilks' statement gave Castus cause for concern. With the graveyard being located away from the temple there was the very real possibility that the vampires could indeed be hiding there.

"What exactly are we looking for?" the lawman asked.

"The men who did this or evidence of their presence. If there are crypts or mausoleums at the graveyard then they are to be searched, if not then I want all fresh or disturbed graves to be dug up and thoroughly searched. Anything that is not meant to be in them is to be burnt."

Wilks' eyes widened in shock. It was considered a sin to insult the dead. To disturb their final resting place was tantamount to heresy, and for a Warrior Priest to suggest it no less…

"Do not fear, your souls will remain clean, for you are doing the work of the just. The evil that might dwell in the dark places or in the depths of the earth is worth the desecration."

"What are we looking for, if we're digging up graves we can't be looking for men? Men need air to survive; they won't get much of that six feet under."

"It is better that you do not know what you hunt, fear has destroyed armies before the blades of their enemies ever touched their flesh. The men of Cabblehiem would be no different," Castus replied swiftly, as if the man's queries were foolish and meant nothing at all.

"Whatever we're hunting massacred the people of this town. Everyone has lost friends or loved ones. No truth about what they are will keep myself or my fellow townsmen from hunting them down. You have my word as a man, we shall not back down." Wilks puffed his chest out, galvanized by his own words and show of bravado.

"Words mean little when confronted with the daemons they describe."

"Well, have my *word* on this, unless you tell me what I am chasing, I won't be chasing anything. You can do this alone." He crossed arms in a show of stubbornness.

"You would refuse the word of the priesthood? Shirk from your duties as both a man and a child of the All-Father? It is well within my power to pass judgment on those who refuse the words of my office," Castus raged.

"Judging by what those men did in the tavern, there's a good chance that those who find them will be torn to bits. Unless you tell me what they are, I don't move. If you want to kill me for that, then go ahead, that will be one life instead of the potential slaughter that could occur upon finding them." Wilks' eyes were locked on Castus.

"Very well, but know this, if ever there is a time that you need the aid of the priesthood, it will be denied you for your affront."

"You say that as if it would be something new. We could've used an extra pair of hands last night, don't think I didn't see you shying away in the shadows."

For the second time that morning, Giento made the potentially fatal decision to assert himself into one of the priest's arguments. "Can the two of you not shut your mouths and get on with helpin' this place? Lawman, you're lookin' for vampires, two of 'em by the sounds of it."

The priest spun on his heel and glared daggers at Giento. If looks could kill, he would have been an unpleasant stain in the lawman's less than pleasant abode.

"Vampires? That's madness, they're stories that you tell to your children to keep off the streets at night," Wilks declared, yet his voice betrayed his words. A part of him knew that what Giento had said was true.

Castus turned back to face Wilks, "They are very real, and as my aide has blurted that fact out, there is no reason for me to pretend otherwise. Rouse your townsmen and arm them as I asked. Anything less will not harm the beasts. Do this now, if you wait to search after dark, every man, woman and child in Cabblehiem will have seen their last sunset."

****

Despite the rising heat of the day, Cabblehiem's temple had a chillness to the air that made Giento shiver. He sat in one of the pews that lined the small temple. He had been there for what felt like an age as Castus prayed to his lord. The priest had not moved since he had begun, remaining knelt before the temple's altar, his heavy earthen-colored trench coat laid out before him. Giento could not make it out from behind, but he was certain the man's pendant had not left his lips.

He had tried to talk to Castus about his temper, but the priest had blown up in his face, chastising him for opening his mouth when he was not asked. It appeared there was a lot of work to be done before he either learned to trust Giento's common sense or learned to show an ounce of respect to his fellow man.

The only reason he intervened when he did was because if it was left for Wilks and Castus to argue until a conclusion was made it would have been nightfall before anything was done. As little as fighting the undead appealed to Giento, doing so in the daylight when the creatures had not a hope of defending themselves was far preferable to stalking them at night.

The lawman had assured them that he would meet them outside the temple come midday, along with the men Castus had asked for. Giento wondered if the townsfolk that were being roped in to help would be made aware of what it was they hunted, and if they were, would they still come?

He fingered the blade of his silver dagger, frustrated at the fact that all he had was such a short blade to defend himself, whereas Castus had a sword edged with silver and a single-shot pistol. The shot was lead and designed to slow the vampires down rather than kill them outright. Either Castus could not afford a projectile weapon that fired silver rounds or he wanted to finish the beasts up close. Knowing of the man's wealth and his fierce pride, Giento assumed it was the latter.

The emergence of this second vampire had complicated matters somewhat. Until now he had been content with the fact that he was on a hunt for *one* of the creatures, while at the same time desperately trying to avoid it. Terrified yet content. Another of the beasts made things difficult, not only did he have to keep an eye out for one vampire, but now he had to watch for a second. It made matters worse that he had not the faintest idea what either creature looked like. All he had was hair color to go by, and he doubted the priest would approve of him sticking every blonde or black-haired man with his dagger as a precaution.

At length, Castus rose from his knees and gathered his trench coat. He moved away from the alter in silence and made to leave the temple.

"It is past noon, vagrant. The lawman will be waiting," he said, so soft was his voice that it was almost a whisper. He may have had little respect for his fellow man, but Castus held any temple of the All-Father within the utmost regard and would not raise his voice while inside its hallowed walls.

Giento rushed off to follow him, places of worship sent shivers down his spine. He was not a particularly pious man, but he always felt as though he was being watched while in a temple.

The light of the midday sun was harsh to their eyes as they strode out from the temple's gloom. True to his word, Harlen Wilks had amassed a group of what must have been Cabblehiem's finest. A shabby-looking bunch of men lead by an even shabbier-looking dwarf of a man. Giento laughed to himself and then remembered his own appearance.

It was obvious the lawman had held nothing back from those he had listed to his cause; each of them had wild eyes and fearful expressions about their faces. Men looked back and forth as if expecting the vampires to come for them before they were hunted themselves. This was precisely the kind of situation Giento enjoyed being part of, one where there was absolutely no threat and where he could look the picture of bravery.

Times like these had served him well throughout his career as a sell-sword. Give the right image of yourself before any action was taken, show your face a bit during, and then so long as you're alive at the climax, and on the winning end of the struggle, you appear a hero. With the sun high atop its zenith, Giento puffed his chest out and swaggered after Castus, twirling his silver dagger in his hand in an attempt to look as dashing and heroic as he could.

The priest stopped a few feet before Wilks and looked the group he had with him up and down, shaking his head and sighing as he did so. Giento tried to suppress a grin, for it was the leader's job to rally his troops, not to make them feel worthless before he had had the chance to make use of them. The priest's utter lack of personal skills amused Giento, he felt like he would almost miss them when the day came that he was rid of the man.

Almost.

"I trust each of you knows the manner of evil that you hunt?" The question was answered by a low murmur and an assortment of nodding heads, none of which looked too enthusiastic at the prospect of hunting the undead.

"Do not look so afraid." Castus pointed to the sky. "You have the blessing of the All-Father and more importantly, you have the sun on your backs. The fiends are powerless during daylight. If they are exposed to the sun, they will burn."

The crowd of men were noticeably more at ease, yet the fearful looks remained. It was one thing to know you had the advantage but another thing entirely to know you might come face to face with the undead. Creatures that until a few hours ago they no doubt thought of as nothing but old wives' tales.

"I ask only two things of you this day. The first is to remain calm and resolute in your task and know that the All-Father gives you his blessing to do anything that is deemed necessary to destroy this evil. The second, if you find them, is to make your strikes count. Wound them at all costs, and kill them if you are able. The heart, neck and skull are the most vulnerable parts of a vampire. Anywhere else and they may recover and regenerate. Remember, if struck by silver they will fall. If burned with fire they cannot heal."

Giento watched as the men turned their weapons over in their hands, no doubt running through potential scenarios. The majority of them were equipped with burning torches and iron brands. Few had weapons of silver, those that did could not really be said to have weapons in the conventional sense. They clutched at cutlery, candlesticks and other such implements. Heat was far easier to come by than precious metals, it seemed.

Castus strode over to Wilks and said a few words into his ear before returning to Giento.

"The lawman and half of his number shall search the graves, the rest shall search the wagons and surrounding area," he said to Giento.

"What about the store rooms?" Giento asked, already regretting having done so.

"You and I, vagrant. You and I."

Chapter Three

Sallus had watched as the Warrior Priest gave his orders to his group of makeshift hunters. The fear and trepidation in the men's eyes had been a sight to behold; it had made him wish he had chosen one of the places they were tasked with searching to shelter from the sun.

The priest had sent them off to places that would be otherwise vacant, a wise plan of action. It was what any man would have done, which was precisely why Sallus had chosen to hide in plain sight where he would be least likely to be disturbed.

He and Conrad had slipped into one of the homes a short distance from the *Broken Goblet;* the old wives' tale that a vampire was unable to cross the threshold of the living was merely that, a tale. Superstitions had never proved effective in protecting the cattle from their kind.

They had slaughtered the occupants upon their return and he had let Conrad drink deeply of their blood. The emaciated corpses were still scattered about the floor. Their skin was sallow and sunken in places, it looked as though the ravages of death had been at work for many weeks rather than a handful of hours.

Their deaths were laced with a delicious irony that had made Sallus salivate. The couple had been up all night, tirelessly fighting to save their home from the touch of the flames, only to return to find that it was their home that held their demise, not the fires that threatened it. He cast his gaze towards Conrad and doubted whether his son-in-death had appreciated the irony of the couple.

The newborn was less than Sallus had hoped he would have been. He did, at times, live up to Sallus' expectations and had an air of the aristocrat about him, but it did not last. When it was time to feed he would lapse back into the uncouth brute he had been in life. The thrill of the chase and of the feed was to be savored, not rushed. There was a distinct finery to unlife, one that Conrad *would* come to understand and respect.

The last of the sun's light had faded and dusk had settled over Cabblehiem, and with the light went Conrad's restraint. He paced the floor in anticipation of slaughter and bloodshed. The sadistic glint in his eyes intensified with every step he took, as though his frustration at being caged within the home was fuelling his own personal fire.

Newborns were seldom easily trained, and this one did not look as though he would prove any different. If he was to learn to appreciate the art of the chase and of the execution, he would have to be starved of it. If given freely, one could never learn. After all, how could anyone learn to appreciate something if it was taken for granted?

"Conrad, come here."

The order stopped him mid-step and he turned his head to regard his sire. Their faces were of stark contrast; Sallus looked calm and serene where Conrad's eyes were wild and agitated.

"You are my get, and as such you must learn to appreciate your new life. I will not tolerate blind rage. I am going to impose a rule upon you that my sire never had the sense to impose upon me."

Conrad raised an eyebrow at this. He knew Sallus was his better, for the foreseeable future at least. He had told him of the links the newborns shared to their sire and the deadly repercussions if the link were to be severed. It took time for a newborn to grow self-sufficient, for the mental link between father and son to fade and for the newborn to become his own man. If it were severed before that time was up, the newborn's mind would shatter, leaving it feral. The mind could heal itself, but it took many decades for that to occur and very few survived due to their vulnerable state.

It was precisely for that reason that he was at the beck and call of his sire. He needed to stay close, to ensure that Sallus remained alive in order for himself to continue to survive.

"I am going to starve you. You may feed one day of every week. When I feel you have grown to appreciate the hunger and have learned to control it rather than it control you, then I shall lift the rule." Conrad's eyes widened and he made to protest but was silenced by the raised hand of his sire. "I do hope you have drunk your fill this day, young one," Sallus said with a smile.

Conrad ran his hands through his hair and pulled at the roots as hard as he could, trying to come to terms with the ban that had been imposed upon his feeding. He spun on his heel, looked at the broken bodies of the young couple and launched himself at them greedily.

"Conrad!" Sallus barked, stopping his get in mid-lunge. "Never drink upon the blood of the dead. It is poison to our kind."

Sallus watched as Conrad dropped to one knee and pummeled the wooden flooring with his fists, the boards splintering beneath the onslaught.

"You will be tempted many times over the course of the coming weeks; the first shall no doubt be the worst. We will be forced to kill, and you will be forced to do so without taking the blood of your victims."

Conrad glared at Sallus, a murderous glint in his cold blue eyes.

"What are you doing to me? I will grow weak! I will become dependent!" he whined.

"You are already weak, you are already dependent! You are weak due to the hold that the blood has over you! The best of our kind can suppress the urge to feed for days and weeks at a time," Sallus snapped back, locking eyes with his get all the while. "You are dependant on me to keep you from harm. Were I not here, your over-eagerness would see you bleed every man, woman and child dry. You would attract unwanted attention to yourself."

"Then I would bleed whoever that might be."

Sallus scoffed at the retort.

"Our kind survives in the shadows for two reasons. For the pain of the sun, and to keep away from the prying eyes of those who would wish us harm. If we announced ourselves, then for all of our strength and cunning we would die. This is the way it has always been because there is no other way, and it is the duty of every sire to teach the ways of unlife to his gets."

"Do you starve all of your sons? Do you invite them to this life and then tell them they cannot have what they need to maintain it?" Conrad's voice dripped with malice.

"Yes, my daughters too," Sallus replied with a smile.

A low guttural growl bubbled in the back of the newborn's throat. He stared longingly at the two corpses before storming off towards the windows, stomping his feet into the lifeless bodies, their bones snapping under the weight of his boots. He stood there, peering through the slits of the shutters, looking out on all that he could not have.

"When the time comes that you can harness your bloodlust, you will thank me for this moment."

Conrad turned to face his sire once more. "And when will that time come? How long am I to remain shackled to your whim?"

"It can take years to overcome the hunger. Nothing of worth can be attained in the blink of an eye. That which we want the most must always be fought for."

"Blood is of worth, and it is the commodity that I desire the most. I can take that in a second," Conrad spat.

"You do not desire blood, you do not *need* blood. It has been mere hours since you last fed; the blood of two humans is enough to keep a newborn sustained for several days," Sallus replied nonchalantly. "You have the mind of an addict, all of us do when we taste blood for the first time. The moment you learned you could not have it freely, you lost all reason."

"It is not I that lost reason. I did not forbid myself sustenance."

"Then why did you not try to leech the blood of the dead before I imposed my rule? Tell me that."

Conrad looked on angrily, he had no answer. Sallus was right and they both knew it, the only difference was that the newborn was not in the right frame of mind to accept the fact. Rather than continue to argue, he turned his attention back to the darkened streets of Cabblehiem.

"The priest," he said.

"What about him?"

"He searches the streets with his man."

Sallus rose from his seat and moved so fluidly it was almost as if his feet did not touch the floor. Within an instant he was by Conrad's side, peering out onto the street.

"The fool knocks at doors? Perhaps he has come to understand that there is only one avenue of thought he did not exhaust?" Sallus mused aloud.

"He will come here, surely?" the younger vampire asked, his voice a mixture of concern and excitement. Sallus had been fleeing this man for the better part of a year. There was a reason why they had not come to blows before, and anything his sire feared quite rightly set him on edge.

With a pang of annoyance, Sallus looked back over towards the corpses lying broken on the floor. He had had such plans for them. They were to be nailed to the front of their home in the dead of night so that come morning, when he and Conrad had moved on, the people of Cabblehiem would witness the corpses as if gifted to them by morning's first light. They would have feared him for many months to come.

"He does not know your face. You will open the door so that we may catch him off his guard."

"Why are we giving this man such respect? Surely he will break as easily as the rest of the cattle?"

"The warrior priests are stubbornly resilient when it comes to fear and pain. Their faith is anathema to us and as such, we are almost on equal footing when confronting them." The eagerness in Conrad's eyes was quickly replaced with a hint of fear.

****

The failed attempts of finding the vampires had left the priest in a sullen, angry mood. It was not only the sting of failure that ate away at him; it was the embarrassment of the whole affair.

He had rallied the townsfolk to rise up and fight the vampires; he had scared them to their wits' end, and for what? All they had found were empty wagons and storehouses. The locals had begun to doubt that he had been telling them the truth and as such had lost what respect they had for him. After all, what proof had he shown them that vampires truly existed, let alone that they were roaming the streets of Cabblehiem?

The eyewitness reports from the *Broken Goblet* were already being dismissed as drunken ramblings. Several graves had been exhumed under his command, all of which had been dead ends. The fresh graves had been those of the victims of the tavern blaze, and, as such, their disinterment had been hard for the townsfolk. Granted, the graves had been little more than shoddily dug holes in the ground where multiple collections of bones and tattered rags had been laid to rest, but it ate away at their consciences. To bury your dead, be it in a mass grave or an individual plot, and have to dig them back up was a difficult task for any man to undertake.

In an effort to regain both his pride and the trust of the townsfolk, he had continued his search along with Giento. Only one stone had been left unturned in his search of the town: the homes of the residents. If anyone were to have gone missing, they would go unnoticed due to the uncertainty of the identities of those who perished in the fire. That made the most obvious places the best ones to seek refuge. Castus chastised himself for not having thought of it sooner. Now dusk had set over Cabblehiem, which meant that the window of opportunity had passed to catch the fiends at their weakest.

Casting his eyes to the heavens, he vowed he would find them regardless; he had chased Sallus for too long without reckoning.

Each home they had called upon thus far had proved fruitless. He did not distrust the people of Cabblehiem, so pressed them with few questions. It was obvious from the fact that they were still alive that the creature was not within their home. Those who had partaken in the day's hunt did not greet him favorably when he called upon them. Several slammed the door in his face when they heard him ask of vampires in their homes. Their lack of faith in him was disturbing, but given the atrocities he had made many of them commit amongst their own dead, he could hardly blame them.

He looked back to Giento; the man was watching the shadows with a fierce attentiveness. His gaze was firmly fixed on the graveyard in the distance, as if he were fearful of the dead rising up to take vengeance for the unearthing of their remains.

Taking a moment to regard the temple, Castus felt his faith bolstered. Nothing unclean or unjust could tread inside its hallowed grounds and as such no evil could come from it. That very fact was proof enough of the righteousness of his mission, for what place did something so abhorred as a vampire have in the world? Castus noticed that his aide had followed his lead and was now watching the temple with accusing eyes.

"You need not fear the temple, vagrant. It is perhaps the only place come nightfall that would not pose you a threat."

"Then why don't we go an' rest our 'eds. We've earned a little kip, and I've got an 'edache too," Giento moaned.

"We have earned nothing for we have attained no success. Your head is not attached to your feet, so following me shall prove no great discomfort," Castus snapped, already moving on towards the next house without waiting for Giento to follow. He did not need to; he knew the man would not risk being left alone in the dark.

Castus rapped his knuckles across the wooden door, the sound seeming deafeningly loud in the darkness. The door opened before he had had chance to take his hand away. It was answered by a man of average height and more than average good looks. He looked too well-dressed to have been a local, his shirt was whiter than white, his face almost as pale. His blue eyes seemed to shine despite the poor light, and he wore his dark blond locks tucked into the back of his shirt.

"My word, a priest. To what do I owe the pleasure?" The man's voice was soft and elegant.

His speech was different, also. It lacked the common edge the locals shared. Castus eyed the man closely without being too obvious, allowing his gaze to trickle over him as he appeared to take in the rest of his surroundings. He noticed a fleck of blood around the man's collar and on the white of his cuffs. His flesh was deathly pale so it was easy to make out blotches that had been wiped away on his hand.

It was his dark blonde hair that gave away his charade. Had Castus not been privy to the eyewitness reports, and had they all not shared that same detail, he might have just passed him off as an incredibly well-to-do trader.

But now he knew better. Or at the very least, he suspected that he did.

"I am searching the town for the fiends that perpetrated the fire. You have seen no suspicious characters around as of late?" He tried to make his question sincere, he could not lie to the man, but he did not want to be entirely truthful either. If the man assumed Castus thought the fire to have been started by men rather than vampires, he might be more easily goaded into making a mistake.

"I can't say as though I have. Although I haven't set foot outside my home since the incident." The man looked disinterested, almost annoyed.

"Then please accept my hand in apology for disturbing you at this hour," said Castus, holding out his right hand while fishing around in his pocket with the other.

"That's not necessary," replied the ashen-faced man.

"You refuse to take the hand of a Warrior Priest? Do you find the thought of my touch so repugnant?"

The man looked to his left, his lips tightened as he did so as if biting back a curse. At length he reached out tentatively and grasped Castus by the hand, shaking it weakly.

The priest refused to let go.

"You look troubled, friend. A penny for your thoughts?" he said, bringing his left hand out of his pocket and slapping it against the back of the man's, sandwiching it between his own.

The man's eyes widened in horror, he struggled to break free of the priest's grip. Castus felt as though his shoulder had been yanked from its socket, such was the supernatural strength of the stranger. A moment later the man released a fierce howl of pain. Without waiting another second, Castus tugged him out of the house and brought his elbow up, striking him across the bridge of the nose. He felt the bone break beneath.

The man pulled his hand free with a sudden surge of strength and fell backwards into the doorframe, clutching at his ruined nose, visibly seething with rage.

Smiling, Castus opened his hand to reveal a small silver coin. The man lowered his hand to look upon the scalding imprint of the coin in his pale flesh. It had emblazoned the shield on the back of the coin perfectly onto his skin.

Within a moment the priest had drawn and leveled his pistol at the wounded vampire. It would not kill him, but it would take him off his feet and allow for the killing blow to be dealt.

"Not a fan of silver? How odd, most men would usually die for it, not because of it."

The man sneered at him; the hatred that burnt behind his eyes fazed Castus for a moment. It was raw and animalistic, bestial in nature. He had heard of the charms a vampire could employ just by staring his victims in the eye, this one was obviously not well-versed in the tactic.

The sound of splintering wood caught his attention. To his right a figure had lunged out of the window and was bearing down upon Giento, broken shutter panes rained down in the being's wake. The vagrant raised his silver dagger high into the air, more on instinct than out of any actual malicious intent.

There was no mistaking the man, his long, flowing black locks betraying his identity.

Sallus.

With a grace that defied logic, he seemed to shirk away from the blade in mid-air, drawing himself backwards so that he landed far enough away from the silver weapon.

Without thinking, Castus made a split-second decision and turned his pistol on Sallus, his thoughts gone from the vampire he had wounded, such was his hatred for his true foe. He fired the single-shot weapon and at such short range his aim was never in any doubt. The shot took Sallus in the chest, pitching the vampire off his feet.

In an instant Castus had drawn his silver-edged sword and was converging on the downed vampire. He stood above the creature he had hunted for the better part of a year as the vampire writhed in agony on the floor.

"A year in the making and it was a silver coin that brought about your downfall," Castus sneered as he stood over Sallus.

"And bloody single-mindedness that spelt the end for you," the vampire replied through gritted teeth.

As if to punctuate the vampire's words, Castus was knocked from his feet a moment later, a blow from behind driving all the air from his lungs. He rolled onto his back to see the blonde accomplice advancing on him, his once cold blue eyes now burning with a fierce anger, his face a mask of purest rage. Castus raised his sword in defense and was greeted with a look of fearful disdain from his would-be killer.

Sallus got to his feet and stood beside his man.

"Your precious metals shall not protect you forever, priest. The next time our paths cross, I assure you, you shall feel the cold kiss of death. Stay in Cabblehiem if you wish to live."

The pain on Sallus' face was evident as he struggled to restrain the vampire at his side, the wound making it all the harder to constrain his get. Castus looked around for Giento and saw the man lying near the wall of the house, he did not remember seeing him get knocked down, but then these fiends were devilishly fast.

The blond-haired vampire fingered the brand on the back of his hand, all the while fixing Castus with a murderous glare. Sallus had chosen not to end his life tonight, he was uncertain as to why, and that uncertainty seemed to be shared by the vampire's accomplice. A length of silver was little protection to a determined vampire. Sallus could have killed him in a variety of ways without the sword ever touching his flesh, and all three of them knew it.

Sallus dragged his accomplice back into the shadows of the homes and disappeared into the night.

Streaks of light played across the dark street. The sound of Castus' pistol had attracted the attention of the townsfolk, and dozens of curious men and women peeked through their shutters as if in an attempt not to be seen. At least the events of this night would prove him right in the eyes of Cabblehiem's residents.

As he forced himself up off the ground he gained a new respect for the vampire's strength. One strike had almost crippled him, he struggled to breathe or gain an even footing, and his shoulder ached numbly from when he had dragged the creature out of the house. The pain forced him to stagger towards the building; he needed to be out of eyesight of the locals. He could not risk them seeing him laid low by one punch. It would be too demoralizing if they saw that none of them had even the slightest hope of combating these fiends. He was not even certain that he had much hope, but then he remembered the broken nose he had dealt the vampire and his spirits returned.

He stumbled past the threshold of the home and the sight that greeted him turned his stomach. His heart sunk as he realized what he would now have to do.

The dead would need cleansing.

****

The remains of the vampires' latest victims had been burnt with little ceremony. Several people had gathered to pay their respects as the flames engulfed the last of their physical remains. The majority of Cabblehiem had opted to remain indoors, some peeking through their windows to show their respect for the unfortunate couple. Many, however, refused to look upon the cremation at all. There had been too much fire gracing the night sky as of late, far too much for many to handle.

Castus was thankful that those who had gathered had not had to bear witness to what he did to the remains before setting them ablaze. They had been dismembered. First the head was severed and then the arms, moving swiftly down to the legs until all that remained was a jumble of body parts. There was very little blood, far too little for a human body. The death kiss of the vampire was evident in that one tell-tale sign.

The mark of the All-Father had then been carved into the flesh of each of the victims' skulls before they were set ablaze. Castus took the cleansing of the dead very seriously and was aggrieved to discover that he had no more white roses. It was customary to place the head of one white rose in each of the victim's mouths prior to cremation. The rose was by no means harmful to a vampire, it was however a symbol of peace.

Glaring off into the distance he was transfixed on the path the vampires had taken when fleeing Cabblehiem. He laughed to himself at the thought. Sallus had not fled, the fiend could have stayed and ravaged the entire town if he so desired.

Castus looked back down at the fire—the flesh that fuelled it had almost burnt away—and wondered just why he stood above the remains instead of laying amongst them. What possible reason could there have been for letting him live?

The uncertainty proved that even after a year of hunting the creature, he was still no closer to unlocking the ways of its mind. He *thought* he knew how its mind worked, but he was wrong.

"Once the fire dies, bury the remains," he uttered.

"Why me? I can 'ardly stand," Giento protested, groping his skull as if to gain sympathy from his paymaster.

He fixed Giento with a penetrating glare that had the man shuffling his feet uneasily. "Because I will not allow you rest until you do."

The emotions that burned within the sell-sword's eyes set him apart from the average folk he was used to dealing with. Most men would do whatever he asked without question, too afraid of the priesthood to defy. Giento, however, was different. On more than one occasion he had openly questioned Castus, not caring whether he made the priest look a fool in front of the common man. As much as he loathed to admit it, it was a quality he liked in the vagrant. No man was so righteous that he could not make a mistake, and it was refreshing for those mistakes to be pointed out so that they might be rectified.

At the same time he would have to keep a firm standing with the man. He could not be allowed to think he was above his station. Castus needed both a guide and tracker, thus far, however, it was proving rather suspect as to whether he truly possessed the ability to sense the undead. Be that as it may, his skills at navigating the lands of the Empire had been invaluable. In that respect alone he had earned his pay.

"We shall bunk down in the home of the deceased, you may sleep once your deed is done," he commanded, leaving Giento to see to the remains.

Chapter Four

They had run for hours, passing dozens of hamlets along the way and pausing to feed at none of them. Sallus had not fed properly for almost a week. The only taste of blood he had had since siring Conrad was what soaked his hands after attacking the men and women of the *Broken Goblet,* but he could resist the urge for now. Although the wound dealt to him by the priest was sapping his strength, he could heal from it. Yet he would need sustenance for it to do so properly.

The most important thing was to get as close to Tilbon as they could before the sun came up. He had matters to deal with in the city, and amongst its sprawling buildings and countless thousands of inhabitants both he and Conrad could truly become lost to their pursuers.

It was well into the night and morning was edging closer and closer by the minute. There were several settlements before they reached Tilbon, one of which they would have to take refuge in. He *could* put off feeding, but it would only make him weaker and that would serve them no purpose if the priest were to catch up to them again. Both of their survivals depended on his strength. It would also prove a suitable exercise in control if Conrad could refrain from feeding while he watched his sire do so.

They had passed through wooded areas which did not allow for their full speed. These forests were blissfully small and soon opened back out onto the open fenlands that surrounded Tilbon.

A fast-flowing river meandered its way through the landscape alongside them. The lamplight of the settlements dotted along the river's edge was visible for miles around due to the low-lying nature of the land and, past them all, in the far-off distance were the high walls of Tilbon and the belt of thick woodland that surrounded the city. The wooded area was dark and oppressive, much like the city that lay within its midst. The trees had been planted shortly after Tilbon's founding, as a natural defense. Even though the walls now offered all the defense that was needed, the woodland was kept as a mark of respect and show of tradition.

Dark and oppressing by day, the black walls of Libetha's second-largest city were almost invisible in the dead of night. Were it not for his unnaturally keen eyesight, Sallus would not have seen the city until morning's light. It was a common thing to hear of travelers passing the city by entirely due to its nightly camouflage.

With every step Sallus felt his muscles tire as the sustenance from his last feeding burned away with his exertions. His body was torn between using what fuel remained within it to either heal his wound or aid his flight. His get was by his side, never losing a step. Sallus grinned as he thought of how the newborn would soon feel the loss of a constant food source. He recalled the time when he had been forced into doing just that and wished that his sire had had the sense to impose the rationing upon him before his captors had ever had the chance. Quickly, he banished the memory from his thoughts and redoubled his efforts in reaching the closest settlement.

Dogs announced their arrival long before any of the slumbering inhabitants knew anything was amiss. It was yet another curse of their kind that animals could see the vampires for what they truly were. Piercing the night sky, the howls of the dogs were soon cut short as Sallus and Conrad quickly silenced them, breaking their necks and leaving them to lie where they fell. It mattered little about being discovered. Sallus needed to feed and he would leave none free of his touch.

Soon the new-found silence was shattered as one by one, curious men and women came to investigate what had disturbed their animals, and one by one they were fed from. Sallus dug his fingers into the soft parts of a man's face and dragged him close, sinking his teeth into the quivering wretch's throat and sapping him of his lifeblood. Conrad broke the legs, arms and spines of those who

Sallus could not get to quickly enough, leaving them to lay and wait for their turn to come.

Grinning with savage delight as he drained one after another, Sallus glutted himself on their blood and savored their fear. He laughed as grown men soiled themselves as they saw him indulge in the blood of their friends and families. Stepping over the bodies of the drained, he stood before the bodies of the broken, rejoicing as their blood burned in his veins. He could feel the wound in his chest slowly re-knitting itself.

The newborn stood to one side, eyes wide with frustration as he watched his sire partake in that which he was forbidden. Sallus noticed this and ensured that each time he suckled on the throat of one of the cattle he did so in full view of his get, occasionally letting blood splash closer and closer to Conrad's feet. Overcoming an addiction got easier, but only if it was made insufferable to begin with.

Only twenty-six called the settlement home and Sallus fed off most of them, those whom he did not were simply killed after being made to watch him feast on those they loved. He toyed with the idea of nailing the corpses to the doors and walls of the huts, but he thought better of it. It was not long before the sun rose. Let the carrion birds have their fun with the bodies and save him the hassle of defiling them himself.

He looked to Conrad; his son-in-death's icy blue eyes had long since lost their shine. They were now dull, devoid of life. The luster would return when he fed once again. It had been over a century since Sallus had last imposed such rules on a newborn; he wondered how his youngest would differ from the others.

"The sun will rise soon. We shall take shelter here and travel to Tilbon come nightfall."

"What business do we have in the city?" Conrad asked.

"Family business," Sallus said curtly.

Making no further attempt to question his sire, Conrad turned and strode off into a nearby hut. Sallus had expected more annoyance, what with his feeding in front of him. He was shocked to see him act so uncaring towards the scene, he would have thought that Conrad would have tried to steal a taste for his own at the very least. Had he not seen the newborn's fists clenched so tightly that they had become a whiter shade of pale, he might have thought that an improvement had been made already. The only improvement seemed to be in the way he expressed his frustration.

****

Sallus had ensured that the solitary window of the small wooden hut they had chosen as shelter was covered before taking a seat in the corner to watch Conrad sleep the day away. He could not sleep himself; he had gorged on too much blood for him to be able to manage that. His body surged with energy, making it impossible for him to rest, his eyes never faltering, remaining wide and alert throughout the day.

Slumber did not come easy for Conrad either. Even in sleep he seemed agitated, his face twitched rapidly at times and remained still at others. It was most certainly not the norm for one of their kind. A vampire literally slept like the dead, never moving, not waking while the sun's harsh rays beat down on the land. There were of course two exceptions to that rule, overfeeding as was the case with Sallus, or deprivation.

The mind of a vampire never truly rested when it was starved of blood, even in sleep it caused its host to suffer incredibly from withdrawal symptoms. It was unusual for a vampire to dream, but for one in Conrad's position it was more than natural for hallucinations to wrack the mind. There was an irony to it all. Conrad had been taken from the life of a mortal, stripping away all weaknesses that the cattle possessed, and with one command Sallus had heaped those weaknesses back upon him.

The day passed slowly, it always did when one was wide awake and eagerly awaiting nightfall. Sallus occupied his time with thoughts of his past, he tried to banish them as quickly as they arose but they would not stay gone for long.

He had stayed away from Libetha for decades, he had returned only once since his incarceration over a century ago. He did not like to think that the memories of his time chained beneath the temple of Nadhaska, Libetha's capital city, fazed him that much, but his avoidance of the country was proof that it had.

For three hundred and twelve years he had been a creature of the night, and for two thirds of that time he had held no control over the way he had fed, taking the throat of any who happened to pass him by if the urge so took him. Sallus had been ill prepared for the starvation he had been forced to endure while in the clutches of the priests. Not only had the thirst plagued him, but so too did the very chamber in which he was held. The prison was situated below the consecrated ground of the temple and as such caused him constant pain. It had been like a burning of both body and mind, yet the agonies never caused a visible display of the pain upon his flesh.

A meager diet of pig's blood or, if he was very lucky, the blood of the condemned had been all that had kept him alive. Once a week he was fed, sometimes not even that. The priests knew what he was and cared little if he died of his starvation. They only fed him enough to get him to answer their questions. He was beaten in between feedings. The priests had enjoyed doing so when they realized that simple physical savagery could not kill him. Little did they know, starvation could not either.

Withdrawal symptoms had gripped him as they now did his get, but he had grown strong of mind if not in body. Gradually the thirst had bothered him less and less, and eventually he was able to capitalize on the limited minds of his captors who had no fear of the dead being able to evolve into something more refined.

The priesthood of Nadhaska had paid dearly for their mistreatment of him.

Sallus shook his head, chasing the thoughts of his past away once again. It was the starvation, even though it was being imposed upon another, it affected him still. It had done with all of his gets.

The thoughts of the past were replaced with the more welcome thoughts of the present and the business he had to attend to in Tilbon. His actions in the dark-stoned city would be the beginning to his campaign. Libetha would drown in its own blood by the time he was through, and all for the actions of four pompous priests. It was ironic that it was now a priest that hounded him. Perhaps that was why he opted against killing the man? He had told himself it would teach Conrad restraint if he could attack without killing, but then he had allowed him to finish off those who he did not intend to feed upon that very night.

Truth be told, he was not always entirely sure why he did certain things. All he knew was that he rarely made mistakes and as such had learned not to question his instincts. The priest had a part to play, the final nail in the coffin, perhaps, when it came to shattering the backbone of this wretched country.

The sound of the newborn stirring roused him from his thoughts. There would be time yet to ponder his future. Sallus had nothing but time.

Sitting bolt upright, the newborn stared intently. His unblinking eyes were bloodshot.

"Rest well?" Sallus asked with a smirk.

The dull blues eyes flared with intensity at his sire's sarcasm. He inclined his head and sniffed, taking in the scent of blood that was still thick on the air. It was perhaps the only time a vampire needed to draw breath. One could survive without breathing, but existing without a sense of smell was detrimental to a hunter.

"Feel free. I said you couldn't taste, I said nothing about enjoying the aroma," Sallus remarked, watching as the hunger in his get's eyes burned ever brighter.

In response to his sire's goading, Conrad stopped breathing. "When do we leave? I do not wish to be surrounded by the dead much longer," he said.

"Why ever not? It will be harder when we reach Tilbon, of that I can assure you. Here you are surrounded by blood that you cannot drink. It is the blood of the living that will tempt you. Your breaking point shall be tested."

"Can we not just leave this place? Blood is in the air, I can smell it, and it sticks to my throat."

"Go ahead, drink it. This I will actually let you sup from freely," Sallus said, his smirk had turned into mocking laughter.

"Fine, we can stay and wait for the priest. Perhaps you have grown a backbone since you last fed," Conrad spat.

Before he was aware of being struck, Conrad was sailing through the air. He crashed into the flimsy wall of the hut with such force that he carried on through it, landing amongst the dead. Within a blink of an eye he was hoisted off the ground, Sallus' hands wrapped tightly around his throat, lifting him several inches off the ground. Were he a mortal man, the strain would have broken his neck instantly.

"Never forget your place!" Sallus hissed in Conrad's face. "I am your better in every way and you shall remember that! If I say the priest lives, he lives. Do not mistake my intent for cowardice." Sallus threw Conrad to the ground as if he were nothing more than a sack of waste. He glared down at him, it was not commonplace for even a vampire to be as quick as he had been when striking Conrad. Had he not glutted himself on the blood of the men, women and children that lay scattered about his feet, such a feat would have been impossible.

"Come, Tilbon awaits."

Sallus launched off at full pace towards the black stone walls of Tilbon, he did not need to look back to know Conrad was following. Despite his hunger, he still pushed himself to match the speed at which Sallus travelled, a foolish mistake for it would only serve to use up his reserves quicker.

Sallus slowed to a stop, holding his hand up to indicate his newborn to do so as well.

"We have a meeting to attend when we reach Tilbon and I refuse to be embarrassed by your madness. I am willing to let you feed before we are inside the city walls."

Conrad's smile touched his ears and his eyes widened with excitement.

"Do not get your hopes up. You will not feed on humans. You may devour whatever animal you find in the woods that surround Tilbon and nothing more."

The smile wavered. "You would have me scavenge rodents?" Conrad asked, his voice thick with displeasure.

"There are wolves to be had. I suggest you hunt those, nothing else will give you more sustenance in the forests of Tilbon." Sallus sped off once more towards the Black City, leaving Conrad before he could further argue the point.

****

It had not taken them long to reach the outskirts of Tilbon's surrounding forests. Sallus had run with speed unparalleled to any other creature and Conrad had struggled to keep up. But keep up he had, for there was the promise of blood to be had in the forests, and despite the fact it would be a poor substitute to the magnificence of human blood, it was blood all the same.

The burning desire to slake his thirst had pushed Conrad on where perhaps had he not been promised a meal he might well have faltered and allowed the starvation to take him. Sallus' words of a meeting rang fresh in his mind and he wondered just who he was being dragged before. Conrad assumed it was someone of import, otherwise Sallus would not have worried about how his bloodlust might cast a negative light on the whole affair.

Letting the thoughts of their work in Tilbon slip from his mind, he took a deep breath as the scents of the forest cascaded forth to meet him. He would let nothing as trivial as his sire's agenda cloud his mind. Not now. He could not wait another week to savor a moment such as this. Conrad was very conscious of the fact that Sallus was watching, no doubt assessing the effect his so-called 'madness' had on his hunting.

He was surprised to find that his overly keen senses had grown even more so now that the time for feeding was near. The moon shone brightly through the treetops, yet his eyes still managed to pick out, in perfect detail, the places its silver light did not reach. The scents that had whipped through the air moments ago were now a hundred times clearer; he could differentiate between each individual smell and the direction from which it had originated.

Craning his neck to the left, his ears picked up the minute sounds of the forest that he imagined even Sallus could not hear. Every rustle of leaves or snap of a twig was like a symphony being directed by the finest of maestros. Within moments he had locked onto a promising scent, it was meaty, powerful, and at the same time unpleasant. Most certainly animal.

There were other scents, the smell of humans was prevalent, which was to be expected being so close to such a large city. The smell of the cattle no doubt wafted over the high black walls of Tilbon and blanketed the forest with its un-cleanliness. He curled his lips in disgust. The fact that he could get so excited at the thought of putting his lips on humans as filthy as the ones he smelt now repulsed him. It was a scent he was all too familiar with, the stink of the slums. Every city lined their more affluent sectors with the protective ring of such lowly places. The districts of a city looked upon from above would have resembled an archery target: the small inner circles being of the rich and powerful, and outer ones being those of the beggars and vagabonds.

The animalistic scent of his prey burned the inside of his nose, but to a man who could have little else it was the sweetest of aromas. Conrad lurched forward, his feet moving so fast and nimbly that he barely disturbed the fallen bracken that lined the forest floor.

The woodlands whipped by at an alarming rate, the ferns that lashed at his face stung momentarily, but his mind had descended into the depths of his own hunger. Outside influence would prove useless until he reached his goal and drank deeply of its blood.

He knew where his prey was before his eyes came across the pack of wolves. The irony of the scene pleased him, they were hunting just as he was. He leapt high into the air, a feral roar escaping his lips as he did so. The startled pack turned to look at their hunter as he launched himself from the trees and fell atop the alpha-male, his teeth ripping its throat out in one swift, savage motion.

A mixture of whimpers and snarls saturated the air and he felt the teeth of a wolf clasp firmly around his right leg as he gorged himself on the blood of the alpha-male. He shook his leg vigorously in an attempt to free it from the wolf's jaws. The animal growled, the sound distorted as it was shaken violently back and forth. For all his strength and fury, the wolf refused to release its lock on his leg.

The attack had galvanized the others and they, too, began to leap forward at Conrad. He snarled, the sound more feral and animalistic than theirs had ever been. He hurled the carcass of the dead wolf to one side and caught another as it leapt for his throat. He snapped the jaws of the beast wide open—far wider than its skull was designed to allow—and let it fall to the ground, writhing in agony at his feet.

Three of the wolves remained, and all were firmly attached to his legs, thoroughly committed to the attack. Conrad chopped one across the back of the neck, snapping its spine at the base of the skull. The wolf fell limp to the floor and remained unmoving. He cursed as he realized he had wasted a potential meal.

Grabbing a second wolf by its hind legs he lifted it off the ground, its jaws still worrying his thigh. Conrad sank his teeth deep into the wolf's side and supped on the blood that flowed from the wound. The neck was preferable—the jugular never failed to unleash a torrent of blood—but cut the body anywhere and it would bleed, and that was all he needed.

The pain in his legs was already dying away and the wounds that the wolves had carved into his shins and thighs would slowly begin to heal. He just had the two wolves left to enjoy before he would have to consign himself to another lengthy period without food.

Groping for the last wolf that tore at his legs he took the creature by the skull and dug his fingers into its soft eyes, forcing them ever further until it released its grip on his limb. It howled in pain and frantically tried to shirk away from his iron grasp. He pushed the wolf back and sucked the juices from his fingers, he mused at how truly demoralizing such a scene was and how such a tactic could never be used to its full effect as the victim would not be able to see it.

The wolf stumbled about blindly, its feet finding every opportunity to trip or become tangled in the flora that lined the forest floor. The creature's howls were ear-splitting and yet at the very same time they were like music to the hunter within him. He hadn't noticed the cries that his first kill had made and had vowed to himself that he would relish those of his future kills.

He sank to his knees and dug his teeth into the blind wolf's neck, sucking the life out of it like some vile parasite. It was different, feeding from an animal. The blood was brackish compared to the glorious taste of humans, but that was tolerable. What really made him gag was the hair that filled his mouth as he dug his teeth deeper and deeper and the feeling as it became matted with blood.

Letting the blind wolf finally have the peace that his actions had shattered, he turned towards the last course of his meal. The creature writhed in pain, its jaw lolled brokenly with every painful motion. He gripped the beast by the scruff of the neck and stood up, hauling it level with his face. The cries of pain were weaker from this one, its pain no doubt too severe to use its mouth in any way.

With a sadistic grin upon his face, Conrad slapped its broken jaw to one side and devoured the warmth that coursed through its veins. He held it up for a moment longer to stare into its eyes. It still lived, barely. Its eyes flickered open, the pain in them was louder than any bestial roar ever could have been.

The unconscious smile that adorned his face quickly faded as he felt a fierce stab of pain through his right hand. He tried to drop the wolf but realized the beast was stuck to him. He saw an arrow jutting out of the back of his hand, his pale skin bubbling as though subjected to immense heat. Immediately he tore the dead wolf free from the arrow and hurled it to the floor, ripping the projectile free of his hand. He grimaced as he saw the tip of the arrow.

Silver.

Sparkling in the soft moonlight, his blackened blood marring the surface of its tip.

The pain refused to go away, his hand burnt as though it had been thrust into a baker's oven. He screamed, the sound was saturated with agony and made the wolf's sound like that of a frightened child.

Beneath the din of his own screaming he could hear something else: the thrum of yet more arrows whistling towards him. He dropped to the floor instinctively as four more of the silver-tipped projectiles pierced the empty space which he had occupied.

Four men, camouflaged in their earthen colors to any with less attuned sight than his, stood twenty paces away half hidden behind the trees. He was thankful of the darkness, it was surely his only savior from the first arrow. No doubt the bulk of the wolf had been the target and his hand had been a fluke shot.

He saw the men reach for their quivers, but their hands never made it. One of them was pitched from his feet, his neck broken from the impact. He was dead before he hit the floor. Sallus was amongst them, knocking them to the ground and ruthlessly finishing them off with stomps to their necks and skulls.

One man rolled away as the vampire ended the lives of his friends, he tried to rise to his feet and flee but all of his courage had sapped from his limbs with Sallus' timely raid.

Conrad leapt to his feet, eager to claim one of their lives for their attack on him.

"No!" Sallus hissed. "This one lives."

Shock and anger burned within him at his sire's bizarre wish. He absentmindedly fingered his cheek, recalling the last time he went against Sallus when he had wanted a man left alive. In a show of submission, Conrad bowed his head briefly and took a step back. The skin of his legs flared white-hot as he moved, looking down he noticed that his clothes had been ripped almost clean off of the lower part of his legs. Staring back at him from under the ruined legs of his trousers, he saw great flaps of flesh hanging from his shins in places and missing in others.

He watched the archer's face, the man was white with fear. He knew what he had stalked through the forest—the silver-tipped arrows were proof of that— but he obviously had never come face to face with a vampire.

Returning his attention to his clothes Conrad sneered, frustrated that a meal of such little worth had cost him such finery. Even his delicately-woven silk shirt had been subject to the razor-sharp fangs of his prey.

Sallus had begun to question the archer and he did not need to move any closer to hear their conversation.

"It is odd for a ranger to arm himself with silver-tipped arrows when the most dangerous creatures in his lands are wolves," Sallus stated.

The ranger stared blankly, his mouth worked frantically but no sound came out. Sallus must have looked like some dark messenger of death with his pallid flesh and locks of midnight black, it was no surprise for one of the cattle, as pitiful as they were, to lose composure.

"Answer me or you shall meet a similar end as your companions." He indicated to the broken bodies of the dead rangers.

The man was trying, but still nothing came from his mouth. Sallus leapt gracefully into the air and landed next to the ranger, he sat down cross-legged next to the man and placed his arm around his shoulders. The ranger shivered at the cold touch.

"I am being more than fair to you, little man. You tell me what I ask and I promise not to kill you. What more could someone in a position such as yours possibly ask for?"

"You…w…w…won't kill me? You'll let me…let me live?" the man stammered.

"I swear to you, I shall not lay a finger on you if you give me what I desire. Now, please answer my previous question."

"We weren't hunting wolves," the man gulped.

"Then what were you hunting? I believe I already know the answer, but I do so love to be proved correct." Sallus still held the man in a friendly embrace, the look in the man's eyes was enough to show that such closeness to a vampire both repulsed and terrified him.

"Vampires."

Sallus reacted with a cheerful smile. "See now, that wasn't so hard. You displease me though, I offer you such sterling conversation and you speak all of five words and expect it to be enough?"

"What else do you want?" The ranger's voice was shrill, as if he expected to be torn to shreds at any moment despite the vampire's promise to the contrary.

"Why, the obvious, of course. How did you know to hunt my kind? You couldn't possibly have foreseen our arrival."

The ranger shook his head, his face had turned bitter and hateful. "Your kind haunts the streets of Tilbon and bleeds our civilians dry. We didn't know you would be in the woods, we heard someone shouting and then we heard the wolves." He looked at Conrad, defeat weighed heavily on the man's face. "But all we found was him."

Sallus remained quiet for a moment, he removed his arm from the ranger's shoulder and rose to his feet.

"My kind haunts the streets of Tilbon, you say?" he said, gazing intently towards the black walls of the city.

The ranger remained silent, Conrad got the impression that he was not meant to answer. The question sounded rhetorical, a hint the ranger picked up on also.

"How odd. It appears our workload has multiplied, young one," Sallus said, staring at Conrad.

"How so?" Conrad asked, well aware of the fact that he was not even privy to the planned tasks that Sallus had for them once inside Tilbon. The fact that they had 'multiplied' meant little to him.

"I will explain once you dispose of my new-found friend," Sallus flashed the ranger a fiendish smile.

"You promised!" the man screamed.

Conrad surged forward and was atop his prey within an instant. "He promised that *he* would not be the one to kill you."

"Kill, not feed," Sallus reminded him.

Ignoring Sallus' annoying reminder, he dashed the ranger's skull against the hard-packed earth of the forest floor until the light faded from his eyes.

"You could have just broken his neck," Sallus said dryly.

Holding his right hand up for Sallus to see, he indicated to the back of his hand where blisters marred the pale flesh, and at the epicenter there lay a blackened hole, the skin raw and scorched.

"You don't seem to have much luck when it comes to silver," Sallus pointed out.

"It hasn't killed me yet," Conrad snarled.

"Take his clothes and put them on, I refuse to have you meet anyone in such a state."

Conrad's snarl intensified at the suggestion. He turned his gaze back to the dead ranger that lay beneath him. His clothes consisted of a dull green shirt and dark, earthen-colored trousers, the fabric as coarse as a hessian sack.

"Who are we meeting that deserves such respect?"

"Our family."

Chapter Five

The night was still young by the time they breached the city walls, but Sallus opted to find shelter immediately. Conrad was disappointed, the city was new to him and he yearned to explore all that it offered.

Tilbon was fashioned from the same smooth, featureless black rock as the high walls that surrounded it. The tallest building in the entire city was the temple. Unlike the rest of the city, the temple was constructed from stone of purest white. It seemed to shine even in the dead of night. Conrad shuddered as he thought of how it must look when the sun was beating down upon it. He was grateful that he would never find out. Just looking at the thing irked him, as though the sheer holiness of it could scald his mind from such a distance as the city limits.

The slums were home to all manners of filth and scum, all of which would go unnoticed if they were to disappear. Each of them stank foully, no better than rats. Conrad wondered if Sallus would see them that way and allow him to feed.

They had taken refuge in a filthy alleyway that was constantly in the shadow of the buildings either side of it. At its worst, the sun would create a divide down the centre of the alley, forcing them to hide in the shadow. Conrad was frustrated that they had to stay in the open amongst the slum dwellers, but Sallus had stated how close they were to their meeting and did not wish to arouse any suspicion by needlessly forcing people out of their homes. Or, indeed, killing them.

As if two pale-faced men hiding in an alleyway, clutching to the shadows for the remainder of the day, would not arouse suspicion? Sallus had laughed at such concerns, telling him that in the slums as long as they were not *doing* anything then they would appear to be model citizens.

The day had passed tediously slow. Conrad had felt weakened, even afraid, by being outdoors while the sun was out. He had not spent time outdoors while the day passed since his rising from the grave, such fears were to be expected for one so unused to unlife. All it would take would be one moment of carelessness for something to go wrong, he was not entirely sure what that would be as he had never witnessed a vampire caught out in the sun. It was an experience he dearly hoped he did not discover firsthand.

His sire had been no help in passing the time, he had merely sat propped against a wall as if the sun beating down across Tilbon, and there being no roof over their head, was of no concern. When asked about the meeting they were to attend he just kept repeating two words: 'our family'. He would divulge nothing of who this 'family' was. Names, appearances, ages, backgrounds, nothing. He had flashed his half smirk, half smile and said that he wanted it to be a surprise, that it would be more fun that way.

The blood of the wolves had done little to keep the madness from Conrad's mind, but he attributed the sun as playing a large part of that. He had been completely lucid before dawn broke across Tilbon, yet now he paced the shadowed section of the alleyway like some felon awaiting his time at the gallows.

"You are making it harder for yourself," Sallus said. "All of this pacing and worrying will do nothing but sap your reserves, and your next feed is a long way off. Do make it last."

Conrad refused to answer with anything other than a snarl as he slumped down beside his sire, gazing at the bright line of sun across the ground mere feet ahead of them. His eyes burned with hatred, he never once took them off the line as if in hope that the sun might shirk away from his gaze.

It did, over time, shy away. Further and further, until the line was swallowed by shadow and twilight fell over Tilbon. With the coming of night so, too, came Conrad's confidence. His fears bled away from him, leaving him free of their touch for another twelve hours.

He followed his father-in-death as he slipped out of the alley and back into the rundown streets of the slums. Beggars still lined the walkways as if glued to their spots permanently. The sight of the poor begging the poor for aid was almost comical. What good was begging in the slums, surely asking for handouts from the wealthy would benefit a man far more?

It did not take long for the gleaming white of the temple to appear in Conrad's peripheral vision. He was glad they were running parallel to it, towards the thing would have been too much to handle. He could not figure out the repulsion that he held for the building. Had he not spent an entire day across from the temple in Cabblehiem? That had not bothered him.

This one, however…

It was like a midnight sun, harsh and threatening to his dead eyes. The moonlight shone gently off of its domed roof, the light cascading down to illuminate all that surrounded it. It truly was as if some higher power was watching over the city. The thought frightened him. He closed his eyes and shook his head slightly as if to chase away his fears, not once did he lose his footing while running blind.

"What makes this temple different from any other? Why am I so affected by it?" Conrad asked, fixing his gaze firmly on his sire's back.

"It's the way it's built. Each stone is blessed by a number of holy men, the ground is consecrated—as you no doubt expected—and silver is used in abundance in both the foundations and the general structure of the building."

"All that effort…for our kind?"

"Not entirely, and that isn't *all* of the effort. There is a great deal more work than that. The catacombs beneath, for instance, and the priestly burial grounds that lie deep in the heart of each temple."

"What did you mean by it not entirely being built for us?" He had not even considered that other legends and myths truly could walk the lands of Taal, but if vampires existed then why not other creatures?

"Silver is believed to be a bane to many evil things, the vast majority of which are merely myth and legend. Most do not exist."

"Most?"

"Yes, most. Do not worry yourself with such trivial nonsense. We have more pressing matters to attend to," Sallus said, stopping short of a three story-building with a dirty black sign hanging limply in the night breeze.

"Another tavern?" Conrad asked. He was somewhat annoyed, it seemed as though taverns and the homes of the poor were all that unlife offered.

"You were expecting something else? A crypt, perhaps?" Sallus flashed his half smile and strode into the *Ferryman's Inn*. The sounds of drunken laughter and, curiously, a beautiful voice singing loudly above the raucous crowd wafted out onto the street.

Conrad sighed but followed eagerly, despite the repetitive environment he was keen to unravel the mystery behind this so-called 'family', and he was somehow drawn by the inviting sound that pervaded the air.

****

Sallus took a seat at a circular table in the far corner of the crowded room, he did not once look back to see if the newborn was following, or if he was keeping to himself with all of the humans around. He had just fed on the blood of animals a day before, and the hunger would not have been sated on such paltry rations. It was akin to a carnivore surviving solely on a diet of shoots and leaves. It did not worry him, though. Conrad feared, and it was that fear that would keep his son-in-death in line.

The sandy-haired vampire fell into a seat at the table a moment later, his eyes surveying the packed room hungrily. Sallus could tell his son's hungered expression was not out of thirst, it was an eagerness to see his family. Withholding information regarding them had been deliberate and was no doubt driving Conrad mad. It was so easy to get beneath the flesh of a newborn, to enrage them to the point where they wanted to act but were too fearful to do anything.

The first floor of the tavern was a communal room where the residents of the slums and of the floors above came together to forget their worries by drowning them in drink and entertainment. It was the one place that the poor would come and willingly throw what little coin they had into the hands of another.

Sallus noticed Conrad's eyes had stopped flittering across the crowd of people and had become fixed on one. The songstress, whose golden voice had welcomed them into the *Ferryman's Inn*, was a captivating creature to behold. Her beauty was unmatched by any of the harlots that frequented the place or indeed anywhere in the city no doubt. And her voice…

Sallus had heard the woman sing on many occasions and yet was still moved by the gentle, yet powerful tone of her vocals. Were his heart still beating he was positive it would be doing so a little faster.

"Captivating, isn't she?"

His son-in-death took his eyes from the golden-haired woman at the centre of the room for a moment. Sallus could see the effort was almost painful to him; his eyes longed to explore every inch of her soft, pale flesh right up to her chocolate-colored eyes.

"She is the most beautiful thing I have ever seen. I died for a woman in Cabblehiem and I thought how weak and human a gesture that was, but now…I would gladly do so again." Conrad's voice was soft and bereft of the anger he had felt since his siring, as though the songstress had washed away all of the resentment he felt merely by existing.

Almost immediately after speaking, he snapped his head back towards the small stage at which she stood. The look upon his face made Sallus wonder if anything could break his concentration. It was an effect he was used to, he had been sitting there many times, watching and listening to her sing, seeing the men around him go weak at the knee when she parted her lips.

Despite his acute hearing, Conrad did not seem to register as a large, well-muscled man with short, dark hair, greased firmly to his head with a touch of animal fat, sat himself down at their table. Nor did he look to the newcomer as the man stared at him.

"*This* is what delayed you?" The man's voice was sharp, a harsh contrast to the beauty of the woman's song.

"Among other things, Nicholas," Sallus replied.

"The priest?" He did not wait for Sallus to reply, there could be no other force of nature that would slow Sallus down. "I don't know why you don't just break that man like a twig and have done with it. Holy blood must be quite a taste," Nicholas mused, licking his lips as if to emphasize the point.

"You're beginning to sound like Conrad, he has learned not to question whom I allow to live. I would've thought you would have by now." The threat in Sallus' voice was by no means subtle. Nicholas shirked away in his seat as if fearful of some form of reproach.

"Do not compare me to…to *that*!" Nicholas spat.

The insult caught the newborn's attention and he turned to face Nicholas, snarling like the wolves of his last meal. Sallus held a hand up to keep his newly sired son from making a scene.

"Gentlemen, can we not act civil? I do hate to see brothers fight amongst one another." The look of shock that flared within the newborn's eyes amused him. Equally as amusing was the contempt written across Nicholas' face.

"*That* is the family you spoke of?" Conrad asked. "I had thought you were just playing with your food."

"Rich words for a man with wolf blood on his breath! There must be less of a requirement these days for siring newborns," Nicholas hissed.

Sallus slammed the heel of his boot into Nicholas' foot, the bones crunched beneath the onslaught, twisting Nicholas' face in agony.

"Do you question my judgment, Nicholas? You dare to disrespect me in such a way?" Sallus twisted the ball of his heel back and forth to apply more pressure, his teeth bared and his eyes wide.

Grinning at the display, Conrad's smile suddenly disappeared as silence descended over the room. The songstress had stopped singing and was nowhere to be seen.

"Miss the pretty woman, wolf boy?" Nicholas laughed through gritted teeth.

Sallus lifted his heel and stood from his seat. "I think we should take this upstairs, I do not trust either of you to behave in public."

Sallus strode off through the packed room with both his sons following swiftly behind. He noticed that Conrad's eyes were locked longingly onto something by the stage; he did not care to look as to what. Carrying on, he turned his back on his sons, trusting them not to draw attention.

Through the noise of the crowd he picked out the uneven footfalls of his sons and smiled to himself. Nicholas was limping, a lesson paid for was a lesson learnt. He continued on up a narrow staircase and along a shabby, ill-maintained hallway. The cattle were no better than dogs, living in such squalor. It was ludicrous to think that such slovenly creatures tasted as gloriously as they did.

A second, equally narrow staircase lay at the end of the hallway. The walls on either side were blackening with grime. The stairs allowed for only single file and were not nearly wide enough to allow its users the comfort of walking without rubbing against the wooden paneling.

The third floor housed only five rooms in contrast to the dozen smaller ones that lined the second level. Two sets of large wooden doors sat opposite one another on either side of the hallway. Sallus walked on past them, leading his sons towards a lone door at the end of the corridor. He opened the door without knocking and led both Conrad and Nicholas into the large living space.

The room was by no means luxurious but when compared to the rest of the building it was fit for royalty. The walls were clean and soft, cheaply made rugs lined the cold wooden floor. A large double bed dominated the centre of the room; the straw of its mattress was in ill repair and stuck jaggedly out of the sides. Sitting on the end of the bed, running a bone-handled brush through her hair, was the bedazzling songstress.

Before Sallus could speak, a harsh snarl ripped from Conrad's throat and in an instant, he was between the woman and his family. His teeth were bared and he was crouched as if ready to strike. His eyes were glazed over with a fury that had not been present even in Cabblehiem.

The room was silent for a moment, Conrad eyeing his family and they him in turn. After a few seconds had passed, both Sallus and Nicholas erupted in laughter.

"What?" Conrad snapped, gritting his teeth and balling his fists.

The laughter stopped almost immediately. Vampiric emotions differed greatly from those of the cattle; they found things amusing, but never so that their laughter was uncontrollable. It had all been for show, to belittle Conrad.

"You would fight your family for a woman?" Sallus asked.

The newborn looked behind him and found nothing there.

"Any man would die for my beauty. Wouldn't you, Sallus? I know Nicholas would."

The voice prompted Conrad to spin his head back to face his family. The woman he had lunged in front of to protect was now standing between Sallus and Nicholas, her slender hand stroking his brother's face.

"What is this?" Conrad demanded.

"Come now, you don't honestly believe something so beautiful could be merely human? That a voice as angelic as hers could ever be produced by the throat of a mortal?" Sallus asked, placing his hand on the woman's shoulder.

"I *am* rather insulted," she said, her voice as melodious as when she sang. "Were he not so handsome I would have taken more offence."

"What is she, if not human?"

"Your sister, of course," Sallus replied with a condescending smile.

He watched Conrad's eyes flitter as his mind worked frantically to process all he had witnessed and learned.

"Stupid newborn, taken in by a pretty face," Nicholas snapped, grinning widely, yet there was no humor in his eyes.

The ravishing blonde turned to face her brother, anger creasing her perfect, pixie-like features. She clasped his jaw with her hand and turned his head to face her.

"*Just* a pretty face? I expect nothing less from a commoner with more muscle than he has sense!" she snapped, her perfect voice still bewildering even when raised in anger.

"Not *just* a pretty face, you have nice legs too," Nicholas winked, guffawing loudly.

She pushed him away, so strong for one so slight of frame and fragile-looking.

"At least he has his perspective right, it's nice to have a protective brother instead of a lecherous one for a change!"

Sallus moved between the two, placing a hand on both their shoulders and forcing them back in an effort to restore some semblance of peace.

"Can we cease this incessant prattling and just get on with business? You're confusing the young one," he said coolly, motioning towards Conrad as if to highlight the fact.

Nicholas leant against a wall, a smirk on his face as he took in the annoyed look of his sister. She stormed back towards the bed and sat on the end once more, fingering the brush absentmindedly as she glared murderously at Nicholas.

"Thank you. Now, before we discuss our ongoing quest, I would like to know which one of you has been openly hunting within the city." Sallus' accusing glare washed over the room causing both of his children-in-death to forget their mutual animosity. "Vitria, I do hope your hands are clean. I would so hate to mar your heavenly features." The woman looked hurt by his accusation.

"We're both clean this time. We're not alone in Tilbon." Her soft, velvet voice had the harsh edge of uncertainty to it.

"She's right, we've been scouring the city but we can't find where they nest. We're sure that they're here in numbers, though. Looks like a whole coven," Nicholas offered.

Sallus took a moment to ponder the information. A whole coven? Tilbon had never been home to vampires in the past, not in his memory. Scarce few of his kind came to the lands of Libetha at all, were it not for his incarceration he would have no business here and would likely be haunting the lands of Gurdalin or Gremecia like the majority of his kind.

"How long have they been here?" he said at length.

"As long as we've been here, so that's six months at the very least. They're sloppy, though, they think they're alone and don't even try to hide their actions." Nicholas was frustrated, that much was evident from the tone of his voice. No doubt the man had made hunting them a personal vendetta and his failure was stinging him worse than any blade of silver ever could.

"Yet you have captured none," Sallus said, a statement rather than a question.

"It's not like we haven't had the chance, Sallus," Vitria cut in. "Numbers are just not on our side. There were two of us and who knows how many of them. We didn't want to expose ourselves until you arrived, but we've been watching."

One of Sallus' eyebrows rose in curiosity. "What have you seen?"

"That whoever's at the top of the coven has a warped mind. Don't see many adults hunting, all we've seen is small children leeching the life out of whoever they get their hands on first," Vitria said, her words laced with both disdain and pity.

"Children, you say? That would explain their utter disregard for the rules of secrecy," Sallus furrowed his brow. "I want one, alive."

Conrad gave his sire an incredulous look.

"What?" Sallus asked pointedly.

"You talk of secrecy, yet if I remember correctly, you allowed people to escape solely for the fact that survivors spread fear. If you were concerned with secrecy, then why not just let them all burn in Cabblehiem?"

Sallus shared an amused look with Vitria and Nicholas. Conrad had been one of their kind for less than a week, it was all too easy to forget that he did not know the inner workings of vampire politics.

"A small town, miles from anywhere of any import is of little concern. Yet if it were known that we stalked the streets of a city as large as Tilbon, a city with its own militia, that would be an entirely different scenario," Sallus answered, ignoring the look of confusion that remained on his youngest son's face.

"What daddy is trying to say, newborn," Nicholas spat the word as though it were some form of insult, "is that farmers with pitchforks can do little to worry us. An army with fire and silver could cause a problem."

"Thank you, Nicholas." Sallus shot him a cautioning glance. "We pick our moments. The world is not oblivious to our existence; the majority do, however, like to pretend that we are nothing more than a fairytale."

Walking over to the room's only window, he flung open the shutters and let the evening wind rush through his hair. He gazed out onto the marketplace below, multiple plans of action flittering through his mind. Centuries ago his sire had said that there had been heads of covens that had displayed bizarre fetishes in their selection of those they sired. Sallus had never paid too much attention to such talks at the time—the politics of his kind had not interested him as a newborn—yet he was certain the mention of a coven of children was there somewhere in the depths of his mind.

He had not encountered a child that had been sired into unlife before and was at a loss to provide any information on their strengths or weaknesses. As a rule, a vampire would only sire those he thought would bring something to his family: strength, speed or intelligence. The whole point of a coven was for a show of strength. To have such a large number of vampires in one place always drew the attention of other families.

On several occasions, covens had battled one another, it had usually been for territory or simply through the fear that the rival might attack first. All of the evidence he had seen in his unnaturally long life had shown that covens were made for war and war alone.

To create a coven of children seemed a preposterous idea, but if it had indeed been around for at least as long as he, then there had to be something to the idea. Maybe immortal children did not have the same disadvantage when fighting an adult vampire that a mortal child would have fighting a grown man. It was all so unclear and he yearned to discover just what made these children worthy of siring.

His thoughts were abruptly cut short as Nicholas' fierce growling ripped through the blissful silence.

"What is your problem, newborn? You now know she is not one of them, yet you do not take your eyes off of her!" he roared, moving to stand between Vitria and Conrad.

Growling in reply, Conrad dropped into a defensive crouch.

"I can't help being so beautiful, you *can* help being so jealous, though, Nicholas," Vitria teased.

Nicholas snarled in reply to her mocking tone and took a step closer to his brother, balling his fists, his knuckles cracking with the effort.

"Is that meant to scare me?"

"Not at all! It's so I don't break my knuckles on your jaw," he snapped.

"If either of you throws a fist, I shall break it myself," Sallus threatened. "Now sit down, I do not have the time nor the patience for your temper, Nicholas."

Chastised, the brute eyed his sire furiously. "Look at him! Look at how he stares, as if she is the only thing in the room."

"There is a reason for his obsession. He died trying to gain the affection of a young lady," Sallus explained.

Nicholas loosened his posture upon hearing the words, but his face was still twisted with rage. He took a step back and turned his gaze back to Conrad.

"That explains it," he said. "Just because I understand why doesn't mean I have to like it."

As was the trend of the evening, the newborn looked on in confusion as Nicholas retreated after hearing how he had died. Conrad turned to Sallus for an explanation.

"Of course, I have told you little. When a man is sired, he takes with him into unlife the emotions and reasons for his death. You died for a woman, therefore physical attraction will still be a problem for you."

"Problem? I don't mind it in the least," Conrad said, staring dreamily at Vitria. A growl bubbled in the depths of his brother's throat.

"It is a problem indeed, pretty women will have a hold over you. You will not feed on them, even if they are all that is available."

"That's not true, I fed off the woman whose affections I sought. She was my first. You know, you were there."

"You fed on her as she was the reason for your death. Vengeance is an emotion that suppresses all others for our kind." Sallus looked to Vitria. "If Vitria begged you to kill me, if she promised herself to you in exchange for my head, you would do everything within your power to lay me low."

It was frustrating that there was the threat of a coven of unknown strength in the very same city as they, yet at the same time he had to nurse a newborn. There was so much he needed to teach Conrad, so much to explain before he would get a thorough grasp on his new existence. It was worrying to think that if they were drawn into a fight with this coven, they would have to watch out for him also. Siring him had been necessary in his game of cat and mouse with the priest, yet in this unforeseen circumstance it could prove to be a costly decision.

Were it any other man hunting him, he would simply kill him as both Conrad and Nicholas had suggested. Yet there was some part of him deep inside that quite literally begged with his sense of reason to let the man live. Sallus could not say for what reason, but there *was* a reason. He had been a great believer in destiny as a mortal, perhaps that aspect of his past life had clung to him. Perhaps the priest had some vital part to play in the drama that was his existence?

"I tire of this room!" Nicholas moaned. "I want to stretch my legs, I want to slake my thirst. You would have us capture one of these children? I can do that, Sallus."

"I want to see them before giving you the chance to blunder anything. I will observe these children tonight. I doubt they will be too difficult to find."

"We have watched them for almost six months, we can snare one tonight," Nicholas protested.

"I said no," Sallus snapped. "Take Vitria and feed. Do not disobey me, Nicholas."

****

Conrad followed Sallus swiftly over the flat rooftops of the slums as he led the way to the more affluent districts of Tilbon. It was obvious when they shifted from poor to wealthy; the rooftops, for one, became more elegant, sloping and perfectly tiled as opposed to flat and incomplete. Small spires threatened the clouds impotently and wall flowers climbed most of the tall buildings, transforming the endless black into a sea of color.

Conrad had had a lot to think about since leaving the *Ferryman's Inn*. The reason he was drawn to pretty women, to Vitria, despite the fact that she was one of his kind. It had not solely been Vitria who had his heart threatening to beat once more. There had been another.

As he had sat listening to Vitria's song, his eyes had caught onto a creature of unparalleled beauty. Unlike Vitria she had no fine clothes, nor did she have objects of value from what he could see. She had been sitting in the corner of the room, her eyes similarly fixed lovingly on another. To his annoyance, that other had not been himself.

The woman had chestnut hair that matched her eyes and lightly tanned flesh. There was nothing overtly special about the way she held herself, but there was an allure to her. Other men had not cast a second glance in her direction—certainly not the clumsy barman she had adored from afar—yet to him it was as if she were the only thing that existed. The heavenly song Vitria had been singing had only caused him to become more enamored by the simple slum dweller.

When the song had stopped, Nicholas had wrongly assumed it was Vitria's disappearance that had upset him. It was merely the fact that the gentle harmony of her voice was no longer highlighting the woman's beauty. He wanted her more than anything, which was why his sudden defense of Vitria in her room had shocked him. It was to be expected though, he reasoned. After all, would a man not protect his silver as vehemently as his gold?

His sire clung to one of the conical spires, searching the streets of Tilbon's middle district for signs of the children. Conrad could see equally as well as his sire and was not perched nearly as high; over-doing things seemed to be a trait that Sallus found hard to let go.

The streets were full of men and women ambling drunkenly along from one ale-house to the next, laughing merrily to one another and talking in voices too loud for everyday conversation. Even without his keen hearing, Conrad could eavesdrop with little difficulty. He grimaced to himself. Had this been what he had looked like on one of his many drunken outings? The thought was repugnant to him.

Pushing the drunken cattle from his mind he found himself recalling Sallus' words '*when a man is sired, he takes with him into unlife the emotions and reasons for his death'*. The recollection was all the prompt he needed to barrage his sire with the questions that burned in the back of his mind.

"What did you take to unlife from your death? Vitria and Nicholas, what about them?"

Sallus turned sharply to look at Conrad, frustration creasing his handsome face. "Must we discuss this now? There are more pressing things at hand than your curiosities."

"I will watch, you talk," Conrad replied.

"Like I said to Nicholas, I have neither the time nor the patience tonight. You will get your answers, just not now."

"But I want to know, it will drive me insane! There is so much I do not know about this new life, so much you have not told me," he pleaded.

"There is too much to cram into one night, especially when that night already has a principal activity." Sallus turned his attention back to the streets below. "Speculate to yourself."

Conrad snarled beneath his breath in frustration, another thought pushed to the forefront of his mind almost immediately. "What of your main reason for being in Tilbon. The reason we came here to talk to Nicholas and Vitria?"

Sallus remained silent, watching the streets below for any sign of the murderous children as though he had not heard Conrad's question.

"There was something else, before these…children got in the way," he continued.

"Yes, there was, and much like your curiosities of what I brought from my mortal life, it shall have to wait," Sallus replied curtly.

Conrad's lips tightened in anger at being denied. He thought to argue, to press the point further, but stopped before he even had the chance to begin. His eyes caught the slightest twitch of Sallus' nose—a scent far too subtle for his own—and then the most minute movement of one of his ears as some distant sound found its way to him.

"Looks like we have a bite." He turned to Conrad. "Be silent, and if it is a child make no move unless I give you permission to first. The coven seems to be unaware of our presence in Tilbon and I would like it to remain so." With that Sallus leapt gracefully into the air and plummeted toward the nearest rooftop, his landing making no more noise than the footfall of an average human.

The urge to ask his sire how he planned on not being seen when clinging to a tendril-thin spire was overwhelming. He restrained himself, however. Sallus did not seem in the mood for sarcasm tonight. Instead he watched as his sire sped off into the night. It mattered little if he lost him by sight, it would be more than easy to follow him by scent alone. Conrad slid down the side of the spire, not trusting himself to make a leap of faith as Sallus had and land it as silently. Slinking from rooftop to rooftop with effortless grace yet in a fashion that appeared clumsy compared to Sallus, he followed his sire on the trail of the undying children.

Chapter Six

It had been almost a week since they'd left Cabblehiem, and it had taken them the best part of four days to reach the first hamlet on the road to Tilbon. It had not proved difficult to ascertain just where it was the vampires were headed, there was little of interest in the direction they had fled other than Libetha's second-largest city.

They'd been forced to go it on foot. Had the unnatural presence of the vampires not terrified the horses within Cabblehiem so much so that the animals had broken free of their bonds and fled, they would have had a much easier and far quicker journey.

Giento found himself cursing the horses yet at the same time thanking his lucky stars they had bolted. The fact that they were being made to walk over the uneven country roads had played havoc on his feet—the price one pays for owning shoddy footwear—yet it also gave the vampires four extra days to distance themselves, which in turn gave Giento four extra days of living at the very least.

He shuddered as he relived that fateful night back in Cabblehiem when they had happened across the creatures' stolen dwelling. His spirits had perked up as he watched Castus break the blond vampire's nose—it meant they could indeed be hurt—but the leader of the pair crashing through the window and almost landing atop of him had brought his thoughts back to reality. He had hoped Castus would have learned his lesson after being bested by one strike and just listened to the vampire's warning. Self-preservation obviously ranked just below stubbornness on the priest's scale of importance.

The hamlet of Luth had been good to them. The people there saw those of the priesthood far less occasionally than the townsfolk of Cabblehiem and, as such, had spared no thought to their own wellbeing when it came to housing the pair. They had offered the pick of their food, as much of their ales and wines as both he and Castus had wanted—Castus had politely declined the alcohol, of course—and one man had even offered that his family sleep outside so that he and the priest had some privacy.

Were it not for the fact that they hunted a predator more deadly than Giento had ever imagined existed, he thought he might get used to travelling with a priest. The benefits of such a relationship were far better than any of his previous employers had afforded him.

Castus had refused to allow the man and his family to sleep beneath the stars and had asked that they make no change in their sleeping arrangements for either he or Giento. The answer had astounded him. He could see why a man would not want to take advantage of the poor in such a way, but when it came to the priest, he expected very little common courtesy. At the very least he would have thought taking the offer of sleeping beneath a roof would have been a smart move. Instead, Castus had opted to drag him into a nearby wood and sleep beneath the cover of the trees with only a small fire and the clothes on their backs for warmth. They had food aplenty from Luth but blankets would have been a wise thing to ask for as the ones they already had were filthy from their travels. He glanced at the priest out of the corner of his eye; the man was fast asleep beneath his thick trench coat. The sell-sword grumbled a string of obscenities and shuffled closer to the fire.

When morning came, the fire had died and the air was far cooler than the night before. He shuddered as moisture ran down from his neck to the small of his back. Morning dew. The one thing he hated about a bad night's sleep out in the open was the unwanted coating of moisture you received. *The fire must have died pretty early in the night,* he concluded.

Looking over to where Castus lay, he was certain that beneath his trench coat he was snug and warm, but most of all, he would be dry. Giento continued muttering the obscenities from the night before, frustrated at how self-centered the priest could be. He had long come to terms with the fact that Castus was not used to being polite or in any way nice to those he considered beneath him, but to knowingly allow another man to risk freezing to death, especially one whom he counted on to lead him around the lands he knew nothing about, was madness.

In some ways the two of them were no different. Castus would refuse politeness to Giento—he had yet to hear the priest use his name, anyone who heard them speak would assume he was merely named 'vagrant'—but in return Giento would be as uncaring when it came to anything dangerous. He would do all it took to ensure he survived, even if it meant leaving the priest to be devoured by the vampires. There was no characteristic more important to him than self-preservation. That was where the two men differed.

It was roughly an hour before the break of dawn and Giento refused to stay and wait for the priest to wake. There was no sense in him freezing while he waited for his paymaster to rouse himself. He stood up and gathered what little they had not left in Luth—they had used the generous man's home as a place of storage, some small compensation for not giving him the honor of them using his bed.

A sly thought crossed his mind as he watched Castus sleep; his light snoring was proof enough that he was indeed well and truly unconscious. He crept close to the priest and gently tugged the trench coat off of his face and up over his feet, leaving his extremities exposed to the biting cold. *Not as bad as I've had it, but it'll do*, Giento thought. With his deed done he strolled off smugly, in search of breakfast.

As he began his slow, ponderous walk back to Luth, Giento thought back to Castus and his big heavy boots and how the man would not feel any part of this rocky trail. He grumbled once more, wishing he had done something to cause more discomfort to the priest than merely giving him the chance of catching a head cold.

Gentle wisps of smoke rose from the small homes of Luth. He smiled, knowing the residents were already up and about and, by the looks of it, preparing food. He salivated at the thought. They had been given food to take with them to the woods, but only cold meat and cheese. It had been so long since he had had a good home-cooked meal rather than the meager rations of cured meats, cheese, raw vegetables and other products that were easily prepared or found along a roadside.

Giento fished around in his pocket for a small, worn leather purse that contained all of the earnings he had made from the priest to date. Inside, twelve golden coins and around double the amount of silver glinted dully in the morning gloom. He had been paid ten gold coins just to agree to lead Castus wherever he wanted and had been promised much more of the same along the way. Contrary to the priest's promise, he only received two more pieces and the rest in silver—not that he was displeased as it was still more than many men made, and there *would* be more to come.

Castus had been the main reason behind the people of Luth being so generous, they had only offered the same to him due to the fact that he accompanied the priest and no doubt feared offending him by not offering Giento anything. He was certain he could get a free meal if he so desired, but the people of Luth appeared kind-hearted and seemed to genuinely like both he and Castus. Small towns or hamlets such as these had long memories, if he did manage to give the priest the slip somewhere along the way, he would no doubt be welcomed here if they still thought him in league with Castus. So it might help to be generous to them.

Giento's thoughts of losing Castus, the riches he had and those still to come had taken his mind off the trek back to Luth, and, to his pleasant surprise, he found that he was no more than a few minutes' walk from the hamlet. The scent of eggs already wafted eagerly towards him, making him drool a little more than he already was.

Upon reaching Luth he made straight for the home where his belongings were stored. He reasoned that if it looked as though he was just coming back for his things, it would not look like he was fishing for a meal. To his surprise the homeowner and his wife were waiting for him with two extra places set at the table. *The priest* is *good for something at least*, he thought to himself.

Before he had the chance to shrug his cloak from his shoulders, it was in the hands of the man's wife. She was pleasant-looking, not unattractive but by no means eye-catching.

"Where's the priest? Will he not be joining us for breakfast this morning?" She looked genuinely disappointed. Giento was stunned momentarily, the thought of someone being upset that Castus *was not* present was a hard concept to grasp.

He nodded through the open window toward the small wooded area where they had bedded down. "Still asleep when I left 'im. Didn't wanna wake 'im, he has a temper in the mornin' sometimes."

"Oh," she replied glumly, her shoulders visibly slumped.

"I'm sure he'll be 'ere as soon as he wakes up and smells the spread you put on." He grinned. The woman smiled in reply and hurried over to the small table, pulling a seat close by for him.

Giento feasted on a generous breakfast of eggs and bacon and an assortment of local produce that he was not familiar with.

Mushrooms he recognized, but little else. It was by far an improvement to what he had had to put up with as of late, so he was not at all bothered about what he was eating. Just so long as it was edible and hot, that was enough for him.

He suddenly felt self-conscious as he noticed that the couple were not eating. The man and his wife were standing at the window, gazing out into space. The man had something pressed to his eye.

"Back again. It can't be an animal, otherwise the folk up there would have got rid of the body."

"Well, what is it then, Marren?" the woman asked, jostling for position at the window.

"I don't know, maybe they're taken with them? Maybe they feed them meat?" Marren answered unconvincingly.

"Like pets? Never met anyone who likes crows enough that they'd feed them."

Giento stopped eating and craned his neck to try and see what the couple were arguing about. The word 'crows' had caused him to worry. He had no doubt that if the carrion birds were feasting on something further along the road, it wouldn't be an animal. He just was not that lucky. He got up from his meal and moved to the window. The couple seemed oblivious to him, too caught up in what was happening in the distant sky.

"Mind if I take a look?" he said, forcing himself to the window.

"Of course," Marren said, moving aside. "Take this," he said, offering Giento a spy glass that looked to be worth more than the man's home.

Giento nodded his thanks and placed the instrument to his right eye, forcing his left one shut in order to see better. Dozens of black birds swarmed around a tiny assortment of wooden huts in the distance, diving low and swooping back up high moments later. The scene repeated itself constantly, the birds looking as though they could keep up the aerial dance all day.

"This been goin' on for long?" he asked, reminded of the couple's earlier comments.

"Several days. They come and they go. It looks like there's less of them today," Marren replied.

Giento removed the spyglass from his eye and, as much as it pained him, gave it back to Marren. "I think I best go and tell Castus." He looked at the breakfast table and resisted the urge to force another strip of bacon into his mouth. “I’m sorry, but I don’t think he’ll be stayin’ for breakfast.”

****

They had been fortunate that one of the residents of Luth frequently made trips to and from Tilbon for the purpose of trade, and even more so that the man was taking one such trip that morning. The trader had gladly accepted Castus’ request for them to ride along with him in the back of his wagon.

The priest took in the look of pleasure on Giento’s face, looking at the man’s shoes there was no doubt that he was happy not to be making his way to the site where the carrion birds gathered on foot.

Bottles clinked together in one of the crates the sell-sword was using as a seat. Alcohol or medicines most likely, and with either being in constant demand, and of such high price, the trader would be guaranteed a decent turnaround, even with only four crates of merchandise.

“I ‘ope you’ve got your white roses ready this time. I can’t see them crows bein’ there for the scenery.”

Castus looked at his guide; the man was talking with his eyes closed, not even looking at him while he spoke. He shook his head, frustrated that he was forced to enroll one with such little respect on his payroll.

“The birds have been gathering for several days now, if what the villager says is true. Carrion birds do not bother vampires from my experience, so it is safe to assume we will find only corpses. Rituals will not be necessary, only fire,” he replied somberly.

“Just once I’d like to find a corpse we didn’t ‘ave to burn. It’d be a nice change of pace.”

“I would prefer that we found no corpse at all. Luth was uneventful, I could get used to such boredom,” Castus replied, his words nothing but sincere.

The wagon rocked violently beneath them as they encountered harsh terrain and the trader’s booming voice could be heard yelling at the horses, followed by a sudden slowing as the horse’s reins were firmly yanked.

A small panel was slid back to reveal the trader’s grinning face. “Won’t be long now, the settlement’s coming into view. Just at the top of this hill.” It seemed as though the trader still thought there was a need to yell. He blushed when he saw look of shock on Giento's face as his eyes snapped wide open.

The panel slid shut once more, muffling the sound of hoof beats and mercifully hiding the trader, Saim, from view. The man was annoyingly friendly, if such a trait were possible in men who lived solely for profit. Castus had slammed the panel shut himself when he learned that it existed—the trader having left it open so he could talk to his passengers. The man had opened it once more and tried to make conversation, only to be met by a fierce growl and an even more forceful slamming shut of his panel. He had opened it only to talk of important matters pertaining to their travel ever since.

Giento moaned about the trader but, truth be told, Castus' attention had been taken by the swirling flock of crows that no doubt feasted on the inhabitants of the small hamlet. He thought back to Luth and the carefree people there and found himself feeling thankful that the vampires had not darkened their doors. The one benefit of finding only corpses was that there was no chance to get emotionally attached.

The road beneath gradually inclined ever higher, rattling the contents of the crates more than before as they rolled and settled at the back of their containers. Giento was forced to take a more rigid seating position as opposed to lounging across anything that was fastened down.

Castus took a small parcel of dried meats and cheese from one of the pockets of his trench coat. Marren and his wife had been distraught that he would be missing breakfast—by the look of the food they had prepared for the vagrant, it had been a shame indeed—and in an effort to make up for it in some small way they had prepared some snack food for the journey. He had grown tired of dried meats and cheeses that crumbled when touched, a nice home-cooked breakfast would have done wonders to lift his spirits.

From his seat on the uneven crates, Giento looked on hungrily as he tucked into his meager rations; he turned away from the man so he could see he was welcome to none of it. Giento *had* eaten well that morning after all. Castus stuck a lump of cheese into his mouth before it had a chance to crumble in his hands. He sniffed loudly—his coat had fallen from his face at some point during the night and it seemed as though a cold had worked its way into him. Giento chuckled and went back to pretending to sleep.

The wagon did not level out again as Castus had expected. The trader stopped on the incline and opened the panel once more, announcing that they had reached Graan. Castus made a mental note that he had to be more observant, the trader—whose name he still struggled to remember—had mentioned the name of the settlement multiple times. Perhaps his mind simply refused to listen to those who annoyed him in some way.

Castus was first out of the wagon and was pleasantly surprised to find that they had been taken within a hair's breadth of Graan. He had expected the unease felt by both he and Giento to have affected the driver in some way and made him stop further away. The hill they had stopped on seemed near enough flat when out of the wagon, the fact that the trader's crates of bottled goods had been rocking fiercely back and forth had made him assume the hill to be steeper than it was.

Their arrival seemed to irk the crows somewhat, prompting them to perch atop the huts as opposed to at ground level where their gruesome meal would no doubt be waiting to be discovered. Castus took what he assumed would be his last breath of clean air before making the short walk to Graan.

He had not been wrong in assuming there would be little fresh air to breathe. As they drew closer, the putrid stink of death clung thickly to the air, making it difficult to draw breath without the contents of their stomachs fighting to free themselves. Giento had covered the lower half of his face with his cloak, yet the stench still brought tears to his eyes. Castus refused to disrespect the dead in such a way. He had been around rotting corpses in the past, it was part of his role as a Warrior Priest, and as such he had grown more used to the foulness of it all.

The sight that awaited them amongst the wooden huts of Graan was as repugnant as the stench. An assortment of bodies both young and old lay in crippled heaps, their flesh pecked away in places revealing gore-covered bone beneath. Foul-smelling liquids oozed from the bodies and glistened sickly in the sunlight. Flies buzzed over the deceased, and maggots writhed hungrily in eye sockets, ear holes and any other orifice created by the ravenous crows.

Marren had said the birds had been coming for days, yet with the fierce heat that blazed down from the heavens it was impossible to judge the time of death. Castus had been told that the settlement boasted less than forty inhabitants, but the reeking mess gave the illusion of there being more than there was.

He regarded the scene coolly, his soul hardened to such things. He could not say the same for Giento; the vagrant had vomited upon seeing the bodies, lying broken and ravaged as they were.

"Gather dry wood and start a fire, I shall search the settlement." Giento nodded and rushed off with his hand pressed firmly against his mouth.

As gruesome as the sight of so many men, women and children lying broken and abused was, it was preferable to finding corpses with naught but puncture wounds in their necks. These people would not rise again, the period of time was proof enough for that, as vampires tended to rise within one or two days of their death. Carrion eaters being present also gave credence to that thought, as they only ate the flesh of the dead, not those that would rise again.

The search of Graan proved uneventful; the vampires had moved on, no doubt to Tilbon. The only finding of any interest was in one of the huts. One of the walls looked as though something had crashed through it. Something had fought back, at least.

Returning to the scene of the slaughter, the priest was not surprised to see Giento standing well away. He had brought the wood Castus had asked for and left it as close as he dared move towards the dead.

"You can wait inside the wagon if it pleases you, vagrant. The smell will get no better here." Giento held his hand up in a sign of acknowledgement and rushed off to the wagon. If it were not for the grim circumstances, Castus might have smiled at the man's weak stomach.

****

Giento had taken no time to argue when the priest had suggested that he leave. He had run as fast as his legs could carry him back to the wagon and slammed the door with such force that it awoke Saim, the trader, who had dozed off while waiting for the pair to return. He could still smell the reek of dead and decaying flesh on his clothes, he could *feel* it clinging to his skin and burning the back of his throat.

The first thing he had done upon reaching the safety of the wagon was sit with his head between his legs and try to will what was left of his breakfast to stay down. *Just my luck, get a slap up meal like that and I spend the day bringin' it back up*, he thought to himself. Seeing the dead was nothing new to him, stumbling through life as a sell-sword had given him more sights of corpses than most had of the living. Giento had always been there when the killing happened, though, never afterwards. Never witnessing the effect that the heat of the sun and the appetites of crows had on the bodies.

The wooden panel slid open, revealing Saim's bearded face. With the hat he wore, he almost looked like a dwarf from the fairytales Giento had been told as a child. "Are we leaving? What's with all the noise?" he boomed.

It took Giento a moment to compose himself, he did not want to risk speaking and vomiting at the same time. "No," was all he managed to say before his lurching stomach forced him to thrust his head back between his knees.

"What's the matter with you lad? You've gone pale."

Giento refused to gamble with the contents of his stomach by talking, instead he merely grunted and waved his hand annoyingly at Saim. The trader grunted in return and took the hint, muttering to himself beneath his breath as he closed the panel.

He could not really judge the passage of time when all he thought about was not vomiting; it had not seemed long until the wind brought with it the scent of smoke. Giento took a deep breath, welcoming the scent that would normally send a man into a coughing fit if he inhaled too much.

Despite the cleansing flames and the thick, heady scent of the smoke he could still smell the putrescent odor of rot and decay. It was not as prevalent, but to a man whose stomach was as sensitive as his was at that point in time it was all too easy to pick out.

The panel slid back and Saim pushed his face as close to the opening as he could, no doubt trying to catch some air that was not laced with smoke. "What in the name of the All-Father has that priest done? All of Graan's alight!" he bellowed at Giento.

Giento's eyes widened and he stood bolt upright, rocking gently on his feet as his queasiness reminded him that it had not gone away. "He's done what?"

"Burned the whole bloody place to the ground, that's what he's done!" Saim looked back towards Graan, a coughing fit brought his red face back to the opening, his eyes glistening with tears brought on by the smoke. "Now, I'm not one to talk ill of the priesthood…but…but this is madness!"

Pushing the wagon door open, Giento was greeted by a rush of smoke that poured down towards them, carried by the wind as if it, too, was trying to flee the fire. Castus' silhouette could be seen looming out of the oppressive smoke, walking ponderously towards the wagon like some harbinger of death. *He said the smell wouldn't get any better*, Giento thought to himself, *damn fool could 'ave said he was gonna set the whole place alight!*

Not knowing what else to do, he simply stood there, his face aghast, awaiting the return of his paymaster. There had to be a reason for such destruction. Perhaps Castus had found something amongst the huts? Perhaps there was some taint that was too foul to be left uncleansed? He regained what little composure he had left, determined not to look fazed by the man's actions.

The priest strode towards the wagon, a look of satisfaction about his swagger and a glint of achievement in his unfeeling eyes. He must have found something that demanded purging, why else would he appear so smug?

It seemed to take an eternity for Castus to arrive back at the wagon. He truly looked like some grim reaper emerging from the smoke, his hat and trench coat did him no favors in that instance.

A thousand questions bounced around in Giento's mind, yet the image of this holy warrior striding forth from the flames quelled his curiosity. Did he really want to ask questions he probably did not want to hear the answer to? Was sating his curiosity worth the risk of angering a man who had just burned an entire settlement to the ground? He had to remind himself that the settlement was already dead; burning it did no real damage. After all, what use were homes to people who were dust and less than dust?

"You look unwell." Giento blinked in surprise, he had been too wrapped up in his own thoughts. So much so that he had not noticed that the priest was standing mere feet away.

"The smell," Giento said. He tried swallowing but found that his mouth was dry. Had he not argued point blank with the priest before? Why was he finding it so difficult to find the courage to do so now? The answer would be as clear as day if it were not covered in so much smoke. Never before had he witnessed the callous nature of his paymaster, not on this scale.

"It was repugnant, was it not? It had seeped into the settlement. The huts were laced with the putrescence, the very walls reeked. You were wise to leave when you did, vagrant." Castus nodded his head to Giento and turned to face Saim, who was trying to hide the fact that he was eavesdropping. “Ready your horses, trader. We leave as soon as you are able.”

Saim nodded. “Just as well, all this smoke was starting to bother the horses. Can’t push a horse to run if it’s got no air to breathe,” he joked in his booming tone.

“Quite,” Castus replied before disappearing into the wagon.

The smell? *That* was the reason he had set fire to the village? Giento shuddered at the thought that something as trivial as a bad smell could drive a man to burn an entire settlement. He resolved to probe a little harder and see if the stench was the primary reason behind the priest’s burning of Graan. The ways of the priesthood were unknown to him. Such extremes might well be commonplace.

Saim cleared his throat a little too loudly for it to be simply an everyday gesture. His chubby red face was poking around the edge of the driver’s compartment; his beard had caught a few specks of ash that had blown over on the wind. Giento took the hint and got back in the cabin.

They rode in silence for the most part. Castus had informed him that they would be entering the city via the main trade road. Giento had been stationed at Tilbon for many weeks with a previous employer; he had found that it was relatively easy—as far as cities went—to find your way. The main trade road soon became the South Road which, when one travelled far enough, became the North Road and was the main route through the centre of the city. The streets were numbered and helpfully followed on from one another. He smiled to himself. This was why the priest was paying him, for his knowledge of the Empire.

“You’re curious.” Castus’ voice startled Giento. The tone of his voice was not a questioning one; there would be no point in lying to the man now. He doubted he could if he wanted to. Castus had proved to be a perceptive individual and not one easily taken with lies. He wondered if the priest had already arrived at the conclusion that his guide was not some illustrious mercenary, that in actual fact he was being led by a coward.

“Why burn a place just for the smell?” Try as he might, Giento could not mask the distaste in his voice.

“That is what you worry over? You don’t care what I did, merely my reasons for doing so?”

“It wasn’t needed. Why do it? Fun?”

Castus' eyes darkened. "Nothing I do is for my own enjoyment, vagrant. I need not tell you why I do anything, but I believe that it is important to gain the trust of a man I expect to lead my way.

"Among the first things we are taught upon becoming postulants is that evil leaves behind hints of its passing. My mentor likened it to a fingerprint of damnation. The foulness of the stench was proof enough to my eyes—and to my nostrils—that no matter how many years pass by, the repugnance of Graan will only fester. It will never die.

"It is the belief of the temple that evildoers are born from evil lands, and as such it is the duty of my order to purify potential moral threats such as Graan."

Giento gulped without realizing it, the sound seemed unnaturally loud now that Castus had finished talking. "And fire is the only way?" he asked.

Castus shook his head. "It is merely the quickest. Cities need cleansing far more often than small hamlets in the middle of the country. Prayers and rituals are used to rid them of what taint they harbor."

"Could you not have prayed for Graan?" Giento asked.

"The correct prayers need to be recited by a pair of priests, and the proper rituals take days to enact. Destruction is never my preferred route, but we are pressed for time. I would rather destroy one hamlet that is of no use to anyone," Castus lowered his head as if in respect, his eyes seemingly saddened by his words, "than allow for others to be ravaged by the creatures we hunt."

The wooden panel slid open and for once, Giento noted, Castus didn't look annoyed by the occurrence.

"We're coming up to the city gates. Anywhere in particular you want me to take you? I could recommend a good bath house." Saim's booming laughter followed the quip.

"I think a hot bath would do us the world of good," Castus replied.

The wagon continued on at a lively pace. The road beneath the wheels became gradually smoother as they got closer to the city—for which Giento was eternally grateful as he still felt queasy.

Unsure of what further questions to ask, he resolved to ask none. Silence was better than any inane conversation he could start. He had just been told all that he desired, perhaps more than he deserved to know. The workings of the priesthood were the business of the priesthood, after all. He should feel privileged that he had had the knowledge imparted to him. Yet all he felt was sick.

After what felt like an unnatural length of time, the wagon ground to a halt. Castus made to exit the vehicle but stopped upon hearing Saim's raised voice echoing loudly. He was shouting at someone. Before Giento had the chance to stand, Castus had flung himself out of the wagon, his sword drawn and his trench coat flapping ominously behind him. Giento reluctantly grasped for the silver dagger at his waist and slowly followed his paymaster out of the wagon.

To his surprise there were no vampires standing between them and the city gates. Just why that conclusion had seemed the most plausible what with the sun beating down from high above was beyond him. Three men stood atop the gates shaking their heads. They wore blood-red cloaks that fluttered gently in the breeze. They were the City Guard; their principal role was to filter who they let into the city. Giento looked to the large black gates. It was unusual for them to be closed. As far as he remembered, he had only ever seen them wide open with a barrier across the mouth of the entranceway at the very most.

"I got a priest in that there wagon. You can't turn away a priest!" Saim yelled to the men stationed atop the wall.

The guards looked down towards where Castus stood. One man tried to shield his eyes from the glare of the sun, but Giento expected that was more for show so that he had a good reason for detaining a priest for longer than was necessary. From their body language it was easy to tell that they could see Castus for what he was. Whether Tilbon was under lockdown or not, no man could refuse the will of the priesthood. After all, whatever they were trying to keep in—or out—was most certainly not going to be a warrior priest. Not if they valued their lives.

At length, the black gates of Tilbon slid open wide enough for the wagon to trundle through. The guards gestured frantically for them to hurry up so they could close the gates once the priest's retinue had passed. Giento suspected he knew the reason for the lockdown, and he was almost certain that no vampire would be held by high walls.

Hopefully the fiends had already left.

Chapter Seven

Finding the undying children was easy. Keeping track of them was a different matter entirely. It was not because they had any skill in evasion, they were not even aware that they were being watched. It was because Conrad's attention was taken by something of far more interest to him than mere children.

For the past three nights he and his family had tracked the vampire children and watched their feeding habits; how they chose their prey, how little they kept themselves hidden from view of the cattle. Each of those nights Conrad had waited patiently. He had waited for Sallus to order them to split up and assess the level of destruction being caused by these abhorrations. Each time the order came, he made the most of his solitude.

The very moment he was free of his family, he sped off towards the slums, noting any instance of vampire feeding along the way so that he did not return empty-handed. His priority, of course, was the woman whose beauty had drowned out that of Vitria. The simple slum dweller that had been sitting mere feet from his sister-in-death.

The woman—he had found her name to be Jessamine—was easy to find. Her scent called out to him, burying all others beneath the weight of its intoxicating aroma. Not once did he approach her. He simply watched from afar, judging her actions in order to make some sort of image in his mind as to the person she was. When the time came, and it would come, for him to reach out to her, he would have nothing tarnish the experience. Every whim would be catered for. If he found her to be fond of roses, then he would lure her to a place brimming with them. If she enjoyed an evening meal surrounded by beauty and tranquility, then he would take her to a midnight garden where she could feast beside a pond or gently flowing river. Whatever desire her heart held would be catered for.

It would be perfect.

Perfection came at a cost. The pain of seeing her but not being able to reach out and feel the warmth of her flesh, the delicate thrumming of her pulse beneath his lifeless fingers, was infuriating. To have her so close and not be able to utter a single word in her ear.

She would be his first. His first get. He wondered if Sallus would allow it, he had heard no word of either Nicholas or Vitria siring another. Were Sallus' children allowed to create their own? It mattered not to him, no man, be he living or undead would keep him from Jessamine. Sallus had said that there was perfection in unlife, but he was wrong. There *would* be perfection in unlife, and its name would be Jessamine.

Merely thinking about siring her brought the bloodlust to the forefront of his mind. There were still two more nights before he could feed once more, yet oddly enough he did not feel the thirst as much when he was near the beautiful slum-girl. Perhaps it was his thoughts of the woman that drove all lesser feelings—and everything else *was* a lesser feeling compared to what he felt for her—to the back of his mind? Or was it the thought of tasting blood so close to her and not being able to control himself?

No!

She would be safe as long as he was close. Nothing would harm her, not even him. Thoughts of the few vampire children that hunted in the slums came to him. Sallus had decreed that they were not to reveal themselves to this coven until the time was right. Until they had formed some kind of plan to combat them. But killing them would not reveal anything. None would survive in order to spread word that other vampires were in the city. Their deaths would be passed off as an unlikely victory on the part of the City Guard.

His thoughts trailed from the children to his new family and how he rued their decision to move their lair from the *Ferryman's Inn* to an abandoned butchery a fair distance from the slums. It meant that protecting Jessamine was far more difficult than he would have liked, yet at the same time it meant that there were three fewer vampires close to her that he had to worry about. The mere thought of one of them breaking her luscious skin and draining the blood from her neck set his mind alight with anger.

Conrad was certain that he could defend her from Sallus; his sire was reasonable and could no doubt be bargained with. He could not kill Sallus for fear of losing his mind and hurting Jessamine himself, but he could do everything short of killing him to protect her. He was beyond certain that he could defend her from Nicholas. Nothing would keep him from ripping his brother-in-death apart if he so much as looked in her general direction. The hatred he felt for Nicholas made him almost want for his brother to try and take her from him.

Almost.

Vitria, now she was another matter entirely. He could not say whether or not he could raise a hand in anger against such a lovely creature. She was prone to jealousy when her beauty was in question, and if she thought a mere mortal threatened her status in some way…

He shook the thought of him standing impotently as Vitria killed the one he loved from his mind.

"If she tries I shall maim her!" he told himself, not entirely believing the conviction of his own words.

It frustrated him, as he sat at the same table as when he had first laid eyes on her, that she favored another with her attention. It was not the fact that she was oblivious to his existence that irked him; it was the fact that the object of her affection seemed oblivious to her. How undeserving! To have such a wondrous creature as Jessamine drooling over a man, only for the fool not to notice!

A lowly barman, of all things, held a higher place in her heart than he! Even in his most embarrassing moments—Conrad had witnessed the man fall and spill the contents of his tray on many an occasion—she beamed at him with loving eyes. *If only she would regard me with such adoration. I would need but a second of her attention, and I would not miss it. Not like this lowlife.*

Conrad wanted nothing more than to call the barman over. What he would do when the man arrived was difficult to say. He was of two minds where that was concerned. He could simply call the man over and enjoy the warmth of Jessamine's gaze as her eyes followed the fool lovingly. Then she would see him. Then she would notice him and see that there was more to life than lusting after a man who didn't know she existed.

The alternative, of course, was to call him over and dash his skull against the table until his heart refused to beat. It had felt empowering to do such a thing to the ranger, but to do it to the object of his love's affection would be gratifying beyond all measure. Of course, her eyes would be locked on the barman, meaning that she would witness his murder as would the entirety of the tavern. Conrad scowled, his forehead creasing with the effort. To kill him now would be detrimental to the veil of secrecy that hung over his family.

He slammed his fist against the table; the noise was muffled almost to the extent of it being non-existent due to the drunken rabble that surrounded him. He would do neither. He could do neither. To kill him—as satisfying as that would be—would be selfish. He might have steeled himself to the possibility that he would kill his family if they endangered her, but they had done nothing yet. Summoning him over to simply bask in Jessamine's gaze was also out of the question. With his competition so close, he was not certain he could keep himself from ripping the man's head from his shoulders. The rationing had taken its toll and only seeing *her* had kept the bloodlust from rising. Even now his fingers dug into the soft wood of the table as he thought of the barman. No, his anger *would* betray him.

Conrad rose to his feet. Sallus would be expecting him to return with news of the undying children and if he was gone for too long, his sire would ask too many questions. He desperately wanted to keep Jessamine a secret from them. He was under no illusions that if they caught wind of his feelings for her, they would kill her. They would see her as a weakness, a liability to his state of mind. Nothing could be further from the truth. She was his strength. The light in the darkness that kept the madness at bay. The proof of that was evident when he was away from her. He would become irritable and irrational, slipping back into the mad, blood-driven mentality that had emerged the very moment Sallus had imposed the rationing on him.

He took a deep breath, taking in the cocktail of scents that filled the *Ferryman's Inn*. Jessamine's aroma was unique and easily picked out. Conrad let the smell of her fill his nostrils as he slipped out of the tavern, still as unnoticed by the one he desired as when he had arrived.

****

"He's late again. You gave him the closest area to survey, and he is late again!" Nicholas moaned. He began pacing the old butcher's shop they now used as their lair. It had fallen into ill repair and had long since been abandoned by its owner. The smell of rotting meat clung to the air despite whatever had created the foul stench having been removed long ago. To a normal man the smell would have been overpowering, to a vampire it was positively rancid.

"He has until the sun comes up before I would consider him late, Nicholas," Sallus said coolly.

"We have stalked these abominations the length and breadth of the city, and here we are. Why, when all you give him is the area surrounding this…this hovel, can he not find his way back before we do?"

Sallus looked around the dank, filth-covered room, his expression thoughtful. "I do not see Vitria either. Why is it that you do not protest her lateness, I wonder?"

"We know we can trust Vitria!" Nicholas snarled.

It amazed Sallus how much sway Vitria held over men, especially her brothers. Nicholas was prone to outbursts. His stance was almost threatening, as if Sallus' words against Vitria had been a personal insult to the man himself.

"So that's what it boils down to? You do not trust your brother?"

"He is no brother of mine!" Nicholas hissed.

"You have no say in who I sire. You have no input on who I bring into this family," Sallus' eyes were locked on Nicholas, the weight of his stare cowing his son-in-death. "You would do well to remember that distrust of my kin is distrust of me. If you seek to cause trouble amongst my family, Nicholas, I shall be forced to interject myself. And make no mistake; it shan't be Conrad who suffers my wrath." He had spoken coolly, yet his words had the desired effect. Nicholas backed down, all trace of aggression had left his body and his eyes had lost their luster.

Sallus watched his son. It would not be long before he tried to stir up trouble again. He had been scalded in such a way before, but it never had any lasting effect. Just as Conrad had an attraction to beautiful women, Nicholas had rage and jealousy. They were perhaps the worst things a vampire could bring with him into unlife. It was remarkable that his combustible personality had not got him killed.

In his infancy, Nicholas had been near-impossible to control. He had forced both Sallus and Vitria to move repeatedly for fear of being discovered. It was ironic that one who had such a troubled time as a newborn was giving one such as Conrad, who was fairing far better, such a difficult time.

"We have roughly three hours of darkness left this night. I think we have all the information we are going to attain on these creatures," Sallus said, a smile crossing his face. "I want you to hunt one and bring it back here. Alive."

Nicholas' sullen expression changed to a grin. He was never more content than when he had the chance to test his strength against another. It was a trait that made him so easy to manipulate and was also the main reason why Sallus had kept him around for so long. Thinkers might opt to take a long view of the situation whereas Nicholas would do no such thing. He would charge head-on toward the enemy rather than slink around like some scheming coward. To Nicholas, nothing was a deterrent. He would gladly fight any foe even if it meant certain death, perhaps even more so in that instance.

"I want you to take Conrad." Those six words were all it took for Nicholas' grin to turn sour.

"What? Why? He will only alert the creatures to our presence. Let me do this for you. Alone," Nicholas pleaded. "Or if I must take someone, let me take Vitria. We have both watched these children since before you arrived, she deserves her share of the glory."

Sallus' expression was unmoving. "You will take Conrad and I expect you to keep him on the straight and narrow. If, for some reason, he does alert our quarry to your presence, then I shall place the blame solely on your shoulders. This is a chance for you to prove yourself to me, Nicholas. I do hope you won't disappoint."

****

The foul smell of the dwelling they had chosen to make their own came to him long before he could see the place. It was one drawback of having such keen senses; the most repugnant of smells were amplified beyond comprehension. Even those that were so weak that they were undetectable to mere mortals were striking to a vampire. Just why ones as strong as they had to lower themselves to squatting in an abandoned butchery was beyond him.

Conrad had found Sallus and Nicholas awaiting his return. Sallus looked smugly pleased with himself whereas Nicholas wore a mask of annoyance. *Nothing new with brother dearest,* he mused to himself.

He was shocked to learn that Sallus wanted them to capture one of the children. Not shocked because it meant he had to spend the remainder of the night alone with Nicholas, but shocked because it meant that he would need to find another reason to wander the streets alone in search of Jessamine. Watching the children had been the perfect cover for his obsession with watching *her*.

Nicholas was standing as far from his brother as possible, his eyes narrowed in accusation. He no doubt wondered what had kept him for such a length of time. He would not find out. He *could not* find out.

Vitria had returned moments after Conrad had made his appearance. Her pixie-like face turned in his direction, her chocolate eyes not leaving his for a moment. Nicholas had not been slow in noticing the fact, his guttural snarls echoed off the walls.

"You have the smell of the slums about you, Conrad. I tasked Vitria with patrolling them, so do tell me why you found it necessary to encroach upon your sister's territory." Sallus' voice was flat and held no emotion. It was the tone of a man who knew he was right and wanted only answers.

Conrad's mind began to race. Vitria had been in the slums? Had she seen him? Did she know about Jessamine? It would explain why she had been staring at him so intently. *If only Jessamine stared at me the way Vitria had just then. If only once...* Conrad shook his head to rid himself of the thoughts. He could not allow his mind to wander now.

"I was following one of the children. I didn't know Vitria was hunting in the slums, otherwise I would have stayed out and left it to her." He hoped his voice did not betray the lie.

"You followed one of the children from the Middle District all the way to the slums? I had not thought they held preference to where they fed. This sheds new light on our quarry. Perhaps they are not as single-minded as we had thought." Sallus' words made Conrad curse himself inwardly. His lie had made the undying children out to be more intelligent than they were. That new information could cause Sallus to misjudge them at a later date and that could cost all four of them.

"I did not see him, so it is a good thing he came into the slums to follow the child. It would have been information we would not have known otherwise." Vitria's stare seemed only to intensify as she spoke. Something in her eyes made Conrad think she was lying. She *had* seen him. He was certain of it.

"Let's go, newborn," Nicholas growled. "We don't have long before the sun comes up." He stormed past Conrad, grabbing him by the arm as he did so, and dragged him from the room.

It pained Conrad to leave without having the opportunity to confront Vitria first. He needed to know what she had seen. It was painstakingly obvious that she had seen him in the slums…but did she know why? What if she did? What if she used the last few hours of darkness to kill Jessamine?

He tried as best he could to remove all such thoughts from his mind. Why could not it be Nicholas that could potentially harm her? Then he would have no problem in choosing a course of action. The only option for him was to find one of the children fast so he could return and ensure Vitria did nothing without his knowledge. Whether he had to make up an excuse or not, he assured himself that he *would* spend each and every night in the slums. It was the only way for her to be safe.

A smile crossed his face. The sole purpose of a vampire was to feed from humans, yet here he was protecting one of them. With his mind being so preoccupied, Conrad had neglected the path he trod. It took a severe amount of effort to keep himself upright after losing his footing on a patch of grime. Nicholas looked back over his shoulder, no doubt angered by the noise.

"Keep quiet, newborn. You will alert the children that we are coming."

Nicholas kept ahead and, surprisingly, kept himself to himself. Conrad had grown used to the seemingly endless rage Nicholas had for him. It felt odd, to say the least, not to have some form of hostility directed his way. He could tell from the way Nicholas clenched his fists and from the tightness of his jaw that he was finding it remarkably difficult to keep the peace. Nicholas had seen how Vitria had done nothing but stare at Conrad since returning, and the fact must have irked him.

Tilbon looked far less confined and imposing as they sped their way across the rooftops of the Middle District. He was glad that Nicholas led the way, for he had done little in the way of spying on their targets. He had seen several on his way to the *Ferryman's Inn*, but going anywhere near the slums was out of the question.

Nicholas did nothing but stare dead ahead, his eyes fixed on their path. Conrad wondered if his brother would lose his unnatural self-control if he were to become distracted. He did not test the theory. After all, Conrad had not fed for the better part of a week and could feel himself growing steadily weaker. He had covered a lot of ground since his last feeding and the exertions were starting to show.

He was so lost in his own musings that he barely reacted in time to Nicholas stopping suddenly ahead. He cursed himself for letting his thoughts distract him twice in such a short period of time. His brother held one pale hand up, still not deigning to look at him.

"I smell them. They are close," Nicholas said curtly before dashing over the next rooftop and dropping to the street out of sight.

Conrad sniffed the air. It was there, the unusual smell of unlife. He had grown accustomed to the scents of his family, but the smell of other vampires wrinkled his nose. With the unclean stench of the vampire children came the smell of the cattle. His hunger clawed at his mind ravenously, not allowing him to separate the contrasting scents with any ease. He longed for Jessamine to be near. Having her close was like having his own personal drug. While she was present the bloodlust went away, his mind keeping the hunger at bay for fear that he might lose control and feed from her also. When she was away there was no such restraint holding him back.

The urge to follow the predominant scent of the cattle was almost too strong to deny, but deny it he must. To falter now would do nothing but prove Nicholas right. It would show Sallus that he was wrong in bestowing the gift of unlife onto him. Conrad did not care how much he suffered for his hunger, he would not allow Nicholas one moment of satisfaction.

He found himself to be alone when he dropped from the rooftops. Nicholas was out of sight but not hard to find. His scent was too familiar to Conrad to become lost amongst others. Sallus had once remarked that blindness to a vampire was considered a loss of scent rather than sight. At first the notion had sounded ridiculous, but now he truly understood what his sire meant. He could pick out the exact path his brother-in-death had taken. If he had given Nicholas a two-hour head start, he would still be able to find his way by scent alone.

A shrill scream pierced the silence.

Conrad's head snapped to the left instinctively. They were making it all too easy to be found. This same area was frequented by the children on an almost nightly basis, despite the ever-growing chance that armed guards would eventually be placed to police such areas rife with murder. Conrad thought back to the ranger Sallus had questioned in the woods. The man had stated that the authorities of Tilbon were well aware of the acts of vampirism occurring within their city, so why was nothing being done to counter it? On their nightly vigils they had seen the occasional priest patrolling the streets of the Upper District, but the men had none of the zeal or determination that Sallus' tormenter possessed. It was as though Tilbon feared the evil that lurked within its dark walls.

Eagerly following his brother's scent, Conrad stalked his way closer to the source of the scream. *Not long now*, he thought. Soon they could return and he could refocus on Vitria and what she knew.

Nicholas' scent led him to a small series of winding alleyways. His brother was camped in the shadows, watching as one of the children drained the life out of a fat, balding man whose once prominent screams had slowly and painfully turned into a drowning gurgle. Long curls of auburn hair hung down to the child's waist and a little red bow was stationed atop its head, a fashion sense the majority of the female children seemed to have adopted. The child wore a white dress that reached to her ankles and gore-splattered black shoes adorned her tiny feet. Amazingly, the white of her clothes seemed to be free of blood, a feat Conrad was still unsuccessful in emulating.

Nicholas held his hand up to indicate silence. It frustrated Conrad that the brute thought he needed to be told. The shadows hugged the walls of the buildings that lined the alleyway. Nicholas crept forward, keeping himself out of sight of his prey. Conrad noticed that not for a second did he lower his hand. It was not just silence that he wanted; it was for Conrad to keep out of the action. He wanted to snarl in frustration but fought back the urge to do so. Instead he satisfied himself by hoping that the child tore Nicholas' arms off and beat him to death with them.

In a motion that was almost too fast for Conrad to follow, Nicholas lunged at the child as it made to drop the dried-out body of its prey. His momentum took the child clean off its feet. It screamed in pain and shock, the sound it made was unlike anything a human throat could ever hope to reproduce.

Conrad watched as the child thrashed violently beneath Nicholas' iron grip. He thought of how the scene might look to people looking in: a brute of a man assaulting a girl who looked no older than five years of age. No man would think the girl had the strength to tear his head from his shoulders.

Nicholas grinned sadistically as he forced the child's arms to its sides. He turned his head toward Conrad. "You can come out now, newborn," he called mockingly.

Conrad did nothing to stifle the snarl that leapt from his throat. The look of disgust that crossed his face easily matched the look of hatred worn by the girl. It was hard to conceive that such an angelic-looking creature could be so dangerous. His mind flicked back to Vitria and how he had thought the same upon discovering her true nature.

"We haven't time for your bravado. Let's just—" Conrad was pitched from his feet as something crashed hard into his spine. The sound of his head thudding against a nearby wall was drowned out by yet more inhuman screaming.

"There's another! Kill it, newborn. Kill it!" Nicholas shouted, refusing to release his grip on the girl.

Conrad barely had time to turn his head to his attacker before the child had leapt at him, forcing him to the ground with his momentum. The child began hammering its tiny fists into his face. Had it not been for the fact that he was starved of blood, he would have been able to fight off his assailant with ease. The child— who could have been the girl's identical twin, were it not for his closely-cropped hair and opposing gender—felt uncommonly strong as it sat atop him, thrashing about with its fists and feet. The boy had no flair for fighting; it was obvious he was getting by on blind rage rather than any semblance of skill.

Rage enough to mirror that of the child flared up within him and he slammed his knee into the boy's back, sending him hurtling into the same wall he himself had been dashed against moments before. He leapt to his feet the moment he was free of the child, ignoring the way his nose hung limply or how puffed-up his left eye socket felt. They would heal. Both the priest and Sallus had proved that with their beatings.

The child was on its feet staring at Conrad, a smile flickering across its gentle-looking face. It looked as though it wanted to taunt him, as though it was mulling over just how to insult his weaknesses.

Conrad did not give it the chance.

He lunged forward, hand outstretched and ready to grasp the boy's skull. The child saw the move ahead of time and danced out of his reach, its laughter tinkling like wind chimes.

"Newborn, what are you waiting for? Kill it! It is just a child!" Nicholas shouted in frustration.

Conrad regarded his brother with a wicked glare. "This is what happens when you starve a man! He weakens," Conrad spat back.

The child's laughter grew in its intensity and for the first time since he had laid eyes on the abominations, he heard one speak. "Hungry, are we? Child's play." The boy's voice was a harsh contrast to his heavenly laughter. His voice was not as light and soft as Conrad had imagined. It sounded pained and distorted. Disturbingly so.

"The blood of a rat would give me more than enough energy to best a child!" Conrad hissed.

The child looked around mockingly. "How sad, then, that you don't have a rat."

Conrad roared in anger and quickly closed the gap between him and the boy. Still wearing its smug smile, the child tried to evade him once more but Conrad was ready. He grasped the child's wrist as it attempted to spin out of his reach, lifted it into the air with a sudden yank of his arm and slammed it back down to the stone ground beneath. The sound of the impact was sickening, like meat slapping against a wall.

Conrad wasted no time in digging his knee into the boy's chest, hearing bones snap beneath his weight. He looked into the child's eyes. Where he would have expected to see pain or fear he only saw anger and the burning desire to kill.

"Kill it, you have it where you want it," Nicholas shouted, holding the girl tightly in a massive bear hug.

In that moment the realization dawned on him. He did not know how to kill a vampire, not without fire or silver at least. The thought had not crossed his mind until now and he cursed himself for that fact. He was certain that if he let the child go he would not get this opportunity again. As prideful as he was, Conrad could not hide the fact that he was running on empty. If the child escaped now it would have little trouble finishing him off.

"What are you waiting for, newborn? Kill it!" Nicholas shouted, impatience thick in his voice.

"I don't know how." Conrad's face twisted in a mixture of annoyance and embarrassment.

The boy's face split in a grin and his efforts at struggling to break free redoubled. His tinkling laughter cut through the silence caused by Conrad's words. He could not see his brother-in-death, his eyes firmly fixed on the writhing child beneath him, but he was certain that Nicholas was either stunned into silence or shaking his head in disgust.

"Tell me how! Before this thing breaks free," Conrad shouted.

The only answer that came was a high-pitched scream that seemed to last for eternity, never really quietening. Without warning the wailing stopped as suddenly as it had started, a dull *thud thud* was the only noise distinguishable in the darkness. Conrad wanted to crane his neck to see what had happened but he did not dare take his eyes off the child. The boy, however, had no choice but to witness what had occurred. Conrad's smile grew as the boy's disappeared, his eyes seemed to retreat further back into their sockets, terror wrought across his tiny face.

"It doesn't matter, newborn. We shall just take the boy." Conrad turned upon hearing Nicholas' voice, satisfied that the boy had ceased his writhing. He saw the body of the girl and several feet beyond, a mass of hair. It did not take much imagination to guess what Nicholas had done. He had torn her head from her shoulders with his bare hands.

"I'll carry the child, I don't trust you not to lose him."

For once Conrad found himself in agreement with one of Nicholas' barbed comments. The struggle to best the child had been fought on a knife's edge. He was so weak that the battle could have gone either way, neither he nor the child were ever truly in control. He dug his knee a little harder into the child's chest, eliciting a gulp of pain before he stood up to allow Nicholas to take the boy.

"This would have been different had it happened tomorrow night. I would have fed and this child would have been no match."

"Tomorrow? You can't feed for three nights. Don't you remember the wolves you feasted on? Sallus gives nothing away for free." There was no emotion in Nicholas' voice although Conrad was sure he detected the hint of a smile as his brother turned away from him.

He tugged at his hair, tearing thin strands of blonde from his scalp. The struggle with the boy had sapped the majority of his reserves. If Sallus needed him to do *anything* physical in the near future, he would have to feed. He doubted he would have the strength to best a human in combat now, let alone another of these vampire children. Conrad shuddered despite himself as he thought of the priest. If the man had followed them despite the warning Sallus had given, Conrad was certain there would be no surviving a fight with him. The priest was different to the average mortal man, the gifts of speed and immense strength seemed to be rendered almost inert when faced with the priesthood's zealous nature. The blow Conrad had struck had been at the base of the spine, a normal man would have been snapped in two without a doubt.

Sallus would have answers to his questions, answers that Conrad resolved to seek out as soon as he found himself alone with his sire. Sallus had, of course, mentioned how weakened a vampire became when fighting one of the priesthood, but he had left so much more untold.

Despite it being painfully obvious that he knew little of his new life, he did not want the others hearing of his worries. He was far too proud to give too much away to anyone other than Sallus. His sire would expect questions where his siblings would expect knowledge. Nicholas had been witness to his shortcomings with a mere child, and he would allow the man no more such scenes if he could help it.

Chapter Eight

Castus had reluctantly agreed with Giento to spend their first evening inside Tilbon resting. The vagrant had argued that they had not slept well since leaving Cabblehiem a week previous, and hunting the vampires fatigued would do nothing but give the creatures an easy time.

They had been informed by members of the City Guard—after much apologizing for first being refused entry—that vampires had plagued the city for well over a month now. The news was grim, indeed, for it meant that Sallus and his newly-sired accomplice were not the only fiends within the black walls of Tilbon. There was no concrete evidence as to their numbers, but murder victims had been found across all sectors of the city with puncture wounds across the length of their body and very little blood remaining within on an almost nightly basis.

The priest's fears had escalated after their first night in Tilbon. A messenger had been sent by the City Guard to inform him of what was described by those in the area as 'horrific screaming' in the city's Middle District. Upon hearing the news, Castus had shot a fierce glance towards his guide for his suggestion of rest.

The messenger led the pair to the Middle District and left them to search the area alone, presumably the man was not paid enough to hunt the undead. Castus found himself wondering if, now that he was present, the City Guard would offload the majority of the vampire-related workload onto him. They were frightened of the beasts, that much had been evident from the conversations he had had with members of the guard. They were also shocked by the fact that he was actively hunting the creatures down, for as far as he could discern, the resident priests of Tilbon had wanted little to do with the matter outside of the wealthier sectors of the city. He had come across priests with such attitudes in his home city of Gurdalin. Many believed their priorities were to those who donated to their coffers, and since slum dwellers had no money to feed themselves, let alone donate to the temple, they were not worthy of the priesthood's time.

It was attitudes like that that damned the whole Empire. To allow a vampire to feed was to allow it to grow stronger and become a real threat to the security of the city. The fact that the priests seemed to be turning a blind eye to the matter for fear of associating with commoners was beyond infuriating. What made matters worse was that if his brethren had done their job within Tilbon, hunting down Sallus and his accomplice would be nowhere near as difficult as it now was. Instead of two vampires to worry about, he now had an unknown number to be wary of. If Sallus were to flee the city, Castus would find himself torn. Would he abandon Tilbon to its fate and rush off in pursuit of his own personal vendetta? Or would his sense of duty make him see reason and force him to stay and deal with the more pressing issues of a potential nest of the creatures?

Truth be told, he could not say. He dearly wished that crossroad would not present itself. Sallus had stayed in Gurdalin for a good length of time after all; perhaps he would do so again now that he had reached another city. Castus forced the thoughts of Sallus and his future choices from his mind. He needed to have a clear head to analyze the streets of Tilbon for a sign of the prior night's occurrences. He was under no illusion as to what he would eventually find: a body.

As the search wore on, more and more of the City Guard began to lend their aid. He was certain he knew where their apparent bravery stemmed from. Looking up at the sun, he wondered if they would have been so eager to offer help were it dark out. The answer was obvious from considering the bodies turning up drained of blood. Even frightened men armed with fire and silver would deter a vampire. The guard no doubt kept to their high walls and their patrol rooms during the twilight hours, too afraid of what they did not understand. In a sense, the guards were no different from the uncaring priests of Tilbon. Be it inaction or fear, they were as deadly a weapon as a sharpened blade.

"How many you reckon there is in Tilbon, then?" Giento's words brought Castus from his thoughts.

"Well, we know for certain there are two at the very least. The murders are so widespread; that indicates a nest."

"Which are we after? The nest or Sallus?" Giento asked and, by the sound of his voice, either answer was not the one he was looking for.

"The priesthood have forced our hand. They are doing nothing to combat the threat in the less affluent districts of the city, so I'm afraid we must."

Giento gulped. "Both, then?"

"Indeed." Castus looked towards the shining white of the temple, so tall that it was viewable from almost any point in the city. "We have business at the temple also," he said bitterly.

"You're not gonna start trouble with 'em, are you?"

"I will say what needs to be said."

A surge of guardsmen rushing past them took away the chance for Giento to add anything further. Castus thrust his arm out and grabbed hold of one of the red cloaks fluttering past, nearly wrenching its wearer from his feet.

"Has something been found?" he demanded.

The Guardsman fingered his throat in an attempt to try and loosen his cloak which was now choking him because of the force Castus used in restraining him. The priest noted the man's discomfort and released his hold on the garment. The sudden jolt and breathlessness had brought tears to the man's eyes.

He nodded, trying to regain his composure before answering properly. "You could have just followed, your holiness," he managed to say.

Annoyed at the frankness of the man's reply, Castus waved him on with a sharp flick of his hand. The guardsman took the message and carried on after his peers, both Castus and Giento in tow.

The dull black of the buildings reflected little sunlight as they sped past. Castus had grown to like the dimness of the local stone. It was a pleasant contrast to the glaring white of the temples which he was so used to frequenting. He had encountered scarce few temples that did not blind a man when the sun was out. The black of Tilbon was soothing in comparison. It did, however, all look the same save for the minor alterations to the shapes of the buildings themselves. Very little effort had gone into making each dwelling, tavern or place of business stand out. Castus had been told upon arriving that he might need a local to show him the way around Tilbon. The city's confusing nature was by no means friendly to non-natives.

Giento had mentioned that Tilbon had been fashioned that way so as to confuse attackers if ever the city was besieged. It was, for all intents and purposes, a labyrinthine city, and was best navigated by memory alone.

The procession of guardsmen stopped outside an indistinct alleyway that would have been far too easily missed had they not been led there. Castus' brow creased in frustration. *Black walls and shadows. How am I to effectively search such a place without fear of missing most of it?*

Three men strode from the mouth of the alley. Castus noticed only one wore his cloak of office, yet the other two were clearly guardsmen, their tunics showed as much. The foremost held up a hand, two fingers raised and his head hung low in sadness.

"One is a child," he said, voice trembling with a mixture of shock and grief.

Castus pushed through the assembled guardsmen, dragging Giento by the wrist behind him. The sea of red parted to allow him entrance. Although they had all flocked to witness the findings, none wished to see the lifeless body of a child. Many of them must have been parents themselves, it would be too difficult for some to bear.

They were stopped by the guardsman who had first spoken, his hand pressed firmly to his mouth as if to stop himself from vomiting.

"I warn you, priest. It's not a pretty sight. So young, so young," he said, shaking his head as he stood aside to allow them through.

The buzzing of flies echoed as they made their way through the alley and into the circular space beyond. It was a filthy place surrounded by tall, curved walls. An oil lamp that had long burned out would have been the only source of light in this dank place come nightfall.

"What an 'orrid place to meet your end, eh?" Giento said.

"There is no good place to die, vagrant."

Castus saw immediately why the two Guardsmen had returned without their cloaks. The two blood-red garments were laid across what must have been the bodies. One of them was so large that it did not entirely fit beneath the cloak, its podgy limbs sprawling out on either side. Even from this distance Castus could make out bite marks on the wrists. The man's flesh was deathly pale, more so than an average corpse.

"Go and inspect the large one. I shall see to the child," Castus told Giento.

"Are we gonna be burnin' 'em?"

"I expect so, yes."

"Try not to set fire to the whole city, eh?"

Castus let the comment wash over him without reacting. He had not expected the man to warm to the idea of burning the dead again so soon after the incident at Graan. He had told him the reasons, but to one who had not been schooled in the ways of evil and how to effectively combat it, the methods would have a lasting effect.

Flies buzzed eagerly around the red cloaks, furious at having been denied their meal. Castus waved his hand to shoo them away but with little success. The stench of death was too much to keep them gone for long.

He stood above the small body, paying his respects to the dead child beneath the cloak. He had seen too many corpses to count in his tenure as a warrior priest; it was an almost everyday occurrence. But the bodies of children never failed to evoke emotion. The thought that one with so much life ahead of them could have it snatched away so cruelly and at such a young age was despicable.

Castus took hold of the cloak and cast it off the child. His eyes widened in shock as he took in the sight beneath the cloak.

Revulsion coursed through his body. The child's headless corpse lay motionless on the ground. The Guardsmen had gathered the head and laid it beside the body, its dead, glassy eyes staring ever upward.

Somewhere behind him he heard Giento vomit.

He turned to check the condition of the corpse his aide was inspecting, to see how mutilated it must have been to cause such a reaction. The cloak had yet to be taken from the body, instead he found Giento watching what he was doing. It was the headless child that had affected him so.

"How could someone do that to a kid?" he asked.

Castus paid him no attention. Instead he went back to surveying the headless body before him.

"The cause of death was decapitation," he said coolly to himself.

"You don't say? I coulda told you that."

Castus motioned for Giento to come closer.

"I'd rather not, if you don't mind."

"There are no marks of any kind across her body. No puncture wounds on the neck, wrists, legs or anywhere."

Giento started to cough and spat great wads of phlegm onto the floor. "So you're sayin' it wasn't vampires that did her in?" he asked.

"It most certainly was," Castus indicated to the neck and then to the severed head. "There is nothing to suggest the head has been cut. It has been torn from her shoulders with great force."

The sell-sword swayed a little, almost drunkenly. He stumbled to a nearby wall to steady himself.

"Why would a vampire do that?"

"Decapitation is one of the ways in which you can kill a vampire, vagrant."

Giento stood silent in thought for a moment before his eyes suddenly widened with realization. "You're sayin' the kid's a vampire?"

"Was," Castus corrected. "Think about it, it fits perfectly. Sunlight, silver, fire and beheading are all viable ways in which to kill a vampire. Another such creature could hardly use sunlight, fire or silver without fear of injuring or killing itself. That leaves this," he said, pointing to the child's head.

"What do we do now?" Giento asked, his eyes darting wildly from the girl to Castus.

"You burn the bodies, and I shall inform the City Guard that they have no reason to grieve over the girl."

He got to his feet and handed Giento a white rose from within one of his voluminous coat pockets. The petals were crumpled slightly from being confined for so long a time. He pointed with it towards the fat, bloated body beneath the other cloak. He did not need to say anything, it was perfectly clear that he did not wish the vampire child the comforts of a peaceful afterlife.

****

They had not remained in Tilbon's Middle District for long. Castus had returned shortly after Giento had burned the bodies, wanting to leave as soon as possible. The sell-sword was overjoyed at the prospect of leaving the place, yet at the same time a little fearful of where he knew they would be headed next.

The temple.

The priest's expression was grim, it was obvious he tried to keep his emotions hidden, but Giento was used to the gentle nuances of the man's features. He could not help but wonder what was racing through the priest's mind and just what he intended to do when he reached the temple. He could not possibly hope to achieve aid when it was plain to see that he planned on berating them for their inaction.

Questioning Castus would achieve nothing other than scaring himself. The less he knew of his paymaster's intentions the better. At least that way he would not spend the journey to the Upper District fretting over what was going to be said to the priesthood.

To his surprise, the priest had arranged for a carriage to take them to the temple. From the fearful looks of the drivers and the frustrated glares both he and Castus received from several well-dressed men standing at the roadside, he wondered if it had indeed been arranged and not seized.

Castus barked a demand to the driver and then sat, stern-faced, opposite Giento. Although the priest was looking at him, he was sure the man's thoughts were elsewhere. *He probably doesn't even notice I'm here,* Giento thought. Despite the possibility, he felt himself squirming uncomfortably beneath the weight of the priest's gaze.

"Nice carriage, I could get used to travellin' like this," he said sheepishly.

Castus' eyes refocused on Giento. The priest fixed him with an annoyed stare.

He wasn't staring at me after all...and I drew his bloody attention.

"I've never been to the Upper District, never did let me in there. Nice, is it? Luxuries and what not?"

"What are you doing, vagrant?" Castus asked, his eyes intense.

"Just makin' conversation," he replied.

"I have not the time to indulge in small talk."

"Got a little less than an hour at least, or is your bad mood too important to lighten up?" The look in Castus' eyes showed how stunned he was that to be spoken to in such a way. When Giento went back over his words his eyes matched his companion's in shock for a moment.

"I don't pay you to assess my mood, vagrant," Castus growled.

"You don't pay me enough!" Giento retorted despite himself. "In fact, you haven't paid me in ages, and I've done more than my fair share to earn what you gave me last time."

In reply, Castus forced his hand into his pocket, retrieving a small purse tied with drawstrings and tossed it across. The contents chinked together as Giento caught it. The look worn by the priest was anything but charitable.

"There's more ways to pay a man!" Giento hissed, throwing the purse harshly back at the priest's chest. "Like respect, or at the very least tellin' me what it is we're doin'."

Castus sat in silence for a moment, his steely eyes glaring at Giento. At length, when he finally spoke, his voice was hard and threatening.

"How dare you?"

"How dare you?" Giento countered. "You drag me from Gurdalin, across the country and into the lands of Libetha chasin' vampires. I almost get killed by the things in Cabblehiem and no sooner had that 'appened, you drag me off to the next place and make me sleep in the cold and wet, even after one of the villagers offered us a bed!" Giento's face was beet red and all thought of watching what he said had disappeared. "Then you bring me to a hamlet filled with death and make me stand by and watch as you burn the whole place to the ground.

"Tilbon's proved little different. Me leading the way even though I 'ave no idea what you plan on doin'. And now you take me to a group of men who're above the law and can kill a man if they see fit, knowin' that you plan on yellin' at 'em? Forgive me if I don't like the idea."

"Do not for a minute forget that you are expendable to me, vagrant!" Castus stated, his voice cool yet malevolent at the same time.

Giento laughed mockingly. "Really? I doubt you could find anyone else willin' to put up with your company or willin' to chase these things with you. You're nothin' but a hypocrite. All you've done since you've got 'ere is moan that the priests don't care about the poor, yet all you do is belittle us. In Cabblehiem you talked to 'em like they were horse dung and you've not once called me by name. It's always 'filth' or 'vagrant' or some other lowly word used to describe us commoners."

Castus sat in silence, the intensity of his gaze had lessened and Giento noticed his shoulders had drooped a little.

"At least these priests are honest 'bout not wantin' to 'elp. You only wanna 'elp as it'll make you look good when you finish your work. They may be uncarin' heartless swines but at least these people know where they stand with 'em."

Castus tossed the purse back toward Giento, smiling wryly as he did so. It was a smile that chilled Giento's heart. After such a rant he was certain the priest would have struck him at the very least. His payment handed over with a smile was the last thing he expected.

"You know where it is that we go and why it is that we are headed there." Castus regarded Giento coolly, his eyes watching every inch of his aide's body. "Do not for a moment think I will forget this outburst. You will come to wish that you had kept your mouth shut."

Giento tried to remain calm and still. He did not want Castus to know he was shaking like a leaf inside. The only way he felt he could manage that was by carrying on instead of remaining silent.

"After bein' inches from havin' my throat ripped out, confrontin' you don't seem nearly as scary as it used to. The truth had to come out. If the vampires don't do us in, your 'arsh tongue'll 'ave the people risin' up and bayin' for our blood."

The carriage slowed and juddered to halt. Giento was pleased to see that the priest's attention had been taken from him to the reason for the stalling. The raised voice of the driver, a tone unlike anything Saim had used, Giento noted, could be heard calling out to someone up ahead. If they were already at the Northern Gate they were making better time than Giento had thought. He was not used to travelling these streets by cart however, so his judgment was bound to be off. Having a free passage through the Middle District would most certainly be faster than having to slink around in the hope of not being caught and ejected back to the slums. He smiled, thinking that such times were behind him now.

"Stay here," Castus ordered, the tone of his voice anything but polite.

He pushed the carriage door open with such force that Giento was shocked to see that it had not snapped off its fixing. For all his baldness earlier on, he dared not poke his head around to see what the priest was doing. He knew how far he could push the man before he would snap and was fairly certain than an inch more would see him reaching his breaking point.

Giento had not noticed whether or not the streets had been filled with the everyday hustle and bustle of city life as they had meandered their way through. The noise kicked up by the wheels and oppressing weight of the atmosphere inside the carriage had been enough to drown out all outside influences. Regardless of whether or not the streets of Tilbon's Middle District had been alive with chatter before, they were now silent. The sharp intake of breath as someone—most likely the poor fool keeping them from getting to the Upper District—gasped in shock at the emerging warrior priest was the only thing to be heard.

Giento could well imagine Castus' frustration as this was the second time this scene had played out. It was law that all persons and vehicles were to be questioned and even searched when entering a different sector of the city, so such an occurrence was bound to happen all the time when travelling under cover of a vehicle. It was, however, unfortunate for the unlucky soul who was just doing his job.

Moments later Giento truly felt for whoever had stalled the carriage as an audible *slap* rang out throughout the silent city street. Babbling was the next sound to pierce the silence as presumably the stricken man fired off his apologies.

The carriage door was pulled open once more and Castus stepped back inside, a smug look about his face, no doubt pleased at having the opportunity to relieve himself of some of the stress that he had built up. He sat down and stared at Giento.

"Not once have I struck a commoner, yet I just did so to a man of relative wealth and respect. It appears you are not always correct about my character…Giento." It was obvious Castus had to force himself to use Giento's name rather than some derogatory comment as was his norm.

He's making an effort, but it's forced. He wouldn't have bothered if I hadn't taken issue with him. Doesn't really count unless he means to keep it up, otherwise it's just as fake as he is, Giento thought to himself.

"I suppose not, priest." The title sounded like an insult coming out of his mouth, and to his shock Castus merely laughed. *Typical, I work up the nerve to be disrespectful and he finds it amusing.*

The carriage pulled off once more and carried on out of the Middle District into the outskirts of the Upper District. Giento wished there were windows for him to look out of. The most he had seen of the Upper District was the tops of tall buildings that threatened the sky with their spires, and the brief glimpse he had stolen several years back as the Northern Gate opened. Memories of the minutes following that moment flooded back to him, pushing out the beauty of the scene beyond the gates with the pain of the City Guard's truncheons. *At least I'm welcome in the Upper District this time.*

The few seconds in which the gate had been opened had shown him something that he had never truly expected to see in all his born days: the posh, cleanly-kept streets of the Upper District sprawling out before him. It felt bizarre to know that he could step out of the carriage and not worry about being chased away by overzealous guardsmen.

Giento suddenly became aware that Castus was watching him intently. Had he said something without realizing?

The carriage took a sharp turn, jolting both men in their seats.

"You have an excitement about your eyes, an odd occurrence for one so awed by my brethren."

"Never been this far north in the city before. I'm a little curious is all," he replied.

"Do not be. We will see little more than the temple as I do not intend to stay long. The vampires haunt the lower sectors of the city so it is there we must become nightfall."

A lump gathered in Giento's throat. *Of course, why did I think I'd get to spend a night in safety when I have a madman holding my reins?*

A loud knock echoed through the carriage, making Giento jump. The soft voice of the driver swiftly followed. "We're coming up on the temple. Only be a few minutes now."

Castus nodded to the wall of the carriage as though the driver was meant to pick up on his gesture. Giento suddenly felt his stomach turn as the realization dawned that he was mere moments away from perhaps the most terrifying group of people he would ever come across for as long as he lived.

The last few moments before the carriage finally ground to a halt were spent in silence. It was just as well, as Giento was unsure if he could keep his voice from betraying the apprehension he felt. As Castus pushed open the carriage door they were bathed in the warmth of the sun. The smell of freshly baked bread wafted to meet them. Salivating at the thought of fresh bread baked in the most highly regarded District in Tilbon, he suddenly remembered Castus telling him that bread was used in one of the many rituals practiced by the priesthood. A little disheartened, he followed his paymaster out into the sun and was immediately taken aback by the grand scale of the temple.

The building shined purest white in the sun, the fierceness of the light making it impossible for Giento to see without first shading his eyes. The immense building started off as a large rectangular block on top of which sat a dome the likes of which he had seen nowhere else in his lifetime. Archways were carved into the vast walls, beneath which passages led off into the heart of the temple's grounds. Upon closer inspection, Giento realized that indeed each feature of the temple was edged with a mixture of silver and gold. Castus had mentioned such occurrences in other temples, the gold was meant to show wealth and the silver was meant to show modesty. The irony of the fact that no poor man could afford either luxury seemed to be lost on the priesthood.

A large wooden door opened inwards. A heavily muscled man draped in white cloth strode forth to meet the new arrivals. *As if the building itself isn't imposing enough, they have us greeted by this beast of a man?* Giento sighed and dropped his head so that he was not staring. A moment later Castus strode forward, indicating he was to follow. Against his better judgment, he shakily moved forward towards whatever fate these men had in store for him

Chapter Nine

Despite the midmorning sun, the city of Nadhaska, Libetha's capital city and the most northern city before the border, was shrouded in a dim gloom. Smoke rose thickly into the air, blocking out the rays of sunlight from reaching the city streets in their entirety. So vast were the clouds of smoke that hung ominously overhead that it was hard to believe that only one building had suffered during the night.

Long-necked birds that called the skies above Nadhaska their home swooped in and out of view as they struggled to fight their way clear of the city and the enveloping blanket of smoke. The Nadhaskans echoed the frantic nature of the city's avian dwellers, rushing about the streets trying to fetch anything that might aid the plight of the stricken temple.

Kitali—a stout warrior the Empire's newest ally from across the sea—stood on the roof of the building in which he had been permitted to dwell. His black garments fluttered gently in the breeze as he surveyed the damage wrought on the shining beacon of Nadhaska that was the city temple. He had arrived in the city two nights before with a warning that the city's priesthood had failed to heed. His journey across the western ocean to warn his country's new-found allies had proved to be nothing but a waste of time.

To the people of the Empire, Kitali and the land of Assan-Ghur were officially allies. Yet the standoffish manner in which Nadhaska's own priesthood had welcomed him proved that on a base level, he was utterly alien. An unknown that the people of the Empire seemed reluctant to trust. Had it not been for the merit of Assan-Ghur architecture and knowledge of medicine, Kitali doubted the Empire would have been too keen on the idea of forming an alliance at all. *They want us merely for trade. As soon as they learn all that we know, they shall send their ships to conquer us.*

His thoughts were shared by his people, and in an effort to prove their worth as allies, the Assan King had sent Kitali bearing the message that their mystics had divined. The Nadhaskan priests, who claimed that the work of mystics was some form of devilry, had refused to listen to his warning. He suspected that after seeing his words come true, the priesthood would pay him a visit in the near future. Whether or not they would come in peace or anger was another thing entirely. The men's minds seemed incapable of accepting that there might be beings more reputable, more powerful than the All-Father they praised so vehemently. *If they do come to me in peace, they will no doubt want to claim our mystics as their own.* The thought angered him. *And we have not the strength of arms to thwart them if they tried to take all that is dear to Assan-Ghur.*

He sighed as a throng of academics and chroniclers made their way across the rooftop towards him. Try as he might, he found it impossible to escape their curiosities. His short, dwarfish stature and black skin was something these men had never seen before and, as such, they felt it their duty to bother him at all times of the day in order to pry any extra information from him. Even when he spoke in the tongue of his people in an effort to bore and confuse them, it only served to peak their interest. He had been amazed at how fast they had begun to try and scribble down the foreign words that spilled from his mouth in some vain attempt to catalogue and later translate. If they ever did learn to understand the Assan language, they would find only curses and insulting mutterings in what he had said.

The people of the Empire had been astounded at how fast the people of Assan-Ghur had picked up their language. Kitali had failed to mention that the Empire was not the first men to take to the oceans in search of new land. Explorers forced from the safety of their lands by the Empire had settled with the Assan and taught them the ways and tongues of their people in exchange for similar tutoring. The Assan King had ruled that no mention of such prior explorers was to be made. The King in all his wisdom had deduced that being a very proud people, the Empire would no doubt be angered to learn that they were not the first to make the discovery of new lands. The illusion that the Assan had picked up the language of their own accord also served to give the impression that they were a highly intelligent people, a notion that might serve to stall the Empire if ever they did decide to invade and conquer.

The chroniclers gathered some ten feet from where Kitali stood, he assumed they had learned a fearful respect when it came to his personal space. He grimaced when he saw one of them set up a frame and canvas. They intended to sketch him! *This is madness. I should fling them from the rooftops for such an invasion of my privacy.* All too conscious of the political ramifications such an act would have, Kitali turned back to surveying the city of Nadhaska. *Such an odd place, never before have I seen a city set out in such a confusing manner.*

Nadhaska lay before him, a vast ring-work of concentric circles, each circle becoming smaller as it grew closer to the centre of the city. The final circle, despite being the smallest, was still larger than most Assan towns. Within the final ring lay one solitary yet gigantic building, an awesome example of architecture that defied the generic design of the rest of the Nadhaskan buildings: the temple.

Before the destruction, the temple had been an immense dome sitting atop great slabs of white rock easily twice the height of the tallest Nadhaskan man. From what he had learned, even the people of Nadhaska were oblivious as to how such a creation came into being, for it had been constructed many centuries ago and, for some unknown reason, no records had been kept. He knew how such a grand design had been afforded to such a primitive architectural people. It was simple to deduce when one knew what to look for. The temples of the Empire—if they all shared in such grandeur—had been fashioned with the aid of magic. To a people as sensitive as the Assan, even the faintest ripples of magical energy were detectable. The priesthood would know how their temples were constructed, of course, yet none would ever give voice to the truth. Wizards had been outlawed and any with the talent, be it latent or active, were executed as heretics. That much had been taught centuries ago when the first settlers came to Assan-Ghur as they fled from the wrongful accusations of the Empire. Kitali felt something tug at his cloak.

Spinning on his heel, he glared at the young man who had been fondling his garments. Without a second thought to diplomacy, Kitali struck the man hard across the face with the back of his hand.

"Touch me again and I shall ensure you have no hands to grope around with!" He spat the words, each one making the frightened scholar wince with terror.

Kitali hopped from the ledge on which he was perched and strode over towards the canvas. The scholars took several steps back, none willing to risk their good health for their work.

A piece of paper with several hastily scribbled notes, mostly about the clothes Kitali wore and the manner of his stance, fluttered from the canvas. *How very astute, they must have seen I would grow tired of posing and leave at some point.* The canvas itself had a very scruffy outline of Kitali standing close to the building's edge. He took it from the frame and hurled it like a man skimming a stone far off into the distance.

"Any protests and I shall send a man down to collect it." The frightened looks the scholars gave one another suggested they knew he was not talking about sending a man down the way they had come.

Leaving the terrified men and women behind, Kitali made to leave the rooftop. The beast that he had come to warn the priesthood of had come and gone, its destruction plain to see. There was no point in him staying in Nadhaska any longer. As soon as he had visited the priests once more to ensure they saw him as being free from any guilt of what had transpired, he fully intended to follow the creature wherever it might go.

****

Giento felt all fear wash away from him as he entered the temple. He was still in the company of men who could do as they wished with him and face no reprimand, but the sheer beauty of the building took his focus from all thoughts of worldly pain.

A gently rising ramp led them up into the building's maw. The antechamber in which they were made to remove their shoes and travelling clothes was spartanly decorated. There was nothing save the odd footstool or cabinet for housing the possessions of visitors, yet despite the lack of décor it still seemed undeniably grand. From outside, the temple appeared as if it were all one structure; a single dome. Yet on the inside it was clear it was anything but. The antechamber itself was an oddly shaped crescent that should have been instantly recognizable from the exterior.

They were presented with the same white cloths that the heavily muscled priest wore. Before they were allowed to don the light garment, they were taken through a small archway into a washroom. Giento's eyes widened and the ghost of a smile played across his features as he saw half a dozen young maidens kneeling on the floor.

"See that our guests are fit to enter the temple," said the muscled priest.

The women rose to their feet at their master's words and hurried towards Castus and Giento. They divided themselves off, three to each man, and began their task of cleansing. Giento felt his face flush as they stripped off the last of his clothes and began rubbing the length of his body with soft washcloths. He turned to Castus and saw that the priest was starring off into space. *I suppose he's used to this. Don't seem a bad life, being a priest,* he thought to himself.

As the washer-women scrubbed every inch of his naked flesh, Giento found himself amazed at how filthy he had become. He had assumed that all of the travelling had simply afforded him a decent tan, but seeing the water run off his body he now knew that it was merely layers of filth and grime.

His eyes widened ever further as the washer-women set about cleaning his midriff and groin. He felt himself becoming aroused at all of the attention being paid to his lower regions and risked a glance down at the women's faces. To his dismay, none of them seemed particularly bothered, certainly not impressed.

"I think it wise that we visit as few temples as possible, vagrant," Castus said. The hint of jocularity in the man's tone shocked Giento.

"A man 'as urges, priest. A man 'as urges," he replied, smiling broadly.

To Giento's dismay the women abruptly took several steps back.

"You are clean enough to be permitted entrance, masters." Giento cocked an eyebrow; he had never been called master by anyone before.

They donned their white cloths and strode back out to the spartan antechamber where the well-muscled priest stood in waiting, an older man by his side.

"It certainly is an unexpected pleasure to see a brother from distant lands," the older priest said in a frail voice that matched the appearance of his withered body. "I am Brother Jular, I believe you have already met Brother Shayn," he continued, indicating to the well-muscled man at his side.

"My name is Brother Castus, of Gurdalin, and it is with regret that I come to your temple under anything but pleasing circumstances," Castus replied, eyeing the old man fiercely.

The priest seemed genuinely shocked that his kind greeting had been met in such a manner. He was obviously too used to being played to by his sycophants. The old man motioned towards a grand archway, a serpent was carved into the stone in such a way that it appeared to be snaking its way around the length of the opening in pursuit of its own tail.

"Then I bid you follow and speak of your troubles, brother."

The old priest moved slowly, his brittle bones creaking in protest as he began to shuffle through the main archway into the vast central room of the temple. Giento was lost for words to describe the sheer grandeur of the vast domed room they entered. A thick length of luscious red carpet stretched out from the archway for as far as the eye could see, and several tapestries of similar coloring hung all around. The use of gold and silver was far from subtle; the precious metals lined everything from the walls to the dark wooden pews that dominated the majority of the floor space. Giento stood gaping at the ceiling high above him; he tried to count the number of chandeliers but kept losing his place. Each housed well above twenty candles and was fashioned from the precious metals the priests adored.

So enamored was Giento with his surroundings that he was oblivious to the conversation going on around him. It was only when Castus mentioned his name to the pair of priests that he snapped himself out of his awestruck state. The last thing he wanted was for them to ask him a question and for it to come across that he was being ignorant.

"How are our brethren in Gurdalin these days? It seems an age since we last received news from our brothers outside of Libetha," Jular asked.

"I would not know. I have spent the last year of my life pursuing a creature of great evil across the lands of the Empire. The chase has led me to Libetha, and I confess that I do not find your city in a state that pleases me. If I had not been standing here in your presence I would have assumed that the priesthood of Tilbon had long since abandoned its people to their plight." Castus' words took Jular by surprise, his eyes widened at his fellow priest's disrespectful remark.

The anger that flared briefly in Jular's eyes died off as he composed himself. "I shall take your outburst as nothing more than the frustrations of a year-long hunt. Such is to be expected when a man fails in his duty to capture that which he seeks."

Giento noticed his paymaster's eyes took on the same baleful look as the older priest's had. The insult had been subtle yet barbed. Even Giento felt a little angered by the old man's words.

"And I, Brother Jular, shall take that as the response of a man who knows nothing of the perils nor hardships of hunting a vampire. After all, your blatant disregard for those that haunt your own city streets would suggest you know nothing of how to tackle the beasts. There is a fine line between incompetence and failure, Brother Jular, and you tread it with shaky steps."

Jular surged forward a step, the quick movement was made clumsy by his aging bones as they protested against the speed at which he sought to push them. Brother Shayn closed the gap that Jular had left, Giento noticed the man was never more than a handful of steps away from the older priest.

"How dare you accuse me of incompetence?" Jular shouted, spittle spraying from his mouth with every word.

"Your incompetence is plain to see," Castus snapped. "Do you know how many souls have been lost through your inaction? They're claiming children, damn your eyes! Children!" Castus' tirade was having the desired effect, Jular's face saddened at the mention of children being taken by the vampires. Giento thought he noticed the steely features of Shayn drooping momentarily.

"That is regrettable, it is a sad thing indeed to lose the life of a child. Although it cannot be helped. My men are spread thin ensuring the dark ones are not allowed to sup upon the people of this district. I simply cannot afford to send them southward into the lower parts of the city."

The word 'lower' had almost been spoke with contempt. It was plain to see he truly meant 'poorer'. Giento thought back to how Castus had voiced his thoughts on the priesthood's inaction. He had said they would do nothing for the lower districts of Tilbon as they paid very little towards the upkeep of the temple. Being a sell-sword himself, Giento could understand why the priests lavished their protection on those who paid them. Unlike the priests, however, he did not pretend to be a protector of the people. He had seen their kind countless times throughout his checkered past as a mercenary: great protectors in times of peace yet utter cowards in times of peril. He had seen it time and time again due to his own cowardice in times of struggle. Men of his ilk tended to hide in the same sort of places.

"I see where you are coming from, Brother Jular," Castus said thoughtfully, earning a look of approval from the older man. "Why waste time on those who cannot afford to pay for the upkeep of your priesthood?" Jular's approving look faded and was replaced by one of annoyance.

"You dare accuse me of pandering to those with money? You think I would sell my soul so cheaply? That I would hire out my brethren like some band of lowly mercenaries?" Giento winced at the comment and hoped that neither Jular nor Shayn had noticed. Now would be an awkward time for them to learn that he was here on the payroll of the priesthood as opposed to his own free will.

"Quite simply put, Brother Jular, yes, we do," Castus replied.

Giento stared at his paymaster in horror. Why drag him into the firing line? Why risk bringing the wrath of the priesthood down on him? If he managed to get out of the city alive, Giento decided he would demand that his pay was doubled when other priests were involved.

"I think my aide's words best sum up your dire excuse of a priesthood. Uncaring, heartless swines," Castus said each word emphatically, ensuring each syllable was simply dripping with disapproval and malice. The display was more for Giento than it was for the priests, that much was certain.

Giento felt all color drain from his face as the two priests immediately turned to face him, their ire was for him alone, it was almost as if he had spoke the words instead of Castus.

"Is that so?" Jular asked. Despite his weak and frail appearance, Giento felt as if he were in the sights of a hungry beast.

He tried to think of something to say in his defense but nothing came to mind and he was certain if it had that his fear would have made it impossible to speak coherently.

"You prove it is so by your inaction, brothers," Castus stated.

Giento sighed with relief as the attention of the angered priests was drawn back to Castus. The information he knew of the priesthood ran through his mind. The fact that they could not strike a brother in anger yet could string *him* up by his knees and beat him until death took him with no fear of reprimand nagged at him. All hope of leaving Tilbon unscathed—or leaving alive for that matter—suddenly fled from him.

Jular stared levelly at Castus, his expression was pensive yet his eyes betrayed the façade. He was seething; it was a credit to his character that he was able to hide his anger so well. Were it not for the slight reddening of his sunken cheeks his emotion would have been unnoticeable.

"Your presence in this temple is no longer welcome, Brother. I ask that you take your aide and be gone."

For the longest moment Giento held his breath. He had been expecting the hulking form of Shayn to come surging at him or for Jular to simply tell him that he was a dead man. Being asked to leave was a blessing! It was what Giento had wanted more than anything since arriving, with the exception of a few more minutes with the young women who had bathed him.

"It is just as well, my presence is needed in all of the places your brotherhood shuns." Castus turned abruptly and strode from the pair of glowering priests without waiting for Giento.

He watched Castus stride away and became acutely aware of the two pairs of eyes that were staring a hole through him. He smiled weakly before dashing off after Castus, tripping over the long white material covering his body as he went.

****

Castus flashed a malevolent glare at the trio of postulants that now inhabited the antechamber. His hatred was fuelled by the old coward, Jular, but these men were just as guilty of allowing the population of Tilbon to be harvested by the vampires that haunted the city. If it were not against the laws of the priesthood to strike a fellow brother, Castus would have taken out his displeasure on any and all comers.

A wry smile crossed his face as he heard Giento fall down hard on the marble flooring of the temple. The look of horror that had graced the man's face when his own words had been used against him was nothing short of satisfying. He had promised that he would make him regret being so bold on the journey here, and he had proved there was more than one way to punish a man. Giento had expected a beating, but what he received was far worse.

Castus retrieved his clothes and made his way to the carriage, not stopping to change his attire. A few short moments later and the carriage door was pulled open by the panting Giento. Castus expected to receive yet another tirade or at the very least to be stared at murderously by the man. Instead, he took his seat without making eye contact.

The rapping of Castus' knuckle against the carriage's partition was all the prompt the driver needed to be on his way.

"I told you I would make you regret your outburst," Castus said. "I am not so simple that a beating is the only way I can exact punishment."

Giento did not answer. Castus noted his head seemed to droop even lower than he already held it.

"A fist does relatively little damage, yet my words have ensured that you will not be safe unless you are under my protection. You *are* the only one that Jular can exact vengeance on for such a slur."

With that Giento's head shot up, his eyes looked accusingly at Castus. "That's why you did it. You sold me out so you wouldn't 'ave to pay me! Now I 'ave to follow you if I wanna keep my 'ead."

Castus locked eyes with Giento, cowing the man before he could muster any more bravado. Being in the presence of Shayn and Jular seemed to have broken his rebellious nature somewhat. They were two shining examples of how despicable even the most noble of men could be, and he no doubt now attributed similar characteristics to Castus.

"I am a man of my word, vagrant. You shall be paid, and despite your outbursts I shall not diminish your purse. I did not do what I did to save my coin. I did it to send you a message." Castus paused to swat at a fly that had landed on his leg. "I am a dangerous man who owes you nothing, so it would do you well to remember that crossing me is neither clever nor conducive to your good health."

The sell-sword shirked back in his seat.

Giento wanted the man to fear him, he wanted him to know his place. If Giento kept trying to second-guess all of his actions, they would get nowhere fast. As a sell-sword, the man should already have been aware that it was perilous to question the word of your paymaster. If he had not earlier, he had now learnt that it was beyond perilous to question the word of a warrior priest.

****

Giento turned away from Castus; he did not want to see the priest. He knew that if the man kept pushing him, he would eventually do something stupid and, as Castus had put it, 'not conducive to his good health'. Normally such thoughts would not cross his mind, but he knew this instance was different. For all the priest's talk, Giento suspected it was all a bluff. He knew the man needed him a lot more than he needed the coin he was being paid. After all, no amount of money was worth this treatment and a journey that was bound to end in certain death.

One more place had just been added to the ever-growing list that he would not be welcome, or safe, in again. He had refused to aid the townsfolk of Cabblehiem in putting out the tavern fire and had made them violate the graves of their dead for nothing. He had burnt the village of Graan to the ground. It was an uninhabitable place, but such an act would have riled those of the surrounding settlements as in doing so he had destroyed valuable land which those nearby could have used themselves for storage or some other menial pursuit. *And now he's ensured that I can't come back to Tilbon without him unless I want the priests to kill me on sight.*

It was true that he was being paid more than handsomely, but it appeared the price was alienation from the rest of the Empire. If things kept up as they were, sooner or later Giento would be forced to flee the Empire and seek refuge in The Outlands. The rogues, bandits and cut-throats there were preferable to Castus. At least they were his sort of folk. He could fit in there if need be. As likely as him fitting in amongst the scum of The Outlands was, the thought did nothing to comfort him. He very much doubted he would last in a place as lawless as that much longer than he would if he were on the run from the priesthood.

Thoughts of his life ending much sooner than he would have liked filled his mind. His thoughts forced him to make a decision that he both feared and welcomed. He would have to leave Castus. As soon as they were free from Tilbon, he would simply slip away in the night while the priest slept.

With his plan of action set he turned back to face the priest and focused on playing the lowly downtrodden aide that Castus expected him to be.

Chapter Ten

Mercifully the child had not screamed during its interrogation. Sallus was furious with himself for rushing into capturing one of the undying children before arranging a place to keep it without fear of them being discovered. The abandoned butcher's shop was surrounded by dozens of buildings still used for one thing or another, and it would have been only too easy for the child's screams of pain to be heard, especially in the dead of night.

The boy's tight-lipped nature extended to the questions they asked. Not once had it given a complete answer. It would give answers that did not make sense until a later point in time or more often than not never at all. The only pattern Sallus could discern was that it was breaking its answers up and giving random pieces of information so that nothing concrete could be gleaned from its cooperation.

In response to the child's surprising level of intelligence, Sallus had applied a similar method to his questioning. It had not taken long for the manner of his own disjointed interrogatory methods to confuse even himself. The last image he remembered of the child was his own fist impacting into the side of its smirking little face.

Frustration had forced him to leave the child in Nicholas' care; he knew his brutish son would relish the chance to pry information from the abomination. Ordinarily he would not allow Nicholas to conduct an interrogation alone, but Sallus had noticed subtle differences in the character of both Vitria and Conrad and had chosen to look into it more closely.

The newborn had seemed even more on edge than normal and had taken to watching Vitria with hateful eyes when he thought the woman was not watching. That in itself was cause for alarm. If a man whose unlife was governed by his unhealthy attractions to pretty women suddenly showed such a drastic change towards, perhaps, the most beautiful creature on two legs, then there was most certainly something wrong.

Vitria seemed to enjoy Conrad's apparent frustration with her. She was aware of his watching and more often than not would make a point of enraging him further. She was hiding something, that much was evident. Sallus had questioned her on the subject on more than one occasion, and each time she had feigned surprise at hearing of the looks Conrad had been affording her. Vitria was talented at keeping things to herself but had no flair for lying or keeping the fact that she had secrets hidden from others; even Nicholas had noticed a change in her and had sought Sallus out to make his concerns known.

This development had been the reason for Sallus keeping Nicholas occupied with the child and constantly forcing Conrad to entertain himself about the city. Not only did he need them separated, but he needed to speak with Vitria, alone.

"Interrogating something as abhorrent as the child does not pain me in the slightest, but to think that you force me to question something as beautiful as yourself, Vitria, now that weighs down my heart."

She smiled and toyed idly with her luxurious blonde locks. "Then don't question me, Sallus. I know nothing of any importance; you're just wasting your time."

"I think you're lying to me, dear one," he said, stroking her hair with his pale hand. "I've seen the way Conrad glares at you and I've seen the ways in which you react, even if you claim not to have noticed his glances."

"I think you read too much into nothing, Sallus," Vitria replied, removing his hand from her hair and taking hold of it with both of her own.

"Do I, my sweet?" he asked, withdrawing his hand. "Never before have I seen a man look at you with such murderous hate burning behind his eyes. No, not nothing," he said shaking his head. "You've done something or have seen something which Conrad would rather you hadn't."

"Have I? Perhaps we just enjoy making you guess and pushing you to your wits' end?"

"You will tell me what is going on or so help me I—"

"You'll what? You'll make me? How will you do that, I wonder? No man can force my hand, no man can *make* me do anything. You know that," she said, stroking the side of his face.

Sallus pushed her hand away sharply and withdrew back a step. "Don't think to force your charm on me, Vitria. In all my life I have not once paid for a woman and I shall not start now by paying with my self respect."

Her sensual brown eyes darkened at his words. "You wound me."

"I may only be able to wound you with my words, but from the looks of it, Conrad would have no problem doing so with his fists. I would not be surprised if he takes a shot at you when he next feeds and, if he does, I promise I won't stop him. So if I am not to know what is going on between the pair of you, I advise that you make things right with him. He only has two days until he can feed, do keep that in mind."

"You don't honestly think he would dare harm me?" she asked, apprehension creeping into her voice.

"What do I know? I'm just a poor man at his wits' end reading too much into nothing. But I'll tell you this, I'd hate to be a woman who loses her pretty little head over nothing." Sallus winked and left Vitria with her thoughts.

****

Conrad stood in the corner of the empty room, his eyes darting about wildly despite there being nothing to see. He had, once again, travelled to the *Ferryman's Inn*, seeking a night basking in the warmth and beauty of Jessamine's presence. She had been there, as always, yet he found that the hunger clawed at his mind and would not be pushed back. As much as it pained him to do so, he had forced himself to leave her. After all, if the bloodlust took him, she would be the most appealing delicacy by far.

Two more nights and he could sup upon the blood of mankind for a whole evening. Just thinking about how close, yet how so very far away his harshly imposed feeding date was made him contemplate breaking Sallus' rule. It would be all too easy to simply stride back to the common room of the *Ferryman's Inn* and wreak bloody murder upon all who dwelt inside.

Easy, but incredibly hard to hide from Sallus.

Even if his father-in-death did not hear of his bloodletting, he would surely smell the scent on his breath. After all, Nicholas had picked up the smell of wolf blood when they had first met. No, there could be no secrets.

He punched the wall in frustration, his blow splintering the dark wood. It did not matter, the occupant of this room would soon have more pressing things to worry about than the state of his walls.

Conrad had spent his time in the slums well over the past few nights. Sallus had practically forced him from their impromptu dwelling and bade him not to return before sunrise. An order that he was overjoyed to carry out. After having to make excuses to be in this area night after night for so long, he had suddenly been handed a free pass.

He had been overwhelmed with the sensation of being free to do as he pleased, without fear of Sallus or Vitria finding out about Jessamine. Not having to look over his shoulder every moment of the night had made sitting in the *Ferryman's Inn* or slinking in the shadows as Jessamine visited family and friends all too easy. Conrad had the freedom he so desperately craved, and she was the only thing that he desired to fill his time with. Nothing else could hold his attention while he watched her, while he took in the intoxicating scent of perfume that changed nightly.

He had been awakened, however, to another, more pressing concern that demanded his attention. Jealousy consumed him as Jessamine's affections were still drawn to that scrawny buffoon of a barman. It was his jealousy that opened his eyes to what must be done.

Conrad had followed the clumsy barman to the little hovel in which he now stood. It would have been too easy to abduct him then, but he needed a place to hide him until he could feed, a place where he would not be found no matter how hard people searched or how loud the man screamed.

No place in the city provided the shelter he needed, so he had expanded his search outside the city walls. Getting out of Tilbon would prove difficult to a normal citizen. The City Guard stood vigil atop their high walls and inside watch boxes that, despite being crafted of nothing but wood, made the men inside feel safe from the dangers of the undead. Conrad had watched the guard, learning their patrol routes—which never seemed to lead them too far from the 'safety' that their boxes afforded. He very much doubted that if he tried to leave Tilbon via the main gate, dragging the screaming body of the barman behind, the City Guard would dare intervene. They would no doubt see it as a worthy sacrifice. One life so that the monster leaves.

Conrad laughed to himself. The monster would return.

Next time, instead of scaling the walls he might just try to leave by the gate, just to test them. He could use the exercise if they did suddenly develop the urge to try and stop him. And there would be a next time for the building that would serve as the barman's makeshift prison was located deep in the surrounding woodland, a disused ranger outpost that was fast being taken over by the forest.

Conrad's thoughts were cut off as the door slid open. There was little sound, yet to his keen senses the hinges were screaming out to him in the darkness. He recognized the barman instantly. His was the one face that stuck in Conrad's mind, even more so than Jessamine's, for this was the man who unknowingly kept her from him.

The barman moved sluggishly, rubbing his eyes with his knuckles. Conrad stood silent and still, no living thing could keep as motionless as a vampire.

Frustration at the barman's inability to notice the stranger in his abode ate away at him. It took him several moments to remember that mortals could not see in the dark as he could. The shadows of the small room hid him perfectly. He licked his lips as he thought of the man's face upon lighting a candle.

Curiosity got the better of him. He stepped forward in the gloom, looking to test the man's hearing if not his sight, his light footsteps making as much noise as a feather falling to the ground. Conrad's anticipation grew as he watched the barman fumble awkwardly for his candle, the dim light flittering through his open door affording him little aid. Conrad struggled to restrain himself from lunging forward and snapping the man's neck or pulverizing his skull. A red haze seemed to wash over his mind, it tantalized him, and he thought he heard it talk to him, telling him to drink. He thumped his fist into the side of his head to make the voices go away, his eyes widening instantly as he did so. In that brief moment, he had forgotten what he was doing.

The barman's head snapped around to look in the direction of the sound. Although the man did not know it, he was staring directly at the creature that would spell out his doom.

"Hello? I…Is someone there?" the barman asked, his voice trembling.

Conrad bit hard on his bottom lip and glared hungrily at his prey, like a viper regarding a rodent.

The barman's eyes darted around frantically; the vampire could almost tell what the man was thinking. Should he run? Should he ask more questions? Should he light the candle…?

Conrad nodded slowly, answering his own thoughts.

"I…I…I'm armed," the barman stammered while bringing a flame to the candle.

Conrad bit down harder on his lip until it came close to bursting, it was necessary to keep him from barking some condescending retort at the barman's pitiful threat.

The flame flickered weakly before taking to the wick and shedding a little more light. The barman's eyes were fixed on the candle he had been lighting. As if expecting what he was about to see, the man raised his eyes ever so slowly until he was facing ahead. Conrad stood mere inches from the barman's face, the dim light of the candle casting his gaunt yet handsome features in a daemonic visage.

The barman nearly dropped the candle with fright. Instinctively, Conrad shot his hand out to steady the man's arm. He had heard all too well the dangers of fire to his kind and wished not to take even the slightest risk. With his other hand, he raised a finger to his own lips and smiled menacingly.

"Do be quiet, we don't need to make things worse for you," he said.

The barman began to whimper as Conrad unwittingly applied more pressure to the man's arm. He was still new to unlife and had not fully grasped just how much stronger he was than mere mortals.

"W…what do you want?" The barman's eyes were wide with terror.

"What is your name?"

"E…Edward…M…m...my name is Edward."

He released his grip, he was not sure why but he somehow *knew* the barman would not flee. It felt as if he were holding the man in place with his gaze.

"Tell me, Edward, what would you say to a man who threw away a gemstone of great beauty?"

Edward stared at Conrad for a long moment, his face a mask of confusion.

"I don't understand. W…what does that have to d…do with why you're here?"

The vampire's pale, handsome features suddenly morphed into a mask of purest rage. "Answer the question!" he snapped.

Edward cowered and took a step back; Conrad took hold of his arm again in a motion that would have been too fast for Edward to have noticed, even in daylight. The movement extinguished the flame of the candle and left Edward to fumble in the darkness at Conrad's iron grip.

He laughed at the feeble attempt; it was as if a child was trying to break the grip of a man. His mind flashed back to the vampire child and how it had bested him. Despite coming out on top, Conrad still saw his pitiful attempt as a loss. The red haze descended over him once more and he saw nothing but the mocking smile of the child that had made him look so weak. He squeezed Edward's arm in anger; the sound of the bones cracking brought his thoughts back to the present.

The barman slumped to his knees and swayed about limply, groaning and trying desperately not to scream. His efforts were in vain as the pain of his body weight hanging from his broken limb grew to be too much. He hollered out in agony and began to beg his captor to let him go.

Conrad obliged, dropping the man's arm. He slumped in a heap on the floor, cradling his damaged limb close to him as if to protect it from further punishment.

"Answer the question," Conrad said calmly.

The sounds that came from the barman's mouth were not words. All Conrad could discern were sobs and groans of pain.

"What would you say to a man who threw away a gemstone of great beauty?" Conrad repeated, seemingly ignorant of the pain Edward was in. He waited for a moment for the barman to answer. "Answer the question."

He knelt beside Edward and gripped him by the shoulders, hauling him up to his feet. Edward squealed in pain, tears streaming from his eyes. Conrad pushed the barman against the closest wall and held him up by forcing his forearm into the man's chest.

"Would you call such a man a fool, Edward? Would you?" Conrad stroked Edward's broken arm with his free hand, applying only enough pressure so the fool could feel the slightest tickling sensation on his flesh. Just enough to let him know that he could cause more pain if needed.

Edward tried to form a coherent answer but the flares of pain coming from the break of his arm and the force being applied to his chest made it almost impossible. Conrad smiled, knowing the human was in pain and could not do as he asked of him. It meant he would get to hurt him some more until he found a way to answer.

Mere seconds before he had the chance to even think of how he would inflict greater pain, Edward began to thrash his head back and forth, nodding his agreement. Conrad growled, feeling cheated that the human had been able to answer.

"You agree? How odd. How very odd indeed, Edward," he said mockingly.

The barman's eyes bore a look of pained confusion that Conrad had grown used to from the short amount of time he had spent interrogating the man. No doubt he had expected his ordeal to end when he nodded his agreement. Conrad had forgotten just how foolish and slow-witted the cattle truly were.

"Why would you agree when it is something that you have done yourself?" he barked in an accusing tone. "You have been ignorant to a thing of purest beauty and as such have thrown it away!" Edward's eyes widened as Conrad snapped back and hurled him across the room, sending him crashing into a small wooden chest. The barman's moans of pain were louder than ever, Conrad wondered why nobody came. It was no sport simply having his way with one wounded man. He felt elated, unstoppable, as if he could take on an entire army even with his low reserves of strength, and yet no one came!

Not losing a step, he leapt gracefully through the air in a movement that would have awed the downed barman with its impossible fluidity. Conrad cursed the fact that now with the candle drowned out there was next to no light for Edward to see by.

"I bet you don't even know what I speak of, do you?" he said, landing next to the barman in a crouching position.

Edward shook his head and groaned. Despite the near total darkness, he must have realized that Conrad could see perfectly well. Of course he knew that! Conrad had answered the man's nodding. The bloodlust was playing havoc with his mind, making his thought process sluggish as opposed to its normal state of near perfection. His own simple-mindedness was making even the most basic of Edward's actions seem almost staggeringly intelligent.

"She follows you, night in and night out. She adores you as I adore her, and you do not know it! Her eyes..." Conrad closed his eyes and bit his bottom lip. "They never leave you. Such beauty, such unfathomable beauty and warmth. Such a waste!" He smashed what remained of the broken chest beneath his fist.

The barman coughed and shifted himself away from the man causing him so much pain. Conrad did nothing to stop him.

"This…this is about a w…woman?" Edward shrieked once more at the pain of his arm as he set himself against his bed.

"Of course it is, you damned fool! What else would it be about? What else could possibly be worth the suffering you feel now? Why else would I stalk you like a wolf stalks a lamb?" Conrad licked his lips at the thought of a wolf devouring his meal. He thought of the blood he could gorge upon and yet was denied. It would have been too easy to simply feed, but his life would be forfeit. Sallus would kill him for breaking his rules and then who would watch over Jessamine?

"You don't want to rob me?" Edward sounded amazed.

"Oh, I want to steal from you, but I do not want your money. Money comes and money goes, trinkets lose their luster, but love endures. For my kind love *can* last forever, and for me it will."

It was so typical of such an ignorant man to ignore such a beauty as Jessamine even as he was being told the reason for all of his pain. Was money *that* important to the cattle? Had it been that important to him before Sallus had opened his eyes to unlife? No, it never was. He only desired coin so that he could spend it on the favors of pretty women. It was always the love, or more accurately in the case of his pathetic existence as a mortal man, the simulation of love that had driven him on. Now he did not need gold coins or impressive trinkets to impress a woman, he had the gift of ever-lasting youth, of eternal beauty. What woman could truly turn down such an offering?

Conrad regarded the cringing form of his rival in this pathetic little triangle of love. He could feed and he would. Just not now. When the time of his next feed came, he would have a ready supply, and after his thirst was quenched, he would be free to reach out and attain the gemstone that this fool had so callously cast away with his ignorance.

He quickly slipped back to thoughts of Jessamine and how he would woo her. He had had no experience in seeking the affections of someone who he truly felt love for. It had always been so easy when he was one of the cattle. The women he had shared his bed with had been with him purely for the coin he offered them. It could not be the same now. He could and would offer Jessamine the gift of unlife, but that would have to wait. He could not risk scaring her. Perhaps he could console her when news of Edward's disappearance got around. He could even offer to aid her in looking for the wretched whelp.

Suddenly his thoughts turned back to his past, to his rose in Cabblehiem. It was as if the thought of seeking Jessamine had brought back his previous quarries in vivid detail. He found it difficult to remember anything other than his pursuit of beautiful women. His home, his family, everything seemed as though it was never there. Just another question. He assumed he was from Cabblehiem, that was where he was buried after all. It was infuriating! He would need to ask Sallus. Just another part of unlife that he could not begin to understand.

The soft thudding sound of Edward, toppling over unconscious, brought Conrad from his thoughts. He shook his head, smiling widely. The weakness of the cattle was so pathetic. Had he not known it to be true, he would not have believed he could have ever been one of them. As he thought of mortal weaknesses he was drawn back to his own. He was overly conscious of the fact that he had spent a great deal of time awaiting the barman's arrival and was under no illusions that he had little time left before the sun chased the darkness away.

Edward would need to be moved.

****

Sallus stood watching the door to their dwelling, well aware that the sun would arise at any moment. The newborn had yet to return and had never cut it so late as this before. It was not that Sallus was worried for his son-in-death's safety; he was worried that he might have been captured in his weakened state and made to talk. Memories of his own incarceration and subsequent torture beneath the temple of Nadhaska returned to him. He would have his vengeance on that blasted city. He would tear the temple down, brick by cursed brick and stand atop a pile of smoldering rubble.

Pushing his thoughts of vengeance aside, Sallus returned to thinking of possible ways to escape, if indeed Conrad had been made to talk. The City Guard did not worry him, it was the fact that they would come during daylight and the obvious fact that they would not come alone. They would bring priests.

The priesthood was the bane of his kind for they were near impossible to gain an unnatural advantage over. The blessed water they consumed on a daily basis and the sheer faith that they possessed made them almost equal to a vampire. The fact galled Sallus. To think that mere mortals, that their very own food source could be on an equal footing merely because they had holiness coursing through their veins, or because they wore such an amount of their God's trinkets!

It had been one of the prime reasons he had fled the priest that had sought him for so long. A whole year of his existence spent showing his back to one of the cattle. Even in Cabblehiem when he had had the man downed and so obviously dazed by the blow Conrad had somehow managed to land, he chose to flee. Sallus had not truly understood his reasons for doing so then and he was not totally sure he did now. Perhaps he had just been running from the man for so long that it felt natural to let him be and go on his way. Would he miss the pursuit? Would he miss having a blood-thirsty zealot hounding his every step?

Surely not.

No, he did not do this for compassion or for the nostalgia that having the man chase him would bring. Sallus knew all too well the dangers that a priest presented. Even when they were seemingly unaware of a vampire's presence or at their weakest, things never truly went as they were supposed to. Bad things tended to happen when a priest was involved. Sallus could attest to that, having been shot by the wretched man back in Cabblehiem. It would have been all too easy for his unnaturally long life to have come to an end that night. He was lucky that the priest had not been clever enough to arm himself with silver bullets.

The door to the butchery was flung open as a human form dove through it, a thick blanket covering his head and much of his upper body. Thin streaks of early morning light flittered through the door after the tumbling figure.

"You were very nearly late," Sallus said flatly. "What has kept you out this long, I wonder?"

The man rolled away from the invading beams of light and cast the blanket off, revealing a wild-eyed face beneath.

"You don't tell me why you force me out so I will not tell you what I do with my time." Conrad stated.

"That interesting, eh?" Sallus smiled wryly. "You haven't been feeding have you? Is that why you are secretive, young one?" Sallus did not need to ask, he could tell that Conrad had not touched a drop of blood. The crazed, violent look in his eyes was that of a desperate man, yet there was no scent of blood on him. It was truly baffling to think that he had not once made a mistake and given in to the bloodlust, especially now that he was alone each night. Nicholas had failed to keep himself clean for a day at times and yet here was a newborn managing more than a week without the blood of a human. He would have thought the wolf blood would have made him want more, that it would have been nothing more than a tease.

"You know that I haven't!" Conrad snapped almost fearfully.

Another way Sallus could tell Conrad had kept from indulging was the manner in which he presented himself. He was clearly going mad. His eyes never held the same intensity. Filled with rage one moment and constantly flitting from corner to corner, watching shadows for things that were not there, the next. Sallus had also heard him whispering to himself as if in some bizarre conversation with people that only he could see. The fact that Conrad heard voices was proof that he was not feeding. Sallus remembered the first time the bloodlust spoke to him, the first time the voices mocked him and laughed at his predicament. The voices had come for Sallus when he had been shackled beneath the Nadhaskan temple, unable to move his arms and legs. He had truly been at the mercy of his own insanity.

"Where are the others, where is Vitria?" Conrad asked.

Interesting. He asked where they both were but only Vitria by name. I'll walk out into the sunlight if there is not something going on between the pair, thought Sallus.

"They are with the child. Nicholas made it talk and Vitria is ensuring that he does not inflict further horrors upon it. I thought you might enjoy that task."

Conrad smiled widely. "What did he do to the runt?"

"Of course, you no doubt hope it suffered for beating you in a show of strength," Sallus smirked.

Conrad's mad eyes widened and he began to bite his bottom lip. "Tell me that it did! Tell me *how* it did!"

"Oh, it did," Sallus laughed at how enraged Conrad appeared. "He tore off its fingers and toes before he took a stone hammer to its knees. He struck them until the knee caps were dust and less than dust and amidst its cries of pain and anguish it gave us what we wanted."

"And what was that?" Conrad sounded eager, as if he saw this as some form of revenge that he might have on the child by hurting its sire.

"That its lair is in the Upper District and that its mistress has been in Tilbon for some time, gaining the favor of the more affluent of the city's citizens. It even claims that its mistress makes regular payments to the temple in order to seem a charitable noble-woman." Sallus' lip curled upon saying so. "You will stay here while we pay our child-lover a visit."

Conrad stood stunned by his sire's words. Sallus knew that his son-in-death would want to be there with him to destroy all that this child held dear. He knew that vengeance was perhaps the one thing a vampire held dear against all other pursuits, and that the burning desire a newborn has to exact his revenge was almost insatiable.

"No! I need to be there! I will not sit here idly and twiddle my thumbs while you and that...that brute take the lion's share of the victory," Conrad raged.

Conrad's head shot to the right as Nicholas' bellowing laughter echoed throughout the butchery.

"You were too weak to best a child, I will not have you walking into a nest of such creatures and their sire. You would die before you had a chance to land your first blow."

The newborn balled his fists and Sallus could see that his lips were trembling as if he were trying to stifle a torrent of curses.

"You will stay here and entertain yourself with the child, kill it if you must. But beware, it screamed loud enough to wake the dead from their slumber, do not be surprised if the City Guard pay this place a visit."

"Then what do I have to worry of the City Guard? If they come they will do so during the daytime when they think us at our weakest. You and the others will be here until nightfall."

Sallus shook his head and looked towards the thick fur blanket that Conrad had been covered in. “Oh no, young one. We will be leaving as soon as we are ready. You have given me an idea for daylight travel.”

Chapter Eleven

The black rock used in the construction of Tilbon was an assassin's dream. Chan Sweng and his fellows had used the ominous darkness that the city's buildings afforded to rise up through the ranks of Tilbon's underbelly. They had killed high-ranking members of the City Guard, wealthy merchants and unfaithful women, all in the name of gold and prestige.

Today was a first on several fronts for Chan and his illustrious band of blade brothers, for never had they been contracted by a priest to kill a priest.

He had not quite believed the robed figure who had sought him out in the city's slums. However, when the man had expertly broken the nose of one of Chan's fellows before putting another through a tavern wall, he had sat up and taken notice.

All of the violence had been unnecessary. The hefty bag of gold thrust into Chan's eager hands and the promise of twice as much upon completion would have been more than enough to prompt him to forget his morals and consider burying his knife in the back of a priest.

It was not unusual for a client to withhold his name, and this instance had been no different. No doubt the man had known that he dealt with the most fearsome assassins in all of Tilbon and feared repercussions for his unwarranted attack on Chan's men. Identities were not important, though, for Chan had seen the silver pendant hanging from the man's well-muscled neck that pegged him to be one of the priesthood.

It had been wise for the priest to try to avoid letting Chan know who he was, but alas, he had failed and, as such, had sealed his own fate. Chan would fulfill his contract; he had after all never broken his word and had no desire to do so now. A man was nothing if he did not have his word. Afterwards, that would be when the priesthood of Tilbon would see their folly. That would be when the assassins' elite would slip into the pristine white temple and paint it red with the blood of its stewards. He only wanted the muscular man to suffer, but was not averse to silencing anyone who got in his way.

Thoughts of the treasures he could plunder from the temple filled his mind and took his attention away from the task at hand. He scolded himself as he nearly lost his footing on the uneven rooftops above the Middle District.

A quick glance back over his shoulder told him that his two most trusted blade brothers were in place behind him, running in an arrowhead formation. With Lars and Hunter at his side, Chan would make short work of the priest and the vagrant that accompanied him. He almost felt sorry for the pair. They were going to succumb to death from above, and they would not know anything about it, let alone have the chance to defend themselves. Such was the mastery of he and his men with their throwing knives.

Beneath the black cloth that covered the lower part of his face, Chan smiled. Even in the daylight the blackness of the buildings would render them almost invisible. He truly wondered why men took such trouble to establish businesses and work for what little coin they had when hiding in the shadows and killing for payment was by far the easiest job in all of Tilbon.

Of course, he was under no illusions that he and his band of brothers would be unstoppable in any environment. The muscular priest had merely been incredibly lucky when he manhandled Chan's men the way he did. After all, many years of training in The Outlands—the most lawless place known to man—had hardened those under his pay into perfect killing machines.

The targets had annoyingly kept to the well-populated parts of the Middle District, making it next to impossible to launch an attack without anyone witnessing. Normally such thoughts would not concern him, a knife could be thrown from great distances, and in the commotion of a crowd it would be near impossible to see who had actually thrown it. Today, however, was not what he would consider a 'normal' circumstance. If a priest was assassinated in clear view, there would be a manhunt for the culprit. The only thing considered more heinous than killing a priest was killing the Emperor.

For all the martial prowess and skill in evasion that his highly trained blade brothers possessed, he knew there was always the chance—no matter how slim—for error to occur. His client had proved that with the lucky shots he had got in.

He noticed frantic movement out of the corner of his eye. Like the skilled assassin that he was, he ignored it. There was no greater prize than that of his mark. The gasps and shouts of anger from the crowds caught Chan's interest. After all, this could influence what his targets did, so he would be mad not to investigate.

His face scrunched up in confusion as he saw three people running with great furs slung over their heads and torsos. They looked incredibly odd with only their legs on display. There was something bizarre, yet fascinating about the way they ran. Their movements seemed incredibly graceful considering the uneven burdens they carried. Their speed was also rather intriguing, he would have imagined it very difficult to run at average pace with a great length of fur weighing you down and covering your eyes, yet here these people were running at an alarming rate. They even managed to dodge most of the people in their way.

Fascinating.

With his curiosity sated, Chan turned his attention back to the priest and the grubby little man that followed him, only to find that they had noticed the commotion and were heading after it.

Chan smiled broadly, relishing the fact that his targets were leaving the safety of the crowds to follow three people who would neither be able to see nor hear the two men tumble dead behind them. He altered his course across the rooftops to match that of the priest and the odd trio that he now followed.

At the pace they were running, he imagined the priest would be away from the crowds in a matter of moments. His stomach felt as though it was bubbling. It always did just before he made a kill; he assumed it was his body's way of broadcasting its excitement to him.

Taking a gargantuan leap across a gap that normally he would not even consider, Chan came incredibly close to losing his life. He slammed hard against the wall of the building opposite and grasped for purchase over the lip of the rooftop. He praised himself for having such strength in his fingers. To keep a firm grip even while enduring such a bone-shattering impact was not something one could be taught. As he began to haul himself up and over the edge of the rooftop, he heard Lars and Hunter land in the same predicament as he. His heart swelled in his breast at the thought that he commanded men that were almost the equal of their master, for it truly showed that they were a devastating force indeed.

His thoughts of praise died almost immediately as Hunter lost his grip and instinctively grabbed Chan by the leg. He suppressed a scream of terror and was embarrassed that it still came out, yet only as a squeak. He was almost over the edge of the rooftop and now his idiot of a lackey was threatening to pull him back down because of his own selfish fear of death.

Chan made to lash out with his other foot but Hunter had already found purchase and let go of his dangling limb. He wanted to punish the fool there and then but thought better of it once he realized just how long they had spent hanging precariously over the edge of the building. Instead he left Lars and Hunter and took off in pursuit of the priest.

Under any other circumstances, Chan would have been able to run for hours in pursuit of his prey, but the jarring impact of hitting the wall had been absorbed mainly by his knees. He could feel them tremble with every step and was certain the skin was shredded. He felt lucky that his kneecaps had not shattered on impact. Instead of running himself into the ground and risk permanent damage to his legs, Chan resolved to make the kill the very first chance he got.

He removed one of the small, perfectly weighted throwing knives from his belt and eyed the next flat rooftop. He was certain that if he got there quick enough, he would have the time to make ready and aim. Chan had the luxury of a bird's eye view and flat ground, where his targets were now having to navigate the winding alleyways that led ever closer to the main road north.

Even in such a wounded state Chan was able to foresee how the engagement would pan out. His truly was a mind like no other in all of Tilbon. In fact, he was willing to bet the contents of his purse that he was perhaps the greatest tactical thinker in all the lands under the banner of Emperor Beledain.

"Not that it would take much!" he snorted.

Chan immediately flung himself into a crouched position as he reached the edge of the rooftop and sat ready in wait for his target to show himself. The heavy footfalls of Lars and Hunter were so loud that they threatened to shake his concentration. He wanted nothing more than to lose a knife into each of their bellies for being so heavy-footed and risking the entire contract. Had it not been for the speed that his targets had been running, Chan would have done just that.

The fur-covered shapes of the three fast-moving individuals careered around the corner first; Chan let them go without the slightest hesitation. They were no danger, they more likely than not had no idea that the priest was chasing them, so it seemed unlikely they would witness what was about to occur.

The sun glinted off the steel edge of the throwing knife as he tightened his grip. The priest was next to turn the corner, he was noticeably failing to keep up the unnaturally fast pace set by his quarry. That suited Chan just fine, it was far easier to hit a slow-moving target than a fast-moving one. Not that he would find either difficult, for one as skilled as he in the ways of death such things came as naturally as drawing breath.

Chan held his left hand up to signal Lars and Hunter to leave this to him. He could hear them removing their knives from their belts and wanted neither of them to steal his glory. He looked ahead and saw the three unknowns turn another corner. He would have to act now or risk losing his target. He just could not bring himself to run any further!

Without a second thought, he unleashed his steel throwing knife and watched as it sped on its inevitable course to bury itself within…the priest's hat.

He had missed!

How could this be? Chan Sweng did not miss, it was just not heard of. Not unless there was an exceptional reason for his inaccuracy like there surely must have been on this occasion. Perhaps his lackeys had not got the balance of the knives correct. Or maybe they had tinkered with the grip of the handle so that he would surely miss. The grip had felt slightly off, now he thought about it.

Treachery!

It just had to be.

Chan Sweng did not miss.

He watched in annoyance as the hat toppled from the priest's head, causing the man to stop dead in his tracks. He slumped onto his belly so as not to be seen by the searching eyes of his target.

The priest knelt down, picked up his hat and inspected the knife lodged within.

"Assassin! Show yourself and face me as a man of honor would."

Chan bristled at both the comment and the seeming lack of fear the priest showed. If it were him who had just been the subject of a…of a…failed assassination attempt, then he would have darted for cover so that more blades did not quest for his heart. Not only was he unafraid of the danger Chan presented, but he was questioning his honor!

Hurried footsteps pattered off the rooftop behind him. A moment later, Chan saw a black-clothed figure leap from the rooftop beside him. Hunter had answered the priest's challenge!

For the life of him Chan could not understand why he had done so, they were in no danger of being seen and they had plenty of knives left to throw. Perhaps he was attempting to make up for nearly pulling Chan off ledge earlier.

Whatever he was doing, he was going about it all wrong. Hunter had landed awkwardly on a pile of wooden crates below, smashing through them and landing on the stone floor beneath. Chan was amazed the fool had not killed himself with the stupid leap.

He thought of turning to Lars to ask just why Hunter had seen fit to throw himself into harm's way but was prevented from doing so as Lars also leapt from the ledge. Chan shook his head, certain that he was surrounded by fools. Lars had not even tried to aim for anything that could break his fall, instead he had landed flat on the harsh, unforgiving stone floor below. If Lars still lived then Chan would eat his own excrement.

He watched the dazed form of Hunter stand up and grasp hold of the wall for purchase. The fool would die, not even his superior fighting techniques could keep the priest from killing him now.

Chan got up off his belly and took a few paces back. He would ensure that the line of retreat was unwatched by enemy eyes so that in the unlikely event that Hunter did succeed, he would have a way free to escape. At least that was how he would explain it to his fellows back in the slums. After all, this was no fault of his. He had been betrayed by the fool who had armed him and let down by the morons who had accompanied him.

He turned to run but found a tall man clad in a dark green cloak standing before him. How could this be? Chan was the best there was, no man could sneak up on him unless he allowed it. This just simply was not happening. He must have hit his head when struggling for purchase on the side of the building. Yes, that was it, this 'man' was no more than some hallucination brought on by his annoyance at his subordinates and the pain that wracked his body.

Chan squealed in agony as his hallucination struck him in the face with a leather-gloved fist. The man grabbed hold of him, dug a hook into the ledge of the roof and dangled an attached rope down to the street below. Chan's head swam as if drunk. The falling sensation as the man abseiled down the side of the building almost made him vomit.

He felt himself fall for real as the stranger dropped him from a safe distance to the ground below. He struggled to his hands and knees, still not entirely sure what was happening or how his perfectly planned contract had suddenly come crashing down around him. He put his hand in something warm and sticky. Looking down, Chan found that it was blood. Hunter had been cut from ear to ear, his blood still seeping from the wound at his throat.

Pain flashed through his head as he felt something strike the side of his face. He was on his back now and looking up at the man he had been sent to kill. *How ironic*, he thought.

"Who sent you?" asked the priest.

Chan shook his head and tried to spit at the man. His attempt failed and the blood that he spat fell back onto his own chest. He was not about to divulge the nature of his client to his mark. Chan had no love for the priest who had hired him, but he had his own self-respect. His one cardinal rule was that the identity of a client would never be revealed, even under pain of death. He felt distinctively proud of himself for defying such a fearsome man in the face of his own death. It showed strength of character and only served to intensify his greatness.

He thought of his brother back in The Outlands. Chun truly was one of the most talented warriors he had ever laid eyes on. Perhaps even more so than himself. He wished dearly that somehow, someday, Chun could avenge his death and make this wretched priest suffer.

"I said, who sent you?" The priest's voice was harsh as gravel. He backed up the malice in his words by stomping down hard on Chan's chest and then sliding his boot up into his throat.

"All-Father help me, it was a priest!" Chan screamed. He writhed in pain beneath the weight of the priest's boot. The last thing he felt before the darkness took him was the warmth of his own urine as it spread down his legs.

****

Giento had not truly understood what he had witnessed. He could not piece together just how stupid one man had to be in order to merely sit there while someone threw his henchmen off a rooftop. At first he had thought the black-clad man that now lay dead beneath Castus' feet was in league with the stranger in the green cloak. Giento had certainly seen men punish their subordinates in far worse ways during his career as a mercenary. He had been flogged himself, so he knew just how harsh those who thought themselves above everyone could truly be.

The priest had seemed just as perplexed by the display. His concerns, however, did not stop him from ending the man's life with a quick slash from his silver-edged sword. The second man had not been lucky enough to survive the initial drop. Giento winced as he thought back to the sickening *crack* the man's neck had made upon impact with the solid stone floor.

Giento stood behind Castus so that if the newcomer was indeed hostile, he would at least have to deal with Castus first, meaning Giento would have ample time to flee. Not that he would be safe anywhere if he did, what with the way Castus had sold him out to the priesthood. He did not doubt that if it came to it, he would not make it out of Tilbon on his own. Considering Castus was hell-bent on chasing vampires throughout the city, he very much doubted he would make it out alive even with the priest.

"Thank you for your help, I owe you my life," Castus said to the stranger.

The man smiled and laughed quietly to himself. "Trust me, you don't owe me anything. Chan would struggle to stab his way out of a wet paper bag, let alone successfully murder a warrior priest."

"You know the man who was sent to kill me?" The priest sounded shocked, the slightest note of accusation creeping into his voice. A note which the man in green did not fail to spot.

"You can trust me when I say I did not send Chan after you," he said, holding up his hands. "I am rather disappointed you had to kill him though, he was a wonderful source of entertainment."

Giento could not see the priest's face but just by the way he held himself, he could tell how he must look. Utterly confused and no doubt furious that this newcomer spoke of wanting their would-be assassin to have lived.

"Who are you, friend?" Castus asked levelly.

The man held up a finger and then thrust his hand deep inside his tunic. A moment later he produced a shining circle of silver engraved with the Emperor's seal.

"Seeker," Castus uttered.

Giento's eyes widened in shock. He had heard of the Seekers, every man had been told of their legend when they were small children. He had thought it merely a tale to keep him on the straight and narrow. His father had told him of a group of fierce warriors who roamed the land under the direct employ of Emperor Beledain himself. Nobody knew what it was they did exactly, but there was certainly no shortage of theories. Giento's father had told him they took little children who misbehaved and dumped them out at sea. As foolish as the notion seemed, Giento could not quite help but notice how dry his mouth suddenly became now that he was faced with one of the mysterious men who had afforded him so many sleepless nights as a child.

"As you can no doubt see, I would not have needed a bottom-draw assassin if I wished you dead."

"Then why are you here? How did you come to be in the right place at the right time?"

"I am on my way back to Gurdalin and have some business to attend to in the Black City before making my return. I noticed Chan and his bungling henchmen running across the rooftops and thought I would follow them on the off chance they actually managed to do anything other than fail."

Castus nodded briefly. "How do you know of this assassin?"

"It is my job to know of anyone and everyone who could be a risk to the security of the Empire. Chan, however, had proved himself to be nothing more than a damn good laugh. We used to pay him to make a hit on other Seekers when there was more than one of us here at any one time."

Both Giento and Castus stood open-mouthed at the admission. It was insane to think that these men were mad enough to order hits on one another for the sheer fun of it. It simply beggared belief.

The Seeker seemed to find their bemused looks incredibly entertaining; he smiled broadly and waved his hand as though he were dismissing a slave.

"I don't think you fully appreciate just how incompetent Chan Sweng is…was. Some men gamble on games of chance, we Seekers gambled on what the buffoon's excuse would be when he failed. And he did fail, each and every time. My fellow brothers will be most disappointed to learn of his passing."

"I'm sorry that I spoiled your little game," Castus said dryly.

"Tell me, just what is it that brings a priest and his lackey into the firing line of the temple? Was it that which you chased?"

Giento bristled at the term 'lackey'. Were it any other man he might have corrected him, but if there was one thing that was accepted the world over about these Seekers, it was that they were a thing to be feared.

"You will not tell me your business, so I shall not tell you mine," Castus replied.

"With all due respect, priest, I carry with me the authority of the Emperor. When I speak, it is with his voice. When I act, it is with his iron fist that I do so. Normally I would have no need to distrust a priest, yet I have just witnessed your own brethren make an attempt on your life. So please forgive me if I am untrusting of your order."

Castus' face visibly reddened as the man spoke. Giento knew little about the Seekers themselves, but he certainly recognized the Emperor's seal and knew that any man who carried such a thing was not to be denied.

Giento tried to force himself not to laugh at the ire in the priest's voice as he explained their journey from day one. He told of hiring Giento and their encounter with the vampires in Cabblehiem. He explained the events of Graan and the headless corpse of what once had been a vampire child found in the very city in which they stood. Giento was shocked that he had left nothing out, at the very least he would have expected the man to try and make himself seem righteous and glorious in his burning of Graan, but he simply stated that he razed it to the ground. Perhaps the Seeker understood the bizarre situation better than Giento did. Or perhaps Castus already thought himself righteous for doing such things.

Looking at the man and how closely he paid attention to Castus' tale, not once flinching or showing disgust at the more vile or dishonorable parts, Giento was sure the Seeker had committed worse atrocities. What they had been through was probably tame by this man's standards. In that moment he dearly wished that the Seeker would keep from sharing tales of his travels.

The newcomer nodded as Castus told the last of his tale and stood silent for a moment, a thoughtful look upon his face.

"You have indeed travelled far and wide to fulfill this grudge of yours. I commend you for your burning desire to see this fiend destroyed."

"Are the vampires your cause for stopping in Tilbon also?" Castus asked.

The Seeker shook his head. "I'm afraid not. There are more deadly things that roam the world than vampires."

A hint of a smile crossed Castus' face, something Giento did not miss. Did the priest relish the thought of things far worse than what they sought? He imagined the inner workings of the priest's mind and could well believe that what little this Seeker had said had inspired the man. No doubt if they managed to destroy the vampires, Castus would want to be led all over the Empire in search of even greater prey. *Thank the All-Father I plan to cut him as soon as possible.* He had just witnessed a failed attempt on the man's life and could well imagine he himself would fare no better. Perhaps it would be wiser to just slip off in the night when they were free of Tilbon than try anything more…permanent. He had resolved to simply leave while the priest slept once already, why anything more sinister than simple flight had taken his fancy now was unknown to him. "I can see I will get little else out of you, Seeker," Castus said. "However, tell me this, does the man who saved my life have a name?"

"My name is Lucius. Fare well, priest," the man replied before taking his leave.

****

Kitali stood defiantly amidst the bodies of the twice-dead, his twin maces held in a manner that suggested he was by no means finished using them. He had been caught entirely by surprise as what had happened had been missed by even the mystics of Assan-Ghur.

Legions of foul dead things had clawed their way from beneath the ground and had launched themselves upon their living kin. The sight had initially frozen Kitali with fear, for the dead rising from their graves in such numbers was not a sight he had before witnessed.

He had thought it impossible for any creature to emerge from the grave save the beasts that the people of the Empire called vampires.

His moment of fear passed and he had immediately thrust himself at the throng of dead men and women, his maces sending the shambling horrors back to their graves with every savage strike. Where his twin weapons fell, rotten skulls burst like overly ripe fruit. The people of Nadhaska that had refused to flee had congregated around Kitali.

Now so many of those brave men and women lay dead around him, lying amongst the rotten filth that had once been their family and friends. Kitali spat on the nearest rotting corpse and muttered a curse. The sensation of fingers gripping his leg caused him to start. He spun on the spot and raised one of his maces high above his head yet stopped from delivering the killing blow. The woman that held him by the leg was no rotting corpse, she was one of the living who had stood beside him in an effort to repel the walking dead. He remembered the woman with her long, flowing, red hair and fragile-looking features.

Kitali knelt down beside her and offered his hand. The woman was clearly hurt and it was only decent of him to offer aid to a lady in distress. His eyes widened as the woman's mouth sprang open. She lurched forward and tried to take a chunk out of his extended hand. He withdrew his arm and shook his leg free of her grip before bashing her brains out with one of his maces.

He stood in disbelief at what he had just done, yet at the same time, he knew that she was no longer of the right mind and that there was nothing else that could have been done. His thoughts of guilt soon disappeared as all around him the ground began to writhe. Kitali looked on in horror as the rotting corpses of the first assault lay still and motionless. It was the bodies of those who had fought and died only moments before that now dragged their limp, lifeless forms to their feet with hunger gleaming from their dead eyes.

As a son of Assan-Ghur, Kitali had within him the burning desire for combat, for his was a nation built on conquest and war. It took an enormous amount of willpower to restrain himself from wading into the shambling mass of corpses that shuffled inexorably towards him. He had seen the first wave of the dead devour the flesh of the living and was under no illusions as to how he would perish if these things overcame him. He also knew that he would not stay amongst the halls of his ancestors for very long, as death did not seem a permanent thing in Nadhaska this day.

With a force that belied his short stature, Kitali bludgeoned the skull of a young man who got too close with his prying hands, and took a step back. The swing had revitalized the urges for death and bloodshed within him, yet if he stayed and fought there was the very real chance that he would fall. He needed to reach the city's army and tell them what he knew of these beasts. In all likelihood, the army were already aware that the dead only served to swell the ranks of their enemy, yet he could not be sure. The security of Nadhaska came first, he had to put the lives of others before his own selfish desire for combat. With one last almighty swing of one of his maces, he delivered a second death to another of the walking corpses, battering its midsection in order to bring it low enough for him to reach its skull.

Kitali then gazed out at the ever-growing sea of dead and did what he never thought he would.

He turned his back and ran.

Chapter Twelve

Sallus had never been as afraid for his life as he was now. It had been his idea to emulate the frantic method of daylight travel that Conrad had employed in order to return to the butchery, yet that did not stop thoughts of a fiery doom from tugging at his mind. All it would take was for one of them to slip or for the furs they carried to become snagged, and their unnatural existence would come to a horrifying and undignified end.

Perhaps it was that fear that made him incredibly suspicious that they were being followed. Considering the speed at which they travelled, it seemed unlikely that anyone would be able to keep up for long, yet he could not shake the feeling that someone was there. With the sun looming ominously above and that damned priest hounding his every move, he felt he was more than justified in being jumpy. After all, when so many things could go wrong, it was unlikely that everything would go right.

Sallus strained to hear the sound of rushing footfalls in pursuit, yet even with his keen senses he could not pick out the footsteps of a potential stalker from those of the masses of people going about their day. It was like trying to pinpoint a single drop of water in a monsoon.

Taking another lightning-fast glance out from underneath his heavy furs, he committed the path ahead to memory and quickly calculated how many steps it would take for him to reach the relative safety of the alleyways.

Under the loving glow of the moon he would have walked tall and laughed at himself for being fearful that one of the cattle might be the end of him. The harsh, tingling sensation that still lingered across his face and hands from the last time he had peeked from beneath his cover reminded him that he was not under the light of the moon. A second, two at most, and it felt as though someone had scraped at his flesh with a searing hot rock. Sallus shuddered at the thought of the North Gate and wondered just how they would get from the Middle District to the Upper District without being challenged by guards.

The level of sound quickly lessened as they passed from the bustling city streets to the less frequented alleyways that crisscrossed the district like a web of slender veins. He heard his own footsteps echo and could feel that the air creeping up underneath his furs was noticeably cooler. Perhaps his frantic worrying would lessen now that the crowds of peasants had been left behind him. Glancing forth from beneath his furs once more, Sallus cursed beneath his breath. The alleyways were short and winding. He could remember them from his rooftop vigils and could see the way they meandered this way and that in his mind. He would have to keep looking for the path ahead and that meant that he would have to keep allowing the sun to shine on his unprotected flesh.

This was not the first time that Sallus found himself cursing his eagerness to come face to face with the perverse master of the undying children. Just what he hoped to accomplish by travelling by day was beyond him. Of course, it meant that his emergence within the mansion that the children used as their lair would be unexpected. It also meant that there were several dozen things that could go wrong.

Navigating the way ahead was proving to be rather easy, with the pain of the sun being the only real burden. He was certain that things would not continue to stay as easy as this. After all, was it not unnatural for a vampire to travel under the light of the sun? Surely it was inviting death. Mortal men did not breathe under water for the same reason that vampires did not travel under the light of day.

"Assassin!"

The voice came from behind him and sounded alarmingly close. It was not the proximity of the voice that had shocked him; he had, after all, had his suspicions that they were being followed. It was the voice itself. He had been chased for too long, spent far too much of his time lurking in the shadows for fear of action to not know just who that voice belonged to.

The priest.

Of all the potential do-gooders that could be hounding him, why did it have to be the priest? It could have been a member of the City Guard or some low-ranking officer of the Libethan Army looking to advance himself by right of conquest. But no, it had to be the one man in all the Empire that Sallus genuinely felt had the slightest of hopes in destroying the Sovain line. This proved, without a shadow of a doubt, that things went bad whenever the priesthood was involved.

They had had no trouble from the priest since arriving in Tilbon and all of a sudden he appeared when they were at their most vulnerable. If Sallus did not know any better, he would have thought the priest's God of creation had intervened. He scolded himself for such a ridiculous notion. Religion was nothing more than a noose to tie around the neck of the common man in order to keep them in line. Sallus had seen what waited beyond the grave, he had seen it all those years ago when his life had been so cruelly taken and this new existence thrust upon him. There was no holy kingdom, no paradise in which the dead spent eternity. There were no Gods, no divine beings that pulled the strings of mankind like puppets. There was only darkness. Darkness, pain and eternal suffering.

In the week that Sallus lay in his coffin, dead and unmoving, his soul had been locked in the black pits of the Underworld. He remembered all too well the feel of barbed lashes flaying the skin from his back. He remembered the feeling as his own blood seeped from cuts and ran down his raw flesh. Every second had felt like a year's worth of agony. Every day was a new lifetime of torment.

The memories of his time spent beyond the grave had not appeared at first. It had taken centuries after his awakening for the sickeningly painful images to reveal themselves. Sallus was unsure what had triggered them and envied his family for their blissful ignorance of their own time spent in the dark recesses of the unknown.

It was these memories that kept him from acting whenever the chance arose to kill the priest. It had to be, there could be no other reason for him to stay his hand. He knew what awaited him when he died a second death. He could almost see the faces of his former tormenters, their slavering maws gaping hungrily at the thought of visiting unimaginable horrors upon his flesh once more.

Eager to put as much distance between himself and the priest, Sallus forced the thoughts of the Underworld from his mind and pushed onwards with a renewed sense of purpose.

****

The only thing that had kept Conrad from ending the child's miserable existence was the rapid pace at which his mind flickered between thoughts. As soon as he would resolve to hack the child's head from its shoulders with a rusty blade left by the former occupant of the butchery, his mind would suddenly conjure up thoughts of Jessamine. Blissful thoughts of the straw-haired beauty would soon be replaced by ones of the barman she had fallen hopelessly in love with. Those thoughts brought a sick, twisted grin to his pallid face. Simply imagining the suffering he would visit upon the defenseless cretin was *almost* enough to sate his hunger.

Conrad deftly tossed an old cleaver, which looked to be in worse repair than the child's kneecaps, from one hand to the other. The child watched the blunt cleaver with longing in its eyes. It wished to die, to have its pain taken away forever. A few short weeks ago and Conrad would have felt nothing but revulsion towards those who had done such a thing to so small a boy, even if the child *was* evil. Truth be told, he still felt revulsion towards the child's torturer, but not because of the injuries that had been inflicted.

Merely existing had been made harder because of the friction between he and his brother-in-death. It was obvious that the catalyst for their rivalry was Vitria despite neither of them being romantically involved with the woman, although it was perfectly clear that Nicholas yearned to be. Merely thinking about Vitria brought nothing but anger to the forefront of Conrad's mind nowadays. She and she alone held the key to his happiness or his undoing. If only he had been more cautious when stalking Jessamine. If only he had thought to ensure he was not being stalked himself.

"You're weak, that's why you haven't killed me yet. You're afraid that I'll beat you again, even as I am." The child's pained voice brought Conrad from his thoughts of the intrigue within his family.

"Let's see how you fare in combat after being starved for a week," he spat.

The child laughed in response, its usual tinkling laughter was replaced by a rasping noise that sounded as if it were drowning in its own bodily fluids. It hawked a great wad of blackened blood from its mouth. Both the sight and sound reminded Conrad of an old man clearing his throat.

"Just an excuse. You know you're weak, even with the blood of a hundred men. Your family knows it, too. They spoke more of your weakness than of the questions they wanted answered."

Conrad's face bunched up with rage and his hand tightened on the wooden haft of the cleaver, so much so that the heavy metal head fell to the floor as the wood cracked and splintered under his grip.

"You see? You're so easily led. Surely you can see it's a sign of weakness that you're being played by a child?" The boy's smile disappeared in an instant as Conrad launched himself forward and stomped the heel of his boot into one of its ruined kneecaps. The bone had begun to re-knit itself and cracked once more under Conrad's assault. He tossed his head back and took in the sound of pain emitted by the screeching child beneath his boot. It was euphoric to cause pain to one who wanted to die. It was akin to giving a man dying of thirst a tankard of ale with great holes in the bottom. The illusion of what he wants.

"Weak? No." Conrad shook his head. "Mad? Perhaps, but not weak."

"The big one will kill you! You are nothing and he is strong. He will destroy you with all the effort it takes a mortal to swat a fly!" The child's words were screamed in between its agonizing shouts of pain; Conrad was amazed that it could be so coherent after suffering such injuries.

"Nicholas? I do not fear my brother!"

The child smiled, several of its teeth were missing. "Not him. We know of your family and we know of the outcast that your sire created. There's one brother that you should fear."

"How do you know of my family? You did not know we were here! You're lying!" Conrad kicked the child with the point of his boot, causing it to spit up more blood.

"Sallus Sovain sired a monster and let it loose on the world of our kind. A man who creates a force that is deadly to all does not go unknown. Your family will find nothing in the Upper District, we've heeded the signs of his coming and we've left. I'm most likely the only one left in the city."

Conrad took in what the child was telling him. Above all he felt amazed at the child's level of speech; it must have been of a noble family in life, for it spoke as well as any learned man. He thumped his skull to clear his thoughts. What did it matter how elegantly the child spoke? That had no bearing on the words he was hearing. Had Sallus sired some horrifying monster? He could not understand how such a thing could happen, for surely one vampire was as deadly as the next?

Why did he believe the words of a captive who wanted nothing more than to die? Surely this was just some trick designed to anger him and force his hand. Conrad cursed his sire for starving him, without sustenance he could not think straight and thus felt torn. The only thing open to him was to hear the child's tale and judge it in its entirety.

If what the child was saying was true, why had Sallus kept the existence of some great horror a secret? What could one vampire create that would instill fear in all others? The unanswered questions filled him with uncertainty.

"What did he make? Tell me and I shall grant you rest. Tell me and I will kill you as you wanted."

The child nodded, satisfied with the bargain.

"Sallus created a vampire that feeds on other vampires. He takes the strength of the unnaturally strong and adds it to his own. He gains much more strength from one feeding than any of us would from five mortals, and his reserves last for much longer."

"This is nonsense, you feed me lies in hope of a swift end to your pain. A vampire cannot drink the blood of the dead unless he wishes to die himself. I may be young but I am no fool!"

"Vampire blood is not dead, you must be a fool if you think that it is. You said it yourself, newborn. Vampires die if they feed on the blood of the dead. If our blood was dead it would have the same effect on us as that of a corpse" The child shook its head, the effort clearly pained it. "No, our blood is refined, enhanced."

Conrad stood stunned in silence. What the child spoke of made perfect sense. If a vampire's blood was dead, it would act as a poison and would surely destroy him in a matter of moments. Why had Sallus not spoken of this before? Why had he forced Conrad to drink of humans and animals when there was a richer meat out there?

"I see what you're thinking, I thought it too when I learned about this. To drink the blood of our kind is forbidden. It is the one law that our kind abides by, and to break it is to be outcast and hunted to death."

"This…this brother of mine seems to be doing well for himself," Conrad replied angrily.

"He has fed from a lot of our kind and is near unstoppable. Anyone who stands in his way will be added to his strength and used to destroy more of us. He's a plague to which there is slim hope of finding a cure."

Satisfied that he had heard all there was to tell, Conrad turned from the child. What more could the boy possibly know? It had already told him more than his own sire had deigned him worthy of knowing. Of course, he had no way of knowing whether this was a trick, but it mattered not. Even if the child's story had been nothing but fabrications, he had learned something at least. Where tales of some outcast brother might be false, the idea that vampire blood was not dead surely had merit and deserved to be looked into.

He knelt down and scooped up a large blade that had escaped the worst effects of time and neglect. It still looked sharp and was large enough to make easy work of the child. He did not have the brute strength of his brother and highly doubted he could replicate the feat of tearing the thing's head from its shoulders. He turned back and saw a look of smug satisfaction upon its face. It was getting what it wanted, a fact that ate away at Conrad. It almost felt as though the child had won. Only when he reminded himself that he also wanted the child to die and that he wanted nothing more than to have the wretched creature perish by his hand did he come to terms with allowing the boy this small victory.

Conrad drew closer, the blade raised in a savage display of what was to come. This show of malicious intent did nothing but widen the smile of the crippled child.

Angered, he hurled the blade to the ground, the metallic chink resonating throughout the bare room.

"You promised! Kill me," the child begged.

A smile split Conrad's face as he enjoyed the look of fear worn by his captive. This was how it was supposed to be. No creature should be held captive by one of his kind and not feel fear.

Conrad turned and left the child to scream its angered protests at his back. A moment later he reappeared before the abhorration, a thick blanket in his hand.

"I'm not going to kill you. I am going to give you the chance to end your own suffering."

The child looked on with curious eyes. It regarded the blanket with the same look of uncertainty that a newborn babe would afford its toys upon seeing them for the first time.

Without pausing to give the child any answer as to his intent, Conrad knelt down and grabbed the boy by the hair. He dragged it through the butchery, its ruined limbs flailing wildly as his grim plan dawned on the small boy.

"No! No! Not like this! You can't, you promised!" it squealed, clawing at the filth-ridden floor with the stubs of its mutilated fingers.

Conrad ignored the child and continued toward the doorway that led to the street. He glanced down at the child's face and met its panicked expression with one of savage glee.

Dropping the child to the floor, he dug his knee into its neck, pinning it to the ground. He took the blanket and began to wrap the child tightly. The boy's small body was dwarfed by the fabric and before long only its feet poked out from the end.

Despite wanting to die, he knew the child would not want to perish beneath the harsh light of the sun. Sallus had explained the fear of sunlight that was buried deep within the mind of every vampire, and he knew that fear would overtake any wish of death the child harbored. Rolling the boy onto his front, Conrad tied the back of the blanket up as tight as he could so it would not easily slip when he threw the bundle out into the street.

"You have two choices. You can struggle and throw off the cover and allow the sun to roast the flesh from your bones, or you can wait for nightfall for the City Guard to find you. Either way, you will be dead before morning."

With that he hurled the child into the sun-baked street and hastily slammed the butchery door shut.

If the child survived the day, Conrad would take him as close as he dared to one of the sentry boxes of the City Guard so that he would not be discovered so close to the butchery. One way or another, the child would get its wish and Conrad would have deprived it of the small victory he thought he would have had to afford it.

****

The North Gate stood ahead of them imposingly. The gargantuan portal was crafted of thick wood with a coating of steel to ensure that anyone foolish enough to come bearing arms would cause the gate little worry. The gate itself was not the problem for the three vampires, no matter how thick or well-armored, they could scale it as easily as a man could ascend a staircase. It was the host of armed City Guard that stood before it and the scattering of archers that stood atop.

Their blades would do little against the unholy flesh of the undead, and the arrows would fare little better in laying any one of them low, but it would only take one man to grab hold of the furs that covered them and the sun would do all that the steel could not.

The thought of sending Nicholas to kill the guards before the gate was a tempting one. However, such an action would put all on the other side of the gate on alert for their intrusion, and with the temple being in the Upper District, that was something Sallus could not afford. Having one priest hound him for a year had been taxing, having an entire temple's worth hunting him would be the death of him.

It was with great frustration that he gave both Vitria and Nicholas the order to lay low until nightfall. They would lose the element of surprise that arriving in daylight would have given them, however they would lose it anyway if they caused a commotion before the North Gate. Better to go in strong than unexpected.

So as not to arouse suspicion, covered in the furs as they were, Sallus took the initiative and entered a nearby dwelling that lay in the cover of the alleys. He had wanted to be within view of the gate so he could monitor the comings and goings, but constant patrols had made such a room hard to come by.

The building proved to be a poorly kept household with only two rooms and no second floor to speak of. Sallus had been surprised to find such a shabby place so close to the Upper District. The untidiness of the hovel was of no concern to them, however; having spent their time living in a butchery that stank heavily of rotted flesh, this dwelling was a palace in comparison.

The lone occupant of the building—a frail-looking old woman who looked closer to death than Sallus actually was—proved to be of little sustenance. He ignored Nicholas' moans of hunger and took the woman for himself. Her flesh hung from her neck like the waddle of a chicken and it felt disturbingly sickening against his lips. Her blood had been weak and tasted impure as though it was saturated with some sickness. Confident that no mortal ailment could lay him low, he had drunk her lifeblood regardless. He would, after all, need every morsel of strength if things turned sour in the children's nest.

The day passed slowly and with every passing second Nicholas grew more irritable. He would spend hours pacing the floor and staring at the windows, despite the shutters being firmly closed. The sun made any vampire uncomfortable, it was Nicholas' predisposition to anger and violence that made his ordeal all the more difficult to endure. From time to time Sallus noted that his son-in-death would turn his attention to Vitria. He would watch as she ran one of the old woman's combs through her golden hair or rummaged through the perfume boxes.

Sallus scoffed at the thought of the dead old woman even having scented oils or anything of the like. She had smelt repugnant when he had fed off her. He almost felt insulted that she had such items and had not used them, perhaps then he would not have been left with such a foul taste in the back of his throat.

Seeing the look of adoration Nicholas wore whenever his eyes locked on Vitria, Sallus felt compelled to stir the pot. When boredom struck, he always found it important to create his own entertainment.

"Oh, Vitria, have you thought any more about what I asked before?" Sallus noticed Nicholas had turned to him, his interest peaked. "Of you and Conrad?" He fought back a smile as he saw Nicholas' eyes blaze with a fury that had not been present the moment previous.

Vitria noticed her brother's reaction and seemed to take pleasure from his jealousy.

"I just thought I'd enquire, what with Conrad being mere hours from his feeding and having been left alone all day. I imagine he has had nothing else to think about. You have seen how crazed he is, I am just trying to look out for my family," Sallus finished with a warm smile, almost mocking in its sincerity.

"Oh, I've been thinking about Conrad a lot, don't you worry about that, Sallus." Seeing the way Nicholas' posture changed and how he balled his fists by his side at the comment, Sallus could not help but think that her reply had been for Nicholas rather than himself.

Vitria turned her gaze from the two of them, her eyes playful and her expression one of a woman looking for sympathy. "Oh, do calm down, brother of mine. A woman has to have her secrets. Without them I'd be just another pretty face."

"You don't need to be anything other than that," Nicholas growled.

"Stifle your anger, Nicholas. The sun dips, I do not want your temper ruining what we have waited all day to achieve." As if to emphasize his words, Sallus strode over towards the nearest window and pulled back the shutters. The sky above was a dark orange and the sun was nowhere in sight, having passed over their dwelling and almost reaching the end of its arc for the day.

"It's about time!" Nicholas snapped. "I couldn't stay here for a moment longer, I need to kill something."

"You need to deal with your jealousy in better ways," Sallus replied dryly.

Nicholas glared at his father and made to reply but bit back his retort before it could be given form.

Sallus smirked and leapt out of the window into the alleys.

There were only a handful of minutes left before scaling the wall would be achievable. He decided to use that time to search for the best possible place to do so.

Now free of the alleys and back onto the main road approaching the North Gate, Sallus spied the section of wall in the distance where the last of the archers were situated. If they carried on a short distance past that point, they should be able to vault the wall quickly enough not to be seen, and with cover of the darkness that would soon descend across Tilbon, they would be near impossible to spot even to someone standing atop the wall.

Feeling the presence of both Nicholas and Vitria mere feet behind him, Sallus hurried off towards his destination, being careful to keep to the shadows until the last of the day's dying light had dipped past the horizon.

The gloom saturated the sky above Tilbon, the sunlight being chased from the city's skies by the ever-encroaching blanket of darkness. Sallus knew they could now, if need be, scale the walls without any worry of the sun. There was, however, still light enough for the sentries to see their silhouettes. With that in mind he hung back out of view and waited for near total darkness to fall across the Black City.

Chapter Thirteen

Conrad stood watching the City Guard, a furious rage building within him. It was his fault that so many of them were gathered on the streets around the butchery. He thought back to the child's screams as some unknowing young couple had unraveled the blanket in which he had wrapped it.

The sight of the child blackening and bursting into flames had set the streets of the Middle District ablaze with fearful gossip. Conrad had watched helplessly as members of the City Guard gathered to witness the spot where one of the creatures that plagued their city had died. With every passing hour it seemed as though more and more of the cattle flocked to the scene of the child's death. Some were there in an effort to keep the peace and others out of sheer curiosity it seemed.

Regardless of why they were there, none of them seemed intent on leaving. A fact that, as the sunlight wavered and was replaced by darkness, angered him as it meant that the only avenue of escape was blocked by dozens of men and women.

He could almost hear his sire's voice in his head, chastising him for luring such a vast crowd to their door. He fought hard to keep himself from bursting out of the butchery and gorging himself on the blood of those that stood in between him and the barman.

His hunger had slowly driven him to the edge of sanity over the course of the past week, and with Jessamine far from sight or scent, he had nothing to bring him back to his senses. As he surveyed the guardsmen that stood mere feet from the butchery, he wondered why he had brought such a situation upon himself.

The notion that he might have to wait another day before tasting the nectar that he so craved threatened the stability of his already fragile mind. A wicked smile crossed his face as a certain fact dawned upon him: he was allowed to feed.

This was the seventh night since he had supped from the blood of the wolves. He could feed, and there was a plentiful stock of cattle right on his doorstep. Conrad cursed himself as a fool for not realizing sooner. He had not brought trouble to the butchery, he had brought food. A banquet fit for a king.

It was a fitting notion that he would slaughter these people so close to a slaughterhouse. The irony only served to raise his excitement. Was this what Sallus had meant when he had lectured him on the finery of unlife and the subtle joys of engineering the deaths of the cattle?

Refusing to spend a moment longer in thought, Conrad surged out of the butchery and fell atop the nearest living thing in sight. He spared a second to glance up at the horrified faces of those surrounding him. Both men and women stood aghast at the sudden attack, none knowing quite whether to run or stay put. The scene that followed answered any questions as to whether any of them should linger on a moment longer.

He sat atop a young redheaded woman whose hair was matted with blood from the impact on the stone floor. The coppery scent brought forth a week's worth of pent-up hunger and frustration within him. Without giving it a second thought, he sunk his teeth into her neck and tore out her throat, allowing her warm lifeblood to seep into his mouth and course down his gullet.

It was as euphoric as he remembered his first feeding to be. Pulling away momentarily, he saw the face of his first meal, the hurtful young woman who had inadvertently been the death of his mortal self.

His rose.

With his hunger getting the better of him, he cast off the veil of nostalgia and returned to lapping up the woman's blood as it gushed from her ruined neck. Amongst the overwhelming sensation of his feeding, the terrified screams and frantic pounding of feet as the bystanders fled the scene drifted to his ears and served only to heighten the sensation of his feeding. He felt many pairs of hands grab at his arms and grope for purchase around his waist and stomach.

Enraged that his first meal in what felt like an eternity was being interrupted, Conrad raised his head and hungrily tore a chunk of flesh from one of the hands that gripped his shoulder. The action motivated the other do-gooders to release their hold on him for fear of a similar fate.

He used their moment of fear to his advantage. With a thrust of his fist he collapsed the throat of the nearest man. Before his victim had fallen to the ground, he had lunged upon the next, the sound of the dying man's last agonizing breaths spurring him on to further slaughter.

With one hand he reached out and gripped a member of the City Guard by the face and squeezed. The guardsman's body twitched frantically and fell to the floor, his skull crushed inwards. Conrad held his hand up to show the remaining four men the fruits of his labor. He slowly licked his fingers dry of blood and bit his bottom lip hungrily.

The remaining would-be heroes were visibly shaken. They exchanged worried glances and, as one, turned and fled, no doubt hoping against hope that Conrad would not give chase. More out of the need to feed than out of malice, he dashed their hopes. He loped after them, breaking legs and shattering knee caps with well-placed kicks as he went, ensuring that none were killed before they had the chance to savor the sensation of their blood feeding his starved body.

The men screamed as one by one they were devoured. The stench of human waste rose to meet Conrad's keen senses as one of them soiled himself in fright. Refusing to lower himself to such a level as eating from a sullied plate, Conrad stomped angrily on the man's chest, caving it inwards and shattering the ribcage. Twice more he drove the heel of his boot into the pathetic man's chest before he left the broken corpse to rot in peace, its vital organs a pulped mixture of blood and tissue.

Looking up from his slaughter, Conrad was disheartened to find that the rest had fled. He had gorged on the blood of three men and a woman, yet he still felt weak and the touch of madness remained within him, but above all the lingering whisper of the voices in his head were still present.

All of his thoughts went to Jessamine. He longed to be with her, to be near her. Conrad was, for the first time in a long time, totally alone. Free from the prying eyes of Vitria and the inquisitive nature of Sallus, he could spend his night gazing longingly into her eyes, wishing that she would even for the briefest of moments return the gesture.

After this night was done, there would be nothing standing in the way of he and Jessamine. There could be nothing. The barman, that blasted simpleton who cared not whether she existed, would be gone from this world. The very thought of a life without the competition that Edward posed lightened his mood. It felt as if a weight had been lifted from his still heart.

The slaughterhouse was no longer viable as a dwelling now that such a crowd had seen him burst from its confines like the hunger-crazed beast that he was. The priesthood would no doubt be notified, and the place would either be watched or burned to the ground in some bizarre ritual or another.

Sallus crossed his mind, as did Vitria and her oafish admirer Nicholas. They would not know he had blown their cover. They would not know that returning to the butchery meant certain death. Conrad smiled as he pictured Nicholas being set upon by priests of the All-Father and burned alive. He pictured men waiting inside with weapons of silver. Yet at the same time he knew he could not allow such a thing to happen, for he knew if Nicholas was to be destroyed, then in likelihood Sallus would die also. Conrad held no love for either man, but he knew that allowing his sire to die would cause his mind to shatter. He had too much to live for to allow that to happen. By the time his mind became whole again—if he even survived long enough for that to be so—Jessamine would have perished of disease or old age.

He was at a crossroads, utterly torn between what he should and what he wanted to do. Should he rush off into the night and feed on any man, woman or child that crossed his path? Or perhaps return to the ranger's outpost and kill Edward once and for all? There was also his family to think of, should he seek them out and warn them that it was unsafe to return to the butchery?

What he should do was seek out Sallus. But what he wanted to do, what he *yearned* to do, was to kill Edward. The feeding was not important; he could sate his appetite along the way. The thought of drinking Edward's blood was repugnant to him now. Why should he want that filth's lifeblood across his lips when he sought out Jessamine? He wanted nothing of the man to linger on him. Nothing.

Conrad looked up into the night sky, seeing the moon hanging overhead, spilling its loving glow out across the Black City of

Tilbon. That was when he decided that he would do both. The night was young and he was unnaturally fast. He could kill Edward and warn Sallus of the butchery being compromised. It was no longer a case of what he should and what he wanted to do. It was a case of what he *had* to do.

With Edward still alive there was the chance of him being discovered. While the barman breathed, Conrad could never truly have Jessamine. And at the same time, if Sallus were to die, he would still be unable to have her. He had more than enough time to achieve both tasks; he would, however, have to settle for killing Edward quickly for there would be no time to waste. The thought saddened him deeply, for the barman's demise had been something he had been quite looking forward to. He had wanted to sit out the remainder of the night and enjoy every shred of pain that racked the man's worthless body.

Conrad took one last look at the dead bodies around him and savored the scent of freshly spilled blood in the air before bounding off in the direction of the slums. He would snack along the way if the chance arose and then push out of the city and into the surrounding forests towards Edward.

He picked up his pace as he gave thought to the man's name again. A week's worth of fantasizing about killing the man and Conrad was unsure as to how he would go about it. He could not simply snap Edward's neck or run him through with a blade. The barman had to suffer. He had to suffer quickly, but suffer nonetheless.

Putting all of his conscious thought into getting to the forest as quickly as possible, Conrad resolved to find something along his travels to make Edward's last few moments of life unbearable.

****

Vaulting the wall had proved as easy as Sallus had imagined. Their unnatural speed coupled with the darkness of Tilbon's night sky had rendered them practically invisible.

Sallus had spent many nights stalking the rooftops of the various mansions and function halls that littered Tilbon's Upper District when they had first been on the lookout for the nest of the abhorrations, and had found nothing. They had since learned from their captive that a secret passageway leading from a cellar to the city's network of sewers was how the children had been coming and going without arousing suspicion.

Both he and Vitria had immediately turned their nose up at the thought of skulking in the sewers. It had been decided that using the front door would by far be the best route in order to catch their quarry off guard. If they chose to use the sewers, there was the chance that they would run into some of the children and, in doing so, lose the element of surprise. If Sallus could help it, he wanted to come upon the perverse sire of these children first, as with their mistress slain, the newborns would become feral and uncontrollable. With them as likely to attack their own kind as they would the Sovains, the children would be of little concern.

Now that he knew which building to look for, it made spending time so close to the temple almost bearable. Thin white veins streaked through the elegant mansion that stood before him. Sallus stood gazing at the immense iron door for what seemed an age, his acute hearing probing the building for any sign that they had been spotted. His keen senses found only silence beyond the doorway.

Gently, he pried the door open. At first he was surprised to find the door to such a place unlocked, but then he remembered just what waited inside. Any man foolish enough to capitalize on such an opportunity for thieving would find nothing but his own death. After all, what did a nest of vampires have to fear from a common crook?

The interior was as ostentatious as the exterior suggested. The ceiling was domed, something that was not apparent when viewed from the outside, and reached upwards to incredible heights. The floor was smooth and fashioned from the same black rock as the rest of the city, yet was polished to such perfection that it appeared as a different variety of stone entirely. Great busts of gold, studded with rubies, stood on plinths of jade. Silk woven tapestries hung from the walls, and large portraits of small children were set in frames of bronze.

Sallus winced as he heard the footfalls of both his children-in-death resonate softly throughout the entrance hall. Despite treading as gently as a midsummer breeze, the sheer silence of the place highlighted the most minute of sounds. To a mortal man's ears such levels of noise would have gone unheard, but to one such as he, they rang out loud and clear.

He spun on his heel and glared balefully at Nicholas and Vitria. His eyes spoke volumes that his voice would not have managed.

Vitria replied with a playful smile before loping off past her sire. She ignored the twin staircases that rose to the second floor and disappeared through an archway some thirty feet ahead. With every one of her graceful footfalls, Sallus expected a cacophony of warning cries to erupt.

"I think this place is empty," Nicholas whispered.

Sallus thought for a moment. Had the child lied to them? Had he been played by a mere child? The thought enraged him, yet his anger was eclipsed by thoughts of dread as he realized he had told Conrad to kill the child if he wished. In his eagerness, Sallus had thrown away their only lead on where these vampire children nested.

He balled his fists at his side, the cracking of his knuckles sounding impossibly loud in the silence. The scent of blood brought him back to his senses. The luscious aroma saturated the air heavily. The scent was old, that much was certain. Its presence still filled him with a sense of joyous relief, for such a potent smell as that had to be the product of a lot of bloodshed.

Smiling widely, Sallus cursed himself inwardly for allowing his emotions to overpower his senses. He was far too eager to confront the perverse creator of the undead children. After all, had he not seen portraits of dozens of children mere moments before? Each one had the tell-tale red bow in their hair. There was no doubt that he was standing in their lair.

"Sallus," Vitria's cry carried easily despite it being little more than a muttering. "You must see this."

The mixture of fear and revulsion in Vitria's voice had Nicholas moving long before Sallus had even thought of doing so. He hurried after his son-in-death, eager to see what had Vitria so vexed.

They found her standing in the centre of what appeared to be the main living area of the grand home. She stood on a thick rug the color of sapphires, her gaze fixed on a slender wooden chair pushed against the far wall.

All around, Sallus noted small chairs and tables no doubt designed for the children who called this place home. In that moment even his cold heart felt pity for the poor creatures, for these small furnishings displayed just why it was taboo to sire a child. He tried to think what it must be like to live forever and to never grow up, to be so small and underdeveloped for the rest of your existence. He pulled himself out of that train of thought, determined not to feel pity for those whom he had come to slay.

Sallus allowed his eyes to follow Vitria's gaze, he noted Nicholas already stood at her side, his shoulders slumped in a show of fearful submission and his hand tightly clutched by Vitria. *What she sees must truly be vile if she allows herself such a moment of weakness as this,* Sallus mused to himself.

Moving forward to gain an unobstructed view of the chair that had Vitria in such a state of fear, Sallus felt every muscle involuntarily tighten in his body. What he saw had him fighting the urge to turn tail and flee. He wanted nothing more than to take his family and not stop running until they were far away from Tilbon.

A sleek black-feathered raven was perched on the arm of the chair, its gaze not once leaving the three of them. It looked on almost mockingly as they marveled at it. Each of them knew just what this bird heralded.

The moment Sallus locked eyes with the bird he saw flashes of his torments in the Underworld. He felt the sting of every lash as if his wounds had been dealt anew. What followed this bird would be the death of them, there was no stopping him.

"He's here," Vitria whispered, her voice heavy with disbelief.

"Vance," Sallus whispered.

****

Having rushed with all possible haste, Conrad slowed and allowed himself to enjoy the prospect of what was to come. He clutched at four small iron poles, they had been the first objects he had come across upon entering the slums, and he had neglected to trade them for more deadly-looking apparatus.

With the slums long behind him, he felt more relaxed. The concerns of his choices or his duty to his family did not weigh down on him any longer. It was as if the only two people in the entire world were he and Edward. Time would stop and allow him this pleasure, and once Edward had paid for hindering Conrad's chances with Jessamine, things would continue on as normal, the only difference being that Jessamine's eyes would no longer be locked on the imbecilic barman.

It felt too easy.

To think that such an insignificant little man had caused him such heartache and despair was beyond belief. And what was worse, his troubles could have been removed instantly, had he only had the nerve to have done this sooner. It galled him to think that he had only stayed his hand for fear that he might drink of Edward's blood, yet now the thought of allowing even a trickle to pass his lips was abhorrent. He wanted to remove as many traces of Edward from his life as possible, not make him a part of himself.

The forest soon parted to let the ill-maintained outpost come into view, and despite its shabby, dilapidated appearance, he could think of no other place that would fill his heart with such joy this night. Even Jessamine's loving embrace would not tear him away from his appointment in the pitiful little shack.

Edward's dull moans of pain and discomfort were the only sounds that existed to Conrad, all else was of secondary concern and did not register in his mind. He stood in the darkened doorway of the outpost, the small, filthy hut filled mainly with animal droppings and the broken form of the man he had come to kill.

The barman lay bound on the moldy wooden floor, his clothes damp and covered in dirt. Edward's eyes widened in horror as he noticed the vampire. His lips began to quiver as Conrad held out the iron poles.

"What am I to do with you?" he asked mockingly. "I could bludgeon you to death, or shatter each and every bone in your body, starting from your toes and working my way up. But then that would be such a waste, to use only one when I have brought four."

"P…p…please…let me…l…live," Edward begged.

"Oh, but I can't. Even if I had a sudden change of heart, it would simply be impossible. You see, while you still draw breath, Jessamine will look at no other."

"Please. I'll leave. I can go to Nadhaska, or I can travel to Gremecia. I have family in the city of Jaya."

Conrad paused and appeared to consider Edward's words. "But how would you manage such a feat with a broken leg?" Conrad asked as he struck Edward's right shin with one of the iron poles. The barman recoiled and screamed in agony as tears seeped down his cheeks, clearing streaks of grime from his skin.

Conrad smiled and laughed as he watched Edward try to gather his leg to him as if to protect it. Bound as he was, the pitiful excuse for a man could do little more than curl into a slightly lopsided ball and scream his curses.

"How foolish of me, I said I would not bludgeon you to death. Ah well, we all make mistakes, don't we?" Conrad said, smiling as he did so.

He knelt down next to Edward and locked eyes with him. To his credit, the man maintained eye contact. Whether this was out of bravery or fear that an attack would come unseen, Conrad did not know. He eyed Edward's chest as the man took deep breaths in an effort to combat the pain coursing through his body.

"A broken arm and a shattered leg, not much use to anyone, are you? But I'd wager she'd nurse you back to health if given the chance. You'd still be the object of her love and that is why I do what I do.

"I look at you and I see a pitiful wretch who'd give anything so that his life remained intact. We are so different, the contrast is stark and yet she does not see it. She still pines for you." Conrad took Edward's hand and pressed it against his own pale features. "Look at me. I am handsome, beautiful in fact. My looks shall never fade whereas your common appeal would have deteriorated with time. I can give her life anew where all you could offer is life in the slums. And unlike you, I would give my life a hundred times for her. Why she doesn't see that I am right for her and you are nothing more than a passing curiosity, I shall never know."

Conrad kept hold of Edward's hand, got to his feet and forcibly dragged him from the hut. The barman's agonized cries cut through the still night air with ease, and Conrad was under no illusion that they would not be heard by the City Guard. It mattered not whether the last screams of his victim were heard or not, as by the time anyone had gathered the courage to search the forests, he would be long gone and Edward would be beyond saving.

Purposefully, he dragged Edward by his broken arm so that his last night of life would be one of little comfort. He made his way through the forest, pulling his victim along behind him through thorny shrubs and harsh rocky patches of earth. Conrad could smell the barman's blood on the air as the abrasive terrain tore into his flesh.

They emerged on the other side of the forest, the vast expanse of fenland seemed unnatural after being cooped up within the city for the past week. Conrad continued to drag Edward a little further until they were well away from the woodland.

At length, he released Edward from his grip and untied his bonds.

"For the death I have planned, you need to be beneath the open skies," Conrad said.

The barman looked on fearfully as Conrad dropped a pole next to each of his limbs. He tried to roll away but the vampire's boot was quick to pin him to the ground, ensuring that he tried nothing of the sort again.

Conrad clutched at Edward's right arm, his grip as unyielding as iron and as cold as stone. He straightened the arm out so that it was pointing away from Edward's body. So tight was his grip that despite Edward's best efforts, he could not move it an inch.

A thrill of excitement coursed through Conrad's body as he held one of the small poles high above his head as if in offering to the cold night sky. In that moment Edward's eyes flashed with panic as he saw what Conrad intended.

With a strength that belied his slender form, Conrad drove the blunt end of the pole through Edward's elbow and into the hard-packed earth beneath, shattering the bone to nothingness. Edward writhed in pain, screaming into the night sky, begging for his death to come swift and for all pain to be taken away. Conrad ignored the frantic jabbering of his victim and pushed down harder on the pole, forcing it further into the ground so that only a few inches stood above Edward's ruined elbow. He then took the end that protruded from the ground and bent it, as easily as a man would bend straw, to ensure that Edward could not pry himself free of the makeshift stake. All the while his victim's frenzied screams filled the night sky, the thrashing of his body on the earth providing an underlying beat to the symphony that was his agony.

Methodically, Conrad moved on to the next arm and repeated the grotesque act. With both Edward's arms staked to the earth he moved on to the legs, forcing the blunt poles through the man's kneecaps. Blood pooled around the man's limbs as it leaked from the wounds to his joints. With eyes as cold as a practiced killer, Conrad stood gazing into Edward's ever screaming face.

Slowly, Conrad removed a small, slender blade from his belt and held it high so that Edward could see. The steel of the blade glinted in the moonlight.

For a moment Edward's face was no longer a mask of pain. His expression became serene for a split second, as though he knew that

Conrad was going to plunge the blade into his heart and end his suffering. A mocking smile and a slow shake of his head was all it took to transform a moment's serenity back into horror.

"Death will not come so easily for you. Come daybreak you will be food for the carrion birds or whatever animals are hungry enough to venture forth from the forest."

He leaned over Edward's writhing body and tore his grubby shirt from his body. The hair on his chest was slick with blood, sweat and moisture from the forest floor. With the precision of a healer, Conrad took the blade and cut Edward from gut to gullet, deep enough to draw blood but shallow enough to ensure that he remained alive.

Conrad flashed a triumphant smile at Edward's utterly ruined body before turning his back on the screams of anguish to return to Tilbon.

****

As he sped across the low-rise buildings of the slums, a feeling of purest joy spread throughout Conrad's body. The sensation felt almost enough to warm his cold, lifeless form. The very thought that come morning's light, Edward, the only man who stood between him and Jessamine would be no more, made all other things seem less important.

There were still several hours of darkness left and Conrad still had one duty to perform before he could reflect on his night's work. The unenviable task of informing Sallus that he had led Tilbon's authorities to their very door was not something he relished. Conrad could only imagine the things Sallus would do to him as punishment. He shuddered at the thought that additional days might be added on to his starvation period. Having just fed, his mind was clear for the first time in what seemed an age. He remembered how disjointed and irrational his thoughts had been at the height of his deprivation and wanted nothing more than to beat the hunger-induced madness that descended upon him. Increasing the starvation period would be detrimental, and he could only hope that the thought would only cross his mind and not that of his sire.

The sight of dozens of red cloaks flailing in the wind as they rushed towards the city gate brought a smile to his face. No doubt the agonized screams that pierced the night had roused them into action. His smile faded as he spied a sight that would have stopped his heart were it not already incapable of beating. Off in the distance, visible only because of Conrad's higher vantage point, he saw the bane of his sire.

The priest.

Conrad forced back the sudden onset of fear and reminded himself that he had gorged upon many humans this night. He was strong, far stronger than the priest could ever hope to be. It would not only be a pleasure to rid the world of such a troublesome foe, it would also be the perfect excuse for having to leave the butchery. He could blame it on the priest and his filthy-looking lackey.

Moving forward to intercept the priest, Conrad's footwork was so light and quick that it barely looked as if his feet were touching the stone rooftops. With every passing second his anticipation grew and fast outstripped the fear that had initially been present. It was galling, however, to think that such a noble and heroic act on his part would have to take place in such meager surroundings. The small, dingy hovels that were on par with the forest for their level of filth and muck was hardly the place to enact a moment such as this.

Within seconds Conrad had drawn almost level with his prey, not making a sound as he made his approach. With one almighty leap, he propelled himself from the single-storied building and sent himself hurling through the air towards the priest.

The sound of the wind thrashing against Conrad's blood-soaked clothing caused more noise than he would have thought possible. The priest turned, alerted by the sudden blast of sound, and was able to raise his hands in time to lessen the force of Conrad's impact.

Both predator and prey tumbled to the ground, rolling through the muck and grime of the slums. Conrad heard the frantic shouts of the priest's aide as he did whatever it was he was doing. The man's actions were inconsequential, he only had eyes for the priest.

He thundered his fist towards the priest's skull, missing by inches as his prey managed to duck the blow. His fist pummeled the stone floor beneath, the impact sending flares of pain through his hand but not slowing him down in the slightest. His bloodlust was up and pain was secondary to the thrill of the kill. A return blow caught Conrad slightly off-guard and landed just below the ribs.

Barely fazed by the priest's strike, Conrad made to hurl yet another fist. A severe scalding sensation enveloped the hand that held the priest down. He leapt backwards, screeching in pain at the wound dealt to him. Unlike the dull pain of the missed strike, this was a searing, white-hot pain that felt as though it ate away at his very flesh.

A black mark was singed into his flesh and half of the All-Father's symbol was showing like a red-hot brand. A smile of relief split his ashen face, for if he had come away with the mark fully emblazoned upon his flesh then he imagined the pain would be a lasting experience.

He flashed the priest a murderous glare as the man smiled and held up the silver pendant that hung around his neck. The priest barely seemed perturbed by the fact that one such as he had marked him for death. Conrad recalled Sallus speaking of how those of the priesthood somehow negated the awesome strength that a vampire possessed, making any fight *almost* equal.

Such nonsense was unbelievable, but the fact that the priest stood before him, seemingly eager to fight, was making him rethink his stance on the subject. Perhaps these zealots truly did have some sort of mystical quality about them. It mattered not, he had fed well this night and even the bizarre nature of the priest would not be enough to stop him. The fool had demonstrated he could evade attack, but if Conrad could land one strike he was confident that his foe would not get back up.

Thoughts of how Sallus would reward him as he presented the still corpses of both the priest and his aide caused a smile to split his savage face. That one thought pushed all other thoughts of safety and caution aside. He howled into the night and leapt towards the priest.

Mirroring his actions, the priest sped towards Conrad. The man's cumbersome trench coat, catching the wind as he went, made his actions look clumsy and almost comical. Conrad would have smiled, if not for the silver-edged sword that found its way into the priest's hands. He cursed, annoyed that he had been so eager to tackle his foe and had neglected thinking it through. If only he had looked for potential danger, he would have no doubt seen the bulge on the priest's back, indicating a hidden sheath.

Conrad swerved at the last moment to avoid the priest's lunge. He threw his leg out but caught only air as his foe jumped to avoid the crippling blow. He swiped at the priest twice more with kicks and a further three times with fiendishly quick fists, all of which were either dodged or turned aside. The last of Conrad's blows was deflected with the edge of the sword, the keen silver edge slicing into his arm as though it were butter.

Shrieking in pain and anger, he leapt back, yanking his arm from danger. He surveyed the cut, shocked at the sight of his own blood. His night had been filled with the ruby-red blood of the cattle, his own was of stark contrast.

The wound seemed to seep strength from his body. He realized this was a fight he could not win. If the priest was unarmed, perhaps he could have ended this, but as it stood, that damned sword was proving impossible to pass. Not for the first time Conrad found himself despising himself for having such pathetic weaknesses. The very thought of silver scalding the flesh was absurd, yet he had been burned far too many times to know that such a thing was true.

As if hearing his thoughts the priest pressed the advantage, lunging his sword as he closed the gap between them. Conrad was forced to duck and then arch backwards to avoid life-threatening blows from the holy weapon.

"A year of my life spent hunting your fellow," the priest barked, swinging the silver blade for Conrad's neck. "And all I get is his lackey!"

Conrad was not foolish enough to be drawn in by his attacker's taunts. Had he not fed, had this scene occurred prior to supping from the cattle, Conrad would have flung himself on the priest's blade, utterly enraged by his words. But not now. His mind was clear and he would not suffer the weakness of pride while it remained so.

Risking a glance at his surroundings, he spied his next move. The priest might be his match for strength, but there was no chance the man would have any hope in catching him, especially if he made use of the rooftops.

Well aware that the priest had taken in his stolen glance, Conrad gave the illusion that he intended to remain and fight. He leapt high and lashed out with his heel towards the priest's head, catching him on the jaw with a glancing blow. Momentarily, he thought of pressing his advantage and attempting to finish the priest off. All thoughts of victory were soon put aside, though, as his opponent regained his composure and flung himself back into a guard position.

He flashed the priest a smile before turning his back and rushing towards the nearest building. The priest cried out to his aide, and a moment later he felt the air ripple beside him as a silver dagger toppled end over end past his face and clattered harmlessly off of the very building he was fleeing to.

In one fluid motion, Conrad pulled himself atop the building. He looked over his shoulder, taking in the scowl worn by the priest. Any man who claimed it was a coward's way to flee had not seen such a victorious sight.

With the image of the priest seething in anger fresh in his mind, he scaled the next building and sped on across the rooftops to warn Sallus that their lair was no longer safe. His mind flickered back to Edward.

Conrad smiled.

The butchery might be of no use, but the barman would not be using his room any time soon

Chapter Fourteen

Thick smoke hung over the bar making Giento cough. He waved his hand to clear the air in front of him and laid his head back in his arms, utterly tired beyond belief. His sleeping pattern had been drastically altered; what with the nature of the creatures they hunted, Castus had been forcing him to sleep during the day and go about their business at night. It had been difficult adjusting to the different sleep pattern, but a week into the unnatural rhythm and Giento was content with the fact that it would not get any easier. He simply was not one for sleeping during the day. Despite the fatigue that plagued his body and the aches he felt all over, he just could not gain more than a few hours' sleep.

The previous night had proved to be one of the most disturbing he had endured throughout his employment with the priest. It had started with a mad dash to an abandoned butchery where a young woman and several men had been slaughtered. The smell of blood was still stuck inside his nostrils and he very much doubted the image of torn flesh lying discarded in the street would ever leave his mind. Mutilated bodies were getting easier for Giento to deal with, but these had been different. It had looked as though some feral creature had set about them hungrily instead of a vampire. Not that there was much difference, he supposed.

The hours that followed the gruesome discovery outside the butchery were spent searching the surrounding area for any hint on where the dread creature might have fled. Castus had learned that a crowd had gathered outside of the butchery where a child had erupted in flames. It was obvious that the child was one of the things they hunted, but to the townsfolk who had been plagued by these beings for months, such a notion was too hard to stomach. Instead they conjured up tales of sorcery, despite the fact that the practicing of magic had been banned under pain of death for several centuries within the Empire. However, given the fear that saturated their everyday lives, Giento could well understand how they wanted to turn a blind eye to the idea that their own children might also be a threat.

Their searching had led them to the slums, where a trail of bodies had been found atop low-rise buildings and littering the maze of alleyways. Horrified peasants jabbered tales of a handsome savage. A man whose fine clothes and decadent appeal marked him as one of the city's gentry had acted like some depraved beast, slaughtering and drinking the blood of any man, woman or child too slow or foolish to flee.

With an entire network of alleyways and hovels to search, the priest's mood had darkened. Not until the otherworldly screams permeated the night air did he smile.

At first, neither man knew from which direction the screams had originated. Such was the disorientating fashion of the slums that neither Castus nor Giento could find their way back with any ease.

With blind hope being their only guidance, they set off in what they hoped was the right direction to lead them to some sort of main road from where they could gather their bearings. Giento had spent many weeks in these very slums before, but the black stone had a way of dumbfounding all but those who were native to the area. Especially in the dead of night.

It was not long before they happened across a small group of City Guard, their red cloaks fluttering frantically behind them in what looked like some desperate attempt to keep up with their wearers.

Castus had not bothered with questions, he had simply been content to follow the guardsmen, confident that they were running towards the screams and not away from them. Giento recalled how cowardly the guards' actions had been in the past, yet chose not to make his thoughts known to the priest. With any luck, the guards would lead them well away from the sounds of distress.

Of course, as was usually the case, his prayers were ignored. Mere moments after the procession of fluttering red cloaks had led them out of the confusing system of alleys and side streets, Castus was knocked from the ground.

Giento took a long draught of the ale that sat in front of him and shuddered as he remembered seeing the vampire sitting atop his paymaster. Had that beast succeeded in killing the priest, he would most certainly have been quick at his paymaster's heels into the next life. With that thought cemented firmly in his mind, Giento called the barman over and asked for another.

"It's not even midday and you've had three already. It's against the law to send a man out into the city drunk during daylight hours. I'd be fined." The barman shook his head. "It's not gonna happen. It's water or nothing for you, lad."

"It's no different to you wantin' a drink after work," Giento replied drowsily. "I've been busy all night. I just wanna unwind."

"Whether you were awake all night or not isn't my problem, and it don't change the law."

"Half the lowlifes in the slums are drunk all day and night. I won't look outta place."

"I'd watch your tongue if I were you, lad. Them 'lowlifes' are my customers, and they don't appreciate folk from out of town talking down to 'em," the barman retorted, nodding towards the rear of the room. Giento turned and saw a group of five men sitting in the corner, their eyes boring into him with what could only be considered hatred.

"I think it best you leave now and we say no more of this. What says you?" the barman asked, annoyance creeping into his voice.

Giento, being the perpetual coward that he was, had spent most of his time hiding out in places such as this, and he knew when he was not wanted. Yet despite that fact, he was fatigued beyond belief and the three tankards of ale he had drunk had gone down far too fast and had fallen into an empty stomach. Even if he had wanted to move, he would not be able to manage much more than a painful fall from his stool.

"I've 'ad nothing to eat and three of your ales. When ya couple that with bein' awake for the better part of the last week it makes it very 'ard to do anythin'. So I think I'll stay and 'ave a kip if it's all right by you," Giento said, laying his head in his arms.

Evidently, it was not alright by the barman or the thugs glaring from across the room. Mere moments after laying his head down to rest, he felt a pair of hands grab him by the shoulders and haul him from his seat. Instinctively he kicked his feet out and caught the stool he had been sitting on. He heard a grunt of pain followed by a curse behind him. A moment later he was dropped to the ground as the man holding him grabbed at his knee to soothe the pain the lucky shot had caused. Giento smiled at his unexpected accomplishment.

The smile was soon wiped from his face as he felt the point of a boot slam into his side. He tried to roll out of the way but found himself rolling into the bar and leaving himself with nowhere to go.

"Lowlife, eh? You don't look no better!" screamed his attacker before landing another kick into Giento's midriff.

In that moment, he felt like laughing. There he was, in Tilbon for the sole purpose of helping the priest hunt vampires, and he was going to die on some dingy barroom floor. Somehow it did not seem right, it did not seem fair. If he had been a proud man he would have felt cheated that he was being denied an honorable death fighting the Empire's foes. As it was, he just felt cheated that he was going to die. He always envisioned the yellow streak that ran down his spine would keep him alive until he was too old to run away with any great speed.

"I don't want him bleedin' on my bar. It's not good for business."

Giento heard a grunt of annoyance from the man who stood towering above him. The barman's order had obviously not meshed well with his plans.

"It's your lucky day," the man said before lifting Giento to his feet and slamming a knee into his gut. "Now don't come back or else I'll gut ya."

He felt himself being dragged across the barroom, his wheezing coughs the only sound.

As his attacker reached the door, he hurled Giento at the wall and held him by the throat. "You sure I can't bleed him a little?" he shouted towards the barman over his shoulder.

"Just throw him out."

He flinched as the bald, yellow-toothed man flashed a filthy smile.

"I'll help ya get some rest."

Giento's face momentarily scrunched in confusion as he tried to understand what the man meant. A moment later he was dragged from the wall to stand on the threshold. He watched the man wearily and, as he saw the brute's fist hurtling towards his face, did the only thing he could: closed his eyes and hoped for the best.

The impact of the blow sent him tumbling into the street. He slumped against the opposing wall, and despite every bit of common sense he possessed screaming at him to get up and run as far from the bar as possible, he just could not find the energy to move an inch.

Even with the pain he felt comfortable now he was slouched against the wall of some building or another. His eyes began to grow heavy, and even with the sun's light beating brightly upon him, Giento finally managed to fall asleep.

****

The pain-induced slumber proved to be short-lived as, a few hours after drifting off from the fatigue of his week-long adventure, he was rudely awoken by something persistently jabbing at his torso. Refusing to open his eyes, Giento merely rolled onto his other side and grunted in annoyance. His ignorance cost him as the dull prodding vanished and was replaced by something wickedly sharp poking him in the lower back.

Even as tired as he was, the thought that he was being stabbed at enabled him to dig deep into reserves he was not aware he had and leap to his feet in order to put distance between himself and the stranger prodding him.

His eyes widened as they locked onto the small group of guardsmen. The leader stood resplendent in immaculate segmented leather armor, his blood-red cloak flowing from his shoulders. The man was tall and broad of chest; everything about him screamed that he was a warrior with experience. His eyes moved to the halberd clutched at the man's side, the weapon was easily as long as the guardsman was tall. Giento rubbed the small of his back as he took in the spike that protruded from the end of the blade.

He swayed a little, the sudden movement to his feet coupled with the alcohol he had drunk on an empty stomach getting the best of him. He put a hand on the wall to steady himself.

"Fighting and drunk in the street," the lead guardsman intoned.

"You 'ave me all wrong, I wasn't doin' neither," Giento replied, his voice steadier than his legs.

The guardsman glared at Giento. "You are bruised and reek of ale." He turned his head to the guardsmen flanking him and pointed to the bar Giento had been ejected from. "Twenty gold and five silver. If the landlord refuses to pay, close down his establishment until he can." With nothing more than a nod of understanding, two guardsmen carrying short swords moved off towards the bar.

The halberdier returned his gaze to Giento. "You've earned yourself a spot in the city jails. You shall accompany us willingly, or we shall take you by force. For your sake it would be better to remain quiet, lest you say something that might further add to your sentence."

"No, I can't. He'll go spare if I don't get back to 'im."

"Whatever plans you had are not my concern. You shall come with us."

"Wait, you don't understand," was all Giento could say before the halberdier struck him unconscious with the haft of his weapon.

****

Within very few days, the capital city of Nadhaska had been transformed from the crown jewel of Libethan architecture and culture into a rotting charnel house. The city's grand, centuries-old design of concentric circles had been turned from a piece of defensive mastery into a maze of death and damnation.

Men, women and children had been forced to barricade themselves inside their homes for fear of the animated corpses that hungered for the flesh of the living.

The Nadhaskan army had enjoyed initial success at besting their unliving foes in combat, but the battle-hardened warriors soon came to terms with the fact that they fought an interminable foe. With every swing of their blades, with every breath taken, the Nadhaskan defenders saw the stark realization of their predicament. The dead would fight on despite whatever losses were inflicted upon their ranks and, unlike the living, they never slept. For all their ferocity and patriotism, the Nadhaskans knew that defeat loomed on the horizon.

As slow and ponderous as the undead were, they were lethal in numbers. With more and more of the city's dead clawing their way out of their graves on a daily basis, the Nadhaskans soon found themselves to be fighting a battle of attrition.

In open terrain, every man was worth a dozen of the rotten corpses. Yet the defenders' efforts were hampered by the city's narrow streets and tall walls. The compact nature of their surroundings, coupled with the fact that every man who fell only served to swell the ranks of the enemy, had become a serious drain on morale.

The effects of the grotesque nightmare playing out across the city were being felt more by the common folk than those tasked with the city's defense. Men had watched in horror as their loved ones had roused themselves from their eternal slumber. Mothers had been forced to smother their own children and destroy the bodies with cleansing fire rather than see them starve and be born again into such a hellish existence. Whoever dared brave the streets spent their time begging at the gates of the rich for whatever scraps they could spare.

After two days of the dead flooding the streets with their deteriorating forms, the once-pristine city of Nadhaska had become a hotbed of disease. Healers were inundated with a tidal flow of the sick and wounded. More often than not, the only cure to be offered was faith in the All-Father, but with the immense structure of the holy temple lying in ruin, faith was in short supply. After all, if the All-Father would allow his own temple to be sacked, what hope did the common folk have that he would see them safe?

Nadhaska's plight was plain for all to see, perhaps more so to Kitali. Having travelled from across the ocean and spent time within the city's walls, he had witnessed the grandeur of the city and now saw how far into depravity it had fallen in such a short time.

He stood gazing out across the courtyard of the Elector Count's palace. He had never before seen such grandeur used on the housing of one person; in temples and architectural masterpieces, yes, but as someone's personal dwelling it merely seemed pretentious.

The courtyard itself was a vast expanse of concrete that, to the Count's credit, seemed to be more functional than fashionable. Two enormous wrought-iron gates stood at the head of the courtyard, each bar as thick as a man's forearm. The gates were built into high walls that circled the yard and merged with those of the Elector Count's palace. Despite how durable the gates obviously were, Kitali shuddered when he thought about how they were the only thing keeping the dead from coming any closer. He winced and rotated his arm. The heavy fighting in which he had been involved had been an almost constant two-day affair and his shoulders still ached from his exertions.

Armored feet echoed off of the marble interior of the antechamber in which Kitali had been forced to wait. Ever since he had fought his way back to the palace to offer his aid, he had been forced to remain within sight of the Count's guards at all times. He met the gaze of the two men who came to an abrupt stop mere feet away.

"His grace, Henlan Creed, Elector Count of Libetha, shall see you now," one of the heavily armored men said before taking hold of Kitali's shoulder and leading him towards the Count's chamber.

He refused to reply. He had noticed over the past couple of days that he would garner no conversation from the Count's men. They appeared to be nothing more than unthinking brutes kept firmly on their master's leash. To his eyes, the Empire itself seemed to be nothing more than the plaything of one man. In the lands of Assan-Ghur, there was by far more freedom. Not for the first time since setting sail for the lands of his newfound allies, Kitali found himself wishing he was back with his own people. Were it not for the rite of passage that he must complete, he would have been aboard the next available ship bound for Assan-Ghur.

As the two guards led him from the marbled antechamber to the thickly carpeted interior of the Count's inner sanctum, Kitali wondered how such a soft people had grown to hold such power. He found himself asking if he would find the experience in battle that he so needed to pass his rite of passage and become a peer amongst his elders. Surely if such a breed of people who cared more for their own personal wealth than for the wellbeing of their brethren had lasted for so long, there would be little hope of a foe like he had hoped for waiting somewhere in these lands. The undead were taxing, but merely due to their numbers. He sought something to test his very being and not just his stamina.

Such thoughts were ludicrous. Had he not heard of a land to the north of Libetha that no sane man dared tread? Of course, he knew the truth behind the Ash Desert, those who fled to Assan-Ghur centuries previous had told his people of the despicable past of the blighted land to the north. Perhaps, one day, when his duties in this city were done with, he would venture further north in search of this hellish place. He sighed, with things as they were that would not be for a very long time.

Kitali's thoughts were interrupted as one of the guards leading him began to speak. He looked up to find the man making introductions. Not that introductions were needed, Kitali had both heard of and seen the Elector Count and there could be no doubt that the man sitting before him was indeed the ruler of Libetha. No other man would dress so outlandishly during a time of conflict such as this.

Count Creed waved his left hand as if bored of his minion's speech, the sleeve of his voluminous robe seeming to droop so much that it threatened to off-balance him.

The Count was tall and slender, his robes making him appear of far more bulk than he actually possessed. His shaven head was oiled to such an extent that the light gleamed off it, and the makeup he wore about his eyes gave him an effeminate look. As the Count placed his hand back on the arm of his throne, Kitali noticed his fingernails were painted black. They were as shiny as the man's skull.

Having only ever seen the Elector Count from a distance, Kitali had thought of him as nothing more than a bald-headed man, yet up close he saw him as some form of sexual deviant. Was this man so unsure of himself that he tried to appear as a woman? The thought was distasteful and unsettling so Kitali shook it from his mind, forcing himself not to make assumptions before having spoken with the man.

"You are the traveler from across the ocean that came to warn me of my city's doom?" The Count's voice was as soft and delicate as his appearance suggested.

"I am. I came to warn your priesthood of a great evil that was to pass through your city."

The Count raised an eyebrow and raised his left hand to stroke at his cleanly shaven face, as though fondling a beard that he did not possess. "Pass through, you say? To my eyes such an evil has yet to leave."

"This was not what I came to warn you of. The mystics had not foreseen the emergence of your dead."

"Mystics? So, the priesthood were correct in their claims that you engage in some form of daemonancy?" Kitali made to reply but was cut off by the Count. "It is indeed a coincidence that such a horrific thing happens when you appear in Nadhaska. One might almost assume that you brought this hellish nightmare upon my fair city."

Kitali took a step forward, incensed at the Elector Count's words. The Count's eyes widened and he shirked back into his throne as if in an effort to escape the dwarf. Seeing their master's concern, a trio of guardsmen bearing polearms thrust their weapons into the space between he and the Count, makirrg him halt his advance and rethink his actions.

"How dare you accuse me of rousing the dead? How dare you accuse me of tainting the alliance brokered by our peoples?" Kitali spat.

"Because you are an abhorrence!" the Count roared in reply, his confidence brimming once more now that his guards had put an end to Kitali's earlier intents. "You stand no taller than my waist, a child in a world of men. How utterly alien you are to all that this Empire is founded upon. Were it I, and not Emperor Beledain that was in power, such an alliance as we now have would not exist.

"Look at you," the Count continued. "Your skin is black as pitch. *Black* is the color of the Undergods. *Black* is a color not to be trusted. *Black* is the color of evil," the Count intoned, his eyes boring down into Kitali's and his voice growing ever more powerful with each word. "I commend the priesthood for not striking you down upon first sight, for if I were not bound by the laws of the Emperor, I most certainly would have done."

Kitali stood with his fists balled at his sides. He glanced down at his belt to where his maces had once hung. Had the Count's guards not removed them from his possession, he would have been all too tempted to put them to good use.

"Why would I bring this hell down onto your city and remain behind to suffer the consequences? Why would I risk my life and go without sleep in order to battle this unliving menace?" Kitali replied, his words no longer that of a calm diplomat.

"Why not? What have you to lose? You conjure the bones of our dead and throw them against our walls. By staying and fighting them, by surviving with the aid of your fell sorceries, you look the picture of a gallant hero. What do you have to lose when the casualties were never your men to begin with?"

"You are soft, Count. Your high walls have kept your city safe for too long. Without ever facing a threat you have developed nothing in the way of common sense."

"You sack my city and then insult me? What else would you take? You have the livelihoods of my people and my pride, what else is there that your black heart desires?" Kitali noticed the ghost of a smile playing across the Count's feminine features at the remark.

"I would have your apology for your wrongful prejudices. I have done nothing but aid your people and have done nothing to make me suspect."

"That is not what I hear, not what I hear at all. My chroniclers tell me you threatened to throw them from the rooftops if they were to follow you. Is it not the way of a man with something to hide to keep those who wish to delve a little deeper at arm's length?"

"Your chroniclers are incompetent and annoying. My people do not fawn over unknowns like yours seem to. To me it was uncalled for and an invasion of my personal space. I would punish any man who encroached in such a way." Kitali was sure to give his most intimidating glare so that the Count did not miss the fact that he would not think twice about hurting him if it came to it. "Yet in the interest of proving my innocence, I will allow anything that your people wish. I have nothing to hide on this matter."

The Count smiled triumphantly and went back to stroking the beard that he did not have. Kitali looked on with a puzzled expression as the bizarre man then began to sweep his imaginary hair behind his ears. If the Elector Count of Libetha was not perverse, he was indeed quite mad.

"You allow? How very naïve. You mistakenly assume that you have a say in the matter." The Count waved the three polearm-wielding guardsmen away, as if sure Kitali no longer posed a threat. "The priesthood are knowledgeable on the forbidden lore of magic. They have read the grimoires and the scrolls passed down from a time when such practices were legal, and they have methods of rendering someone's magic inert. One way or another I shall be satisfied that you no longer pose a threat to Nadhaska. For the sake of your life and the alliance of our people, I only hope you are telling the truth. Take him to the jails!" the Count snapped, clapping his hands as he did so.

Despite the seeming reassurance from the Count, Kitali sincerely doubted the man held any real hope of his suspect's innocence. In fact, he was almost certain that Count Creed was looking forward to using him as a scapegoat.

Chapter Fifteen

Recently, the black city of Tilbon had lived up to its name in more ways than just its appearance. A wave of despondence had passed over the city, gripping all in its wake. Even the pristine beacon of holiness that was the city temple offered little in the way of cheer.

Despite the gentle flutter of songbirds' wings overhead and the calming rays of the sun washing down across the temple gardens, Jular could not shake the feeling of dread that welled within his stomach. His late afternoon walk had taken him on two complete circuits of the temple grounds, and with enough light left to complete a third, he was strongly considering doing so. After all, if there was one thing he needed, it was to work through the array of depressive thoughts that now lay scattered about his mind.

Wherever he looked there was something wrong with the city he was once proud to consider himself part of. The populace were beginning to lose their faith not only in the priesthood but the All-Father himself, and for the first time in four hundred years, the white birds of Nadhaska had left their dwellings.

Jular had received a message from the Libethan capital of Nadhaska that very morning. What he read had disturbed him deeply, yet he had discounted it as some elaborate hoax that one of the temple's enemies had perpetrated. However, the sight of the Druli—Nadhaska's avian dwellers—flying over Tilbon had quickly dispelled any notion of hoax, for the Druli only ever left Nadhaska when the city was close to collapse.

Since receiving word of Nadhaska's plight, Jular had spoken to no one. The note was a copy and had been sent to ruling bodies all across the Empire and, as such, a few hours of silent thought on the matter would harm nobody.

As a cold wind whipped through the gardens, Jular made the decision to rest while he contemplated the future. Whether it was the wind rattling through his aged bones or the weight of responsibility looming overhead that made him weary, he was not certain.

He all but collapsed onto a stone bench that overlooked the public burial grounds. Despite having his own personal quarters, Jular always came to this spot to do his most profound thinking. It was calm out here amongst the dead of the common folk. Within the temple he was forever reminded of his duties and could never think as straight as he would like.

After almost an hour staring at the crumpled note he held in his hand, Jular had come to no conclusion as to what he should do. Nadhaska, of course, was not his mess to clean up, yet aid would need to be sent. It simply would not do for his temple to be seen to be inactive when his brethren called for aid. He resolved to send a token force of priests and postulants to aid the city and then pushed all thoughts of Nadhaska to the back of his mind. The cry of help seemed to serve only as a reminder that he too had problems, and it was those problems that were important to him.

"You missed ceremony today, Brother Jular."

Jular turned to see the muscled form of his fellow brother, Shayn, standing beside the stone bench. So deep was he in thought that he had not heard the hulking man's approach.

"I have had issues to deal with. Surely the flock is not so misguided that one missed ceremony will affect them?"

"You were not missed by the congregation, Brother Kaleb spoke in your place." Shayn took a seat beside Jular, folding his arms across his chest. "It is almost dark out and I have not laid eyes on you all day. What has you so vexed that you would withdraw from your brethren?"

Jular took a moment to think of how he should word his response. He was a respected voice of reason to the newly initiated such as Shayn and as such could not afford to make himself appear weak.

"The temple is a place for equality, is it not, Brother Shayn?"

"Of course, we are all His children."

"We disciples hold the same rank of Brother, yet despite that I have far more weight behind my words due to age and experience. As the elder of the temple I have a lot on my mind and, as much as it repulses me to admit, I have not been able to deal with my thoughts as swiftly as I once would have."

"It is not that, Brother Jular. The weight of your responsibility is not affecting you; it is the weight of the All-Father's gaze."

Jular shot Shayn a quizzical glance. "What are you talking about?" he demanded.

"I too have been looking for solace by seeking out a place to be alone with my thoughts. I have thought long and hard over our recent actions, and the answers I discovered were not easy to accept." Shayn paused, his head hung in his hands.

"You are making little sense, Brother. Come, out with your thoughts."

"We are treading a dangerous path, Brother. I fear we no longer live for Him, but for ourselves. We no longer judge with His tenets in mind, we act according to our own greed and personal devices."

Jular surged to his feet despite the protest from his pained bones. He stood in silence, his eyes locked onto Shayn's. For all the unofficial power that Jular wielded and the fierceness of his gaze, Shayn would not be cowed.

"You should watch your tongue, Brother Shayn, for it could land you in trouble."

"I have nothing to fear from the mortal world, Brother." Shayn paused for a moment and looked up at the sky briefly. "It is the immaterial world that I fear. No matter how secretive our actions have been, no matter how thick the walls or heavy the locks upon the doors, our conversations are still known to Him. No man in this world can punish us in any way that could come close to what the All-Father can do. We will be judged, Brother. Our sins will be laid out before us, and nothing will be left unseen or unheard."

Jular felt his lips quiver with anger at Shayn's words. All they had done had been to better the temple, to better the city's faith. Yet here his apprentice sat before him, spouting out doubt in their cause. One as young as he could not hope to know even a tenth of what Jular knew. To think that a mere upstart could even claim to know the difference between right or wrong in the eyes of the All-Father was laughable.

"Brother Jular." Shayn got to his feet and stood beside his mentor, his muscular form casting a shadow that engulfed the smaller man. "Today a hunter came to the temple. He carried with him the body of one of the Druli. He claimed to have shot it from the sky and brought it to the temple so that our order might eat well. What would you do with such a man who fires unknowingly on the All-Father's most sacred of birds?"

Jular's eyes widened at the news. He was unsure as to why Shayn had opted to change the subject but was glad that he had. To take the life of one of the Druli was punishable by death. The birds were thought to be the All-Father's favored creations and, as such, were seen as holy creatures. They were to be treated better than a man might treat the Emperor himself!

"Have him hanged for his crime!" Jular spat. "And have him flogged before he dances on the hangman's rope!"

"I am afraid I can do no such thing, Brother."

"You would allow a man who drew the blood of one of the All-Father's favored creatures to live?" Jular demanded in disbelief.

"I would. For it is nothing that we are not guilty of ourselves." Shayn paused, his eyes not for a second leaving Jular's. "We arranged for a fellow priest, a Brother, to be assassinated. This man fired unknowingly upon a creature sacred to us, yet we acted fully aware that to kill a priest was to spit in the All-Father's face."

"What we have done is completely different. We acted to better our faith! Castus was nothing but a troublemaker who would see our beliefs disregarded so that we might do the job of the law."

"Castus was nothing but a man trying to better the quality of life of those too poor to afford our luxuries, and I take great comfort in the fact that our assassin failed."

"You venerate him?" Jular yelled in disbelief, his throat hurting with the effort.

"I do, and so would you if you looked at the situation with clarity as I do now. Castus has travelled from Gurdalin to destroy an evil that now plagues *our* city. Yet we cannot even muster enough interest to step out of the safety of the Upper District to fight the very same evil that he has traversed an entire country to best!"

"How dare you raise your voice to me, Brother Shayn? You first speak of matters that are beyond your comprehension, and then you have the nerve to talk to me as if I were some lowly criminal!"

Jular was seething at how Shayn had spoken to him, his pale face flushed brightest red. He looked at his hands and found them to be trembling, such was the fury that coursed through his veins. He watched as Shayn turned from him, his head shaking in what Jular could only assume was disappointment. *Such a fool! He fills his head with such nonsense and now believes himself to be some kind of enlightened voice of reason.*

"Where are you going, Brother Shayn?" Jular shouted angrily after him. "We are not done here!"

The hulking priest stopped and turned to face his mentor once again, his face firm and unreadable.

"I have nothing more to say. Your mind is closed to all reason, Brother. I am off to try to atone for my sins in whatever small way I can. I would hope that you would do the same when you come around to my way of thought."

With a fierce anger building within him, Jular watched as his protégé walked away. As much respect as he held for Shayn, Jular was not one to become weighed down by emotional attachment. He might have once considered the man a friend, but now it was clear that Shayn had lost himself in whatever madness his mind had conjured. He merely hoped the fool did not do anything reckless. Despite their history, he would have no qualms about removing him if he became a problem.

"I am the instrument of His divine will. His sword, His armor, His voice given flesh," Jular muttered to himself as he continued on his third circuit of the temple grounds.

Chapter Sixteen

The days following Edward's demise had been spent in the man's own home. Conrad was beginning to mirror his brother's frantic behavior, pacing about the small floor-space and crushing what was left of the furnishings beneath his feet. It was not natural for one as unbound as he to be cooped up in a small, dingy room.

Sallus had had to interject between the pair twice already as their cramped conditions only served to intensify the hatred they felt for one another. Conrad had been cowed for the first day after Sallus had admonished him for unveiling their hiding place to the world. It had been a long walk back to the butchery after the confrontation with the priest. He thought back to the shock he had felt when a hand yanked him into an alleyway, only to find Nicholas and Sallus assailing him with questions. He could still picture his sire's face, twisted in anger as the child's death and the crowd of onlookers were explained to him.

Vitria watched her brothers eye one another. Conrad still could not work out what the woman's motives were. Perhaps she held feelings for either he or Nicholas, or perhaps she just enjoyed to watch two men fight over her. Despite the fact that Conrad did not want her nearly as much as he craved Jessamine, Nicholas seemed to see only lust when he glared into his brother's eyes.

The thought amused him. To think that he could, in any way, lust after a woman who was playing him as Vitria was, galled him. The opportunity to speak with her in private had yct to come, and until that moment arrived, he could not be sure how much she knew or what she wanted.

Sallus had relaxed his rationing system, the reason being that he feared attack from one of his gets from the past. Upon hearing this, Conrad had immediately thought of the child and the tale of his estranged, cannibalistic brother. The fact that Sallus feared this man so openly before his family was enough to show Conrad the threat was serious.

Feeding had become the top priority as of late. Sallus wanted each of them to be as strong as possible for when the inevitable happened and this mystery savage found them. None of them was permitted to hunt alone, nor were they to roam out of sight of the dwelling. It was the unknown that had Conrad acting like his brother now did. If Sallus would only enlighten him about what he knew of this beast, he was certain it would ease his nerves.

All three members of his family had, however, remained tight-lipped. None of them had so much as uttered the thing's name, and it was this unspoken fear that was saturating deep into the recesses of Conrad's mind.

How can I prepare for something that I know nothing of? The question had bothered him since he had fed again and his mind had regained its lucidity. He punched the wall in frustration, adding to the many rents already present.

"Come, newborn, you are growing to be worse than Nicholas," Sallus said.

"Maybe that's because you're not keeping anything from him," Conrad replied through gritted teeth.

"You don't need to know. The less about this known by anyone, the better."

"Do you honestly think this bastard child of yours is a secret? The abomination that *you* brought into this world is known by many, and you're hated for it." Conrad had barely finished speaking before he was knocked from his feet. He was thrown into a small bedside table that shattered beneath his momentum. Within moments, Sallus was on top of him, his face mere inches from Conrad's.

"Do not talk about that which you do not understand!"

"Don't get too close," Conrad labored to say as Sallus forced down on his throat. "I might get hungry and take a bite," he yelled, grinning widely despite Sallus' knee pressing down ever harder on his windpipe.

The taunt had his sire stunned momentarily. His eyes seemed to glaze over as he took in his get's words. Slowly but surely, Conrad felt the pressure being applied by his sire fade away.

"What did you say?" Sallus said in disbelief.

Conrad remained silent for a moment. He was as stunned as Sallus was, and he was certain it was for the same reason. Sallus had expected him to be ignorant to the details of his unwanted offspring and Conrad had expected the child to have lied to him.

"Not such a well-kept secret as you might have hoped."

Sallus instinctively turned his head to face Vitria and Nicholas.

"It wasn't them," Conrad said, the sound of his voice snapping Sallus' head back around to face him, his wild, flowing black hair making him look feral.

"Then who?" Sallus demanded.

"The child," Conrad hastily replied. The look worn by his sire suggested that he was in no mood to play games. "It told me that in exchange for an end to its life."

"What else did it tell you?"

"It told me everyone knows it was you who created it. I don't think you're well liked by the rest of our kind. It also said that its coven knew we were here the whole time."

Sallus turned away from Conrad and stormed over towards Vitria and Nicholas. It felt as though a great weight had been lifted from Conrad's shoulders as his sire turned his gaze from him. The sight of his brother shirking away from his sire brought a smile to his face. This was indeed a subject that Sallus took seriously.

"Which of you incompetent fools was discovered? You said that no one knew of your whereabouts within the city!" he roared.

"We couldn't have been…we saw nobody. How could we have known we were being watched?" Nicholas stammered.

Sallus took two steps forward and slapped Nicholas across the face with the back of his hand. Nicholas fell to the floor from the force of the blow and threw his hands up as if to ward off Sallus from striking again.

"Even if they knew we were here, how did they know you were?" Vitria chimed in. "You're just as much at fault in this as we," she finished, standing defiantly before Sallus.

"Do not lay the blame on my head, woman!" Sallus snapped. "This mistake is perhaps more your fault than it is ours. Had you not been singing and playing to your vanity in the public eye we might never have been discovered."

Conrad dragged himself to his feet, pieces of the table scattering across the floor as his movement disturbed the mess. All eyes turned to him.

"What does it matter if our whereabouts are known? It changes nothing, surely?" he asked.

Sallus glared at him condescendingly. "If our enemies within the city know where to find us, it will make escaping Tilbon all the harder. They will come for us and there will be too many of them for us to fight."

"I have no problem trying. I look forward to it, in fact!" said Nicholas, now back on his feet and cracking his knuckles as though he expected a fight.

"You were just knocked to the floor by a slap," Vitria said patronizingly.

"At least I can best a child!" he replied, glaring at Conrad.

"By my count we've both killed one!"

"Quiet!" Sallus screamed, "I need to think."

Both of Sallus' fists were clenched and even though his eyes were fixed upon his children, Conrad knew that his sire was not looking at anything in particular. In all likelihood he was not even aware of where his gaze had landed.

"You won't have to worry about getting out. There's none of our kind left in the city," Conrad said.

Something in Sallus' eyes told Conrad that he was indeed now staring at him even though he had not moved.

"How can you know this?" Sallus asked, his face a mask of anxiety. Conrad was certain that if Sallus had needed to draw breath, his chest would be heaving.

"The child said his coven left when they heard your creation was coming. And with him dead, it's just us and your son."

"Then we leave as soon as possible. We can't stay in Tilbon a moment longer. The ravens...they're everywhere. They'll be his eyes."

A communal surge of terror seemed to flow through the room, the very atmosphere itself felt heavy and oppressive. To Conrad the sensation was almost akin to being back within his grave six feet beneath the earth. Not even Sallus, the one of them who was always unshakably calm, was unaffected. His mind was racing too fast for his mouth to keep up with and not all that came out seemed to have been properly thought about. Normally he was as proud of his vernacular and his intellect as Nicholas was of his muscles. To see him reduced to such a state was mind-numbing to say the very least.

A loud rapping at the door broke the silence that had descended on the room. As one, all four of them turned to face the sound.

"Nicholas," Sallus nodded to the door. "Do something useful for once."

Scowling at the jibe, Nicholas moved towards the door. He pulled it open with a force that suggested he intended to pull it clean off its hinges.

Conrad was stunned by the scent before he even managed to get a glimpse of who stood at the door. The heavenly aroma drowned out his surroundings and for the briefest of moments, he felt as though he was intoxicated and unable to move. The sight of Jessamine standing in the open doorway, trembling with fear and yet still resplendent with beauty and utter perfection, brought him back to his senses.

Jessamine stood gaping at Nicholas. Her mouth moved, yet no sound came from her lips. Conrad thought of Edward—the man Jessamine had expected to answer the door—and forced himself to stifle the grin that yearned to break free. He watched, utterly transfixed by her beauty.

Shock quickly spread across his face as Jessamine's eyes moved from person to person, finally landing on his. This was the moment he had been praying for since he first laid eyes on her. The moment their eyes met and for the first time in what felt like an eternity, she had eyes for him and only him. Conrad drank in the moment, he allowed his mind to wander to the future he had envisioned for them both. He was happier than he had ever been in that instant, and then Jessamine mouthed one word that served to raise his spirits higher still.

"You." Conrad blinked in disbelief. Her voice was so much more perfect when it was addressing him. Somehow it seemed as though every other time he had heard her voice, it had been distorted. But not now. Now it was unleashed upon his senses in all its splendor.

As quickly as Conrad's moment of bliss had come, it was shattered when Nicholas put his hands on the woman he loved and yanked her into the room. He slammed the door and forced her up against it, her feet hovering inches above the ground.

"I was getting ever so peckish," he said, arching his head back to display his razor sharp fangs to his victim.

Jessamine opened her mouth to scream, the sound ringing out louder than any Conrad had heard before. He leapt forward and grabbed Nicholas by the back of the head, the animal fat his brother-in-death used to smear about his hair made it hard for him to gain purchase. Clasping his other hand around Nicholas' throat, he pulled him back from his would-be meal.

Nicholas spun away from Conrad's grip and snarled, baring his fangs at his brother. Conrad paid the menacing gesture no heed and surged forward, darting below a wild right hand and landing one of his own to his brother-in-death's gut. The force of the blow bent Nicholas over. Conrad took full advantage of his brother's plight and hammered his knee into the man's face, breaking his nose in the process and sending him stumbling backwards to crash against the far wall.

Nicholas leapt to his feet, his eyes locked with Conrad's. He took a step forward, a smirk edging across his face. Conrad responded with a guttural snarl that sounded not unlike a wolf that was bearing down on a kill.

Before either man could make another move, Vitria was between them, her hand pressed against Conrad's chest and her teeth bared. She snarled at Nicholas as if daring him to come any closer. Nicholas stood still, the cocky expression gone from his face and replaced with one of betrayal and sadness.

Conrad was lost in his own thoughts and barely noticed anything that was happening outside of the exchange between his siblings. Even Jessamine's presence was forgotten momentarily. Everything he thought he knew about Vitria had suddenly been flipped upside down. He had assumed her to be some evil, conniving bitch whose sole purpose was to make him suffer. Yet here she stood, protecting the woman he loved from Nicholas.

Vitria turned her head to face Conrad and winked.

"This is what you've been keeping from me, Vitria? Conrad's pet?"

"I won't hesitate to kill any of you if she is harmed," Conrad stated.

"We are leaving Tilbon, I care not whether the cattle live or die anymore. Let her go." Sallus waved his hand in annoyance. "Perhaps we'll get lucky and Vance will waste his time on women such as her and allow us to slink away."

Conrad pushed Vitria aside, and stepped forward to address his sire.

"She stays with me."

"I will not have one of the cattle come along with us."

"Then I shall stay with her. I have waited too long for this, I will not throw it away now," Conrad snarled, looking back to the terrified face of Jessamine as he did so.

"Conrad, if you stay in the city, Vance will find you. I don't care whether you live or die, I just care that you are not used to strengthen my enemy."

"Then we shall leave Tilbon. But we shall do so alone, he will never find us."

Sallus' face twisted in anger and he repeatedly ran his hands through his hair.

"I told you that your love of pretty women would get you in trouble." Sallus turned from Conrad and stormed over towards the window. He threw the shutter back and allowed the dusk glow to wash over him. "Nicholas, Vitria, we shall leave for Nadhaska. Conrad, go wherever you want, just do not follow. You have chosen your path and from this point on we shall not see you as family."

Conrad stood and watched as the three beings he had called his family left the room. Vitria was last to leave, but before she did so she held his hand and kissed him gently on the lips.

"See you again, little brother."

Conrad slumped down next to Jessamine and put his arm around her. She flinched at the coldness of his flesh and struggled to free herself from his embrace. After so long of wishing for nothing more than to be with her, he refused to let her leave. He pulled her closer and kissed her gently on the head. The sensation was better than any he could remember.

"Please…let me go," she begged, her eyes wet with tears and her lip quivering with what Conrad assumed was fear.

"Oh no, my sweet. We are going to be together," he kissed her gently once more upon her forehead, "forever.

Chapter Seventeen

Giento stood watching through the barred doors of the communal cell as Castus proceeded to scream his case to the lawmen. He was not certain how long he had been locked up; as daylight was not allowed to shine in sight of the cells, candlelight was all that the condemned were allowed. It had been one day at the very least, he knew that much for he had managed to find sleep once and failed in doing so a second time.

City jails were not an uncommon thing for him. He had spent time in several before and was well used to the cramped, filthy conditions. This time had been different to all the others as he had mentioned the fact that he travelled with a warrior priest. His comments had been ignored by the guards, but they were acted upon by his fellow cellmates.

Every other man, it seemed, had been caught doing something they should not by the priesthood at one time or another. Some even had loved ones hanged as heretics or through some obscure law of treason that many believed the priests made up on the occasions they had nothing else better to do.

As a result, Giento soon found himself out of favor and frequently on the receiving end of treatment far harsher than he had endured in the bar. His face was swollen and bruised from repeated strikes and several of his teeth were either missing or left as jagged stumps. His gums bled and were tender. One of his eyes was swollen shut and the other had a great cut above it that stung as if on fire. Fortunately, his face had not suffered the brunt of the damage, otherwise he most certainly would have been dead. He now sported great bruises across his back and upper legs and was just happy that none of his ribs had been broken. Despite his injuries being mainly superficial, he still found it hard to stand.

His one good eye lit up with hope as he saw one of the lawmen leading Castus over toward the jail cell. The sight of the priest holding his pistol to the man's skull made him smile, his lips cracking with the effort.

Castus' eyes widened as they fell upon Giento.

"You stand in the way of the All-Father's holy work and then return my aide to me in such a state?" Castus roared.

Before the lawman could argue in his defense, Castus rammed his face into the iron bars with such force that it made all within the cell wince. He leaned his head in close to the lawman's whimpering face.

"Which one of them did this?" he snarled.

"I...I...I don't know!" the lawman squealed.

Castus spun the man around and hit him hard across the skull with the butt of his pistol. The lawman's squeal of pain drowned out the *crack* of wood on bone. The priest knelt down besides the fallen lawman and fished the jail keys from his pocket.

"Which one of them," Castus said, his gaze now fixed on Giento, the keys dangling from his hands.

Giento tried to speak but found the effort too painful. Instead he turned, pointed to a tall, heavy-set man with greasy hair and said a single word, "Leader."

The man Giento had fingered as the ringleader began to tremble and soon found himself standing alone against the wall as the rest of the felons shuffled away for fear of being caught in the backlash. The greasy-haired man fell to his knees and put his hands up as if to beg off Castus.

Seeing the man in such a vulnerable position, Giento could not resist. He ran as fast as his aching legs would carry him and landed his boot in his tormentor's gut. Pain flared throughout his body as his abused muscles were forced to work. The sight of the man crumpling to the floor brought yet another painful smile to Giento's face.

He turned as he heard the key scrape in the lock of the cell door. Castus pushed the door open and strode towards Giento and the cowering form of his former tormentor. Despite the priest's back being turned and the cell door being wide open, none of the inmates tried to escape. All were too afraid that the one shot housed inside the priest's pistol would find their back.

"The All-Father sees all sins and punishes all transgressions," Castus said solemnly as he unsheathed a small blade and buried it deep into the man's breast. He then removed the blade and cleaned it on the deceased's clothes.

Giento stood watching in awe as the man who had caused him so much pain had been dealt with as though he was nothing more than a mere annoyance. He had seemed so strong and untouchable when he had been beating Giento for his association with the priesthood, yet now he was simply gone.

The priest turned his gaze to the terrified assembly of criminals that huddled together against the far wall. None of them seemed brave enough to speak, all seemed to wish that the nightmare that was the priest would simply just go away. Seeing the frightened faces of those who had beaten him and the corpse of the man who had led the assaults, Giento truly felt as though he belonged alongside Castus. The priest had done little but work him into the ground and kill his spirit up until now, but this had been a display of affection. He knew Castus would never admit to such feelings as friendship with someone as lowly as he, but there was no denying they existed. The look in the man's eyes as he took in the damage had been proof enough. After all, if it was merely a case of Castus needing someone to guide him on his travels, he could have hired any traveler to do such a job. Whether anyone else would have remained with him for as long was another thing entirely, but he could have tried.

Castus turned from the felons and left the cell with his aide hot on his heels. Giento saw the face of the lawman lying semi-conscious on the stone floor and recognized him as the man who had laughed in his face and turned his back when he had told him of his connection with Castus. There were very few opportunities in a man's life to strike a lawman without being punished for it, and Giento knew that when one came it should be taken. Seeing the priest as his immunity, he seized the opportunity and punted the lawman square in the face, hearing bones shatter beneath his boot.

The keys jangled once more, echoing off of the bare walls as Castus locked the cell door.

"I hope you're capable of travel," he called over. "Vampire activity seems to have ceased over the past couple of days. We leave Tilbon as soon as we get the word."

Giento stared at Castus in what he hoped was a confused expression, yet what with the damage done to his face he would not have been surprised if there was no change at all. The priest certainly did not seem to get the fact that Giento was silently begging him for more information so he forced himself to speak, no matter how painful the experience was.

"Get...what....word?" The words came out slowly over is bloodied, swollen tongue and ruined gums.

"The City Guard is being fractured with half of it sent as part of an expeditionary force to Nadhaska. There is trouble in the city and although it may not be our business, we have no leads to go on here in Tilbon. Perhaps we shall catch wind of our quarry somewhere along the way."

Giento stood in silence, more for the fact that it hurt his lips to speak than because he had nothing to say. Staring down at his legs and feeling the bruises and aches flare up with every movement, he felt as if he could cry at the news. To travel in the back of a wagon as they had been doing thus far was one thing, but to march across the country as part of an army? That would not bode well for his poor aching bones. He could only pray they were given 'the word' at some point in the very distant future.

****

Kitali was jolted awake by ice-cold water washing over his naked body. He had grown used to this rude awakening despite only being held captive by the priests for little more than a day, two at the very most. As far as he could discern, they had taken him somewhere below ground, that much was evident from both the drop in temperature and the dampness that clung to the air.

The room in which he was being held was spacious. He had seen little more than the stone of the walls and the floor, and even that was dependant on whether or not his captives chose to come bearing torches. The immediate area was illuminated by the glowing glyphs that adorned the walls, each of which shed light no further than three feet. His arms were chained to the walls and his feet were bound with coarse rope that dug into his ankles at every slight movement.

As harsh as his confines were, his captors had spoken highly of his progress. One man, a short, pot-bellied priest with dark hair ringing his otherwise bald head, had told Kitali that they held very little suspicion of him possessing magical abilities anymore. The same priest had seemed to have taken a liking to him in the short period of time he had been incarcerated. The man had also stated that situations on the surface had not lessened as the Count thought it might with Kitali being held captive.

He could not help but wonder if his new-found sympathizer was placed there by the priests to give the illusion of friendship. The man seemed genuine, yet Kitali had come across liars of spectacular talent and he would trust none other than himself until he was released.

Gazing around groggily into the darkness, he looked for any sign of a priest after being awoken so. He had been bound and left directly beneath a chute that funneled water from some unknown place at regular intervals and had grown used to it waking him. However, the past couple of times Kitali had awoken to find several robed priests looming over him, empty buckets clutched in their hands. If it was not he that was being subjected to such torment, he would have applauded such tactics, for they were obviously designed to keep a prisoner fatigued and unsure.

Were it not for the stiffness of his back that came from lying in uncomfortable positions on the solid stone flooring, or the raw flesh of his ankles, he would be in almost perfect health. Kitali had come into this place fully expecting to be beaten, and the fact that he had not been subjected to any physical torment was the thing that shocked him the most. As he lay there gazing at the faintly glowing glyphs, he could not help but wonder if they protected him from the advances of the dead. If his suspicions were correct about being below ground, then surely any misshapen corpse could come burrowing through the walls to get at him.

Several glowing balls appeared off in the distance and grew steadily larger and more intense as time passed. As the lights came closer, Kitali heard the soft *slap* of leather-soled feet echoing in the empty space that was his prison. The torchbearers stopped at the edge of the eerie light provided by the glyphs as if they still did not fully trust Kitali's innocence.

"Your trials have come to an end, short one, and we see you to be free of any taint."

Kitali held back the urge to smile, to show relief would only give the priests a valid reason to question him further.

"It is about time," he said, his voice full of annoyance. "These ropes, they eat the flesh from my bones. I would have them off."

Kitali saw a slight movement from one of the priests that he could only assume was a nod. A moment later the pot-bellied priest he had grown used to stepped forward, brandishing a curved blade. He forced himself not to flinch at the sight of the weapon, he sincerely hoped the man would sever his bonds yet if that was not his intent, Kitali would meet death without showing fear.

As the priest knelt beside him and slipped the blade between his numb feet, Kitali felt embarrassed that his mind saw enemies at every turn even when there were none to be found. With his feet free, the priest moved on to the shackles that bound his arms. His bonds were roomy enough to allow circulation, yet not nearly enough for him to have escaped. He wished it had been the other way around with his arms and feet, at least then he would have been able to walk out under his own power. As it was, Kitali very much doubted his ability to stand on his own two legs.

"The Count accepts that you are a friend to his fair city and extends his apology," one of the other priests said, his voice deep yet soft. "Despite your innocence, you are not permitted to stay within the walls of Nadhaska. You will have your belongings returned to you and shall be assigned to a small team of scouts who are being sent to rally aid for the city."

It took a moment for the priest's words to sink in. The privation he had endured had meant little. From the very moment he had spoken with Elector Count Creed, his future had already been decided. If he was found guilty, it was to be death. If innocent, he would be ejected from the city so that the Count would not have to appear weak before his subjects. Either way, Kitali was being used as a scapegoat.

"Our order no longer has any qualms with you, stout one, so it is with great sincerity that we offer this warning. Do not trust whoever the Count assigns you to. He is a petty man driven by greed and power. The life of a foreigner means nothing to him and, as callous as it sounds, you would be far less trouble to him dead than alive."

Kitali truly did not know what to make of these words. Was he being fed lies to fuel his paranoia? Did the priests want him to grow agitated around the men he would be travelling with? Perhaps they wished that he kill his fellows and so ensure his death warrant? He pushed such thoughts aside and thought it through from a logical stand point. As he had learnt from the kindness of the balding priest, not everything was as uncaring in this world as it would seem. Perhaps these men spoke the truth.

"Why do you tell me this? Why do you speak out against your ruler?" Kitali asked, desperate for answers. Even if he was being lied to, he would have as much of the untruths as possible so as to build an appropriate opinion.

"The Elector Count has no say over our temple. By the grace of the All-Father we are permitted to exist outside the reach of the common law. We are held accountable to the All-Father first and the Emperor second. No other being may order us to do anything." Kitali nodded. Such tales had been mentioned by those who fled the Empire many centuries ago and Kitali was shocked to see that they still held true.

He groaned in pain as he was hoisted to his feet. A priest stood on either side with a hand under each of his armpits to hold him up. His feet throbbed, the pain threatening to make him faint. Every step was agonizing, despite his best efforts to keep most of his weight on the priests' hands and off his feet. He did not know just how soon the Count expected him out of Nadhaska but if the pain was any indicator, he would be sticking around for a good few days yet.

****

Any hope of the expeditionary force taking a long time to muster had been dispelled at the sight of an ever-growing horde of armored men. Most wore the blood-red cloaks that marked them as Tilbon's City Guard, yet with every passing moment, groups of men wearing colors unfamiliar to Giento came trickling through the black streets to converge at the city's centre.

As he stood propped against a cart being loaded with supplies for the march, Giento cursed his bad luck. His new-found admiration for Castus was the only thing keeping him from slipping away unnoticed, that and the seething pain that wracked his body. He dabbed at his face with a washcloth and winced at his own touch. He had never suffered such a beating before, his skills of self-preservation had always seen him clear of any such danger in the past, and he found himself wondering just how long it would be until he had his old face back.

Despite the sky above being as black as the city itself, Giento was not the least bit concerned for his safety. He was surrounded by hundreds if not thousands of able-bodied warriors who seemed all too eager to throw their lives away for the greater good of the country of Libetha and the lands of Taal.

Sacrifice never made any sense to him. As a mercenary he had seen his fair share of gallant heroes stay behind and give their lives so that others might live on. To his mind, there was no future if he was not alive to see it, so sacrifice seemed pointless.

As he surveyed the ever-growing throng of warriors that made up the expeditionary force, his heart almost stopped as his eyes flicked across one individual. Giento rubbed the washcloth over his face as if to clear away the horrific vision that stood mere feet away from him.

Looming tall above the mass of warriors stood the one man he dearly wished he would never lay eyes on again. He could not remember the man's name, but his sheer bulk was unforgettable. Even under the heavy cloaks of office that the priest wore, Giento could clearly see masses of muscle that looked as if they had been chiseled by the All-Father himself. Over the man's shoulder, Giento saw what looked like the haft of an oversized blade. Giento shuddered to think how large and deadly the blade actually was.

Forgetting all worldly pain, he pushed himself from the wagon and began his frantic search for Castus. His paymaster had made it perfectly clear that unless he was present, the temple would most certainly kill Giento in revenge for his insults. His mind rushed back to the failed assassination attempt. Perhaps the priests wrongly assumed their man had succeeded. If claiming Giento's head was indeed on the priest's agenda, he would be sorely disappointed.

As much as his fears spurred him on, his injuries held him back. He shuffled along in search of Castus but his progress was halted by the sheer mass of people that had crammed into the city centre. With every step he would receive an elbow to his injured torso or an accidental knee to his legs. He had no clue as to where he was going, Castus had disappeared to speak with city officials and Giento, like the fool he was, had considered himself safe by the wagon.

His ruined face split into a toothless grin as the crowd of people ahead parted. It was rare, but he was thankful that a bit of luck had gone his way at such an opportune time. After taking his first few steps unmolested, his grin faded. A hand clapped down upon his shoulder causing him to stop dead in his tracks.

"Hello, little man."

He did not need to turn around to see who the voice belonged to. There was only one man present who the crowd would part for in such a way.

Giento was turned around quickly by the overly-muscled priest and detected a look of shock as the man laid eyes on his battered features.

"Where is Brother Castus?" The priest's voice was hard as iron and caused Giento to tremble uncontrollably.

As he stood there, clamped in place, thoughts of Castus saving him from a certain death in the city jails filled his mind. Now was his turn to repay the favor. Yet despite his thoughts of selflessness, Giento could not hide the fact that a selfless man did not lurk within him. Cowardice had been his bread and butter throughout life and he was not about to change that now.

"I...I don't know. Oh 'eavens above, please don't 'urt me," Giento begged, closing his eyes and scrunching up his face in an effort to appear even more pathetic than he was. "I'll 'elp you find 'im, though. I'll take you to 'im some'ow. Anythin' you want."

The priest snarled at Giento's response and slapped him hard across the face. He fell to the floor, expecting the attack to continue. After several long, uneventful moments he opened his eyes and was relieved to see that the priest had moved on. Pulling himself to his feet and trying as best he could to ignore the pain lancing through his skull, Giento hobbled off in the opposite direction to the priest, intent on putting as much distance between himself and anything even remotely painful.

Chapter Eighteen

Evenings spent trying to out-drink veteran soldiers had not left his head spinning as much as it was now. Between the blow from the priest—whose name Giento still failed to remember—and his pre-existing injuries from the time spent in Tilbon's jail, he found it incredibly difficult to stand, let alone move in any regular fashion.

Thankfully, the majority of the expeditionary force had gathered a fair distance away from his new-found resting place, which in actual fact just happened to be the spot where he had been knocked down by a passing halberdier and had yet to find the strength to get back to his feet. He dragged himself over to a nearby wall and sat propped up against it, thankful for the rarity of just being able to rest unmolested.

He wiped the filthy sleeve of his shirt across his face and immediately regretted doing so as his broken teeth rubbed against the inside of his mouth. Thin trickles of blood leaked from his gums forcing him to wipe at his face once more. Giento had survived many a campaign through questionable means and knew full well that times of peace were often filled with times of great pain and discomfort. Wounds had to heal and the process was often as painful as receiving them. He was also used to such things happening to other people and usually *after* any form of campaign had ended, not before it had even begun.

Closing his eyes in order to catch a few moments of uninterrupted rest, he found himself reliving the past few weeks under Castus' employ. His opinions of the priest were not yet finalized. The man had, after all, done some despicable things in the pursuit of the vampires, yet at the same time he had saved Giento from certain death in the jails. Try as he might, he could not think of another man in his entire life who had displayed such resentment towards him only to risk his own neck to save his.

His thoughts were interrupted by a sharp jabbing pain in his leg. His eyes shot open to find Castus prodding him with his boot. Giento's eyes watered as with every jab, the point of the priest's toe connected with one of his many livid bruises.

"I'm awake, just stop kickin' me," Giento looked off to his right, taking in the assembly of armored warriors still gathered in the same area as when he last checked. "They ain't ready to go yet, let me 'ave another day's kip. Two at most." He turned back to face Castus, his eyes widening as he saw a large shadow fall across his own legs. Looking to his left he saw the hulking form of the priest who just a short while ago had nearly knocked him unconscious.

"I trust you remember Brother Shayn?" Castus asked.

"We've exchanged pleasantries, Brother Castus," Shayn replied, his tone flat, devoid of any humor despite the fact that he had unwittingly cracked a joke.

Giento stared up at the behemoth and wondered just what he wanted. Why was he here if not to kill them? Perhaps that was his plan and he was just toying with them.

"Brother Shayn has renounced his duties at the temple and has pledged his services to me. He has seen the error of his ways and wishes to atone for his past sins."

The news sent a thrill of fear washing over Giento's body. Travelling with one priest was bad enough, but to travel with two would drive him to his wits' end, especially when one of them had more than enough reason to kill him.

"I seek only to find a glorious death in battle to make up for, in some small way, my wrongs in life," Shayn intoned.

Giento nodded in fearful acceptance. He could scarcely believe what he was hearing. Having travelled alongside suicidal maniacs as a sell-sword, he was well aware of the dangers he would be pitted against. If Shayn was true to his word—and with him being a fanatical zealot, he did not doubt him for a moment—he would be impervious to fear and expect all others around him to be as well.

"I suggest you heal up fast, little man. I hear that we shall be leaving come noon tomorrow." Shayn stared at Giento with eyes as cold and unforgiving as granite. The combination of both his news and his gaze left the sell-sword on the verge of soiling himself.

As the two priests left Giento to his own devices, he allowed himself to drift off to sleep, cursing the fact that Castus could trust this man after he had tried to kill them both in the past, and confident that things could not get any worse.

****

For the first time in his entire existence, both of the living and the dead, Conrad had gotten what he wanted. In life what he had coveted had come with a price. The woman he lusted after so vehemently had cost him dearly and, as a result, he had been transformed into the nightmarish creature that he was today. Despite paying the ultimate price for his advances, Conrad had not gotten what he wanted. His rose had ignored him and left him to the mercies of her other admirers.

This time had been different. This time Conrad *had* attained that which he sought. A prize of such beauty that even his rose paled in comparison. Yet even in success, he had been hit with more disappointment. After learning of the barman's fate, all light seemed to fade from Jessamine's eyes. It was as if upon hearing of Edward's death, a piece of her died with him. She had since devoted her time in equal measure to either staying silent or stating her utter hatred and revulsion towards him. She had even gone as far as to beg that he kill her too.

Conrad had paid her little attention, he had simply dragged her by the arm in his wake. It was only natural for her to grieve after the loss of the man she had mistakenly seen as her soul mate. With time she would grow to understand just what lengths Conrad went to in order to ensure that they be together. Until that time, however, he would drag her to the ends of Taal, kicking and screaming if need be.

His planned route out of the city proved far too treacherous to take with Jessamine being in such an unwilling state of mind. Hundreds of men brandishing blades and finely polished armor strode through Tilbon's slums, cloaks of varying colors fluttering from their backs. The unusual amount of armed guards within the city had forced him to take to the rooftops and slink in the shadows where need be and, as regrettable as such an act was, Conrad had been forced to render Jessamine unconscious.

As much as the thought of harming her tore him apart, he knew that if she had the power to scream out and alert the guards that passed by below, she would do just that. He had come too far to attain his prize and he would not be robbed of her at the last stretch of his journey.

With the southern gate well in sight and his future bride hanging limp over his shoulder, Conrad took one last look at the black city of Tilbon. This place had made up the bulk of his unnatural life and he knew little other than its black walls and confusing networks of alleyways and side streets. As foul a place as the slums were, they had been the place in which his love had been discovered and, for that reason, he would forever remember them fondly.

Turning his eyes back to the southern gate, Conrad spared a thought for the family he had lost and for the kiss he had shared with Vitria only hours before. Her last words still hung in his mind and he truly wondered if he would see them again as she had suggested. He pushed all thoughts of his family from his mind and resolved to leave the memory of them behind with the city.

Beyond the southern gate awaited a whole new chapter in his existence. A new life that he would share with the one woman that ever truly made him feel as if he had a reason for existing.

The only thoughts that filled his mind as he sped off for the gate were of Jessamine and of how wondrous her blood would taste when she finally saw reason and accepted the gift he was offering her. And then, as swiftly as those wonderful thoughts had come, they were replaced with imaginings of his unknown brother and how his appearance would dash all hopes of a happy existence. With those images of utter pleasure and unknowable horrors playing through his mind, Conrad Sovain left the city of Tilbon behind.

ABOUT THE AUTHOR

Aaron lives and works in Melton Mowbray, Leicestershire, UK. When not writing he often spends his time reading, playing pool, snooker or sating his addiction for all things supernatural/paranormal.

www.aaronjbooth.com

18241006R00116

Made in the USA
Charleston, SC
24 March 2013